"How can you hate nature, Jane? You're a deer," Emma said cheerfully.

Emma was my—and I mean this without jealousy—gorgeous cherry-haired best friend. Mythology had a history of making female shapeshifters look gorgeous and male shapeshifters look monstrous, but the former was true. She was tall, curvy, and had that aura men just wanted to be around. That was a shame for them, since her interests were decidedly Sapphic.

Today, she was wearing a pair of shorts and a House Stark t-shirt with the bottom cut off to expose her midriff. Emma was wearing sandals and completely ignoring the fact that we were hiking through poor terrain with way too many bugs. She was also carrying a picnic basket like Little Red Riding Hood.

I, by contrast, was wearing a green fishing hat and a purple tie-dyed shirt over cargo pants. I had a thick backpack on that probably weighed more than I did (never go out hiking unless you are prepared for everything to go wrong) and a wooden staff in hand. The staff was mostly cosmetic since, weighing slightly over a hundred pounds, I still could lift about three or four times that much. It was one of the benefits of being a shapeshifter of Clan Cervid (weredeer, for occult laymen).

# An American Weredeer in Michigan

## Book Two of the Bright Falls Mystery Series

### by C.T. Phipps and Michael Suttkus

# CHAPTER ONE

Iswatted a mosquito from my face and wished I hadn't bothered to come out on this hiking trip with Emma. "I hate nature. I hate nature and nature hates me."

"How can you hate nature, Jane? You're a deer," Emma said cheerfully.

Emma was my—and I mean this without jealousy—gorgeous cherry-haired best friend. Mythology had a history of making female shapeshifters look gorgeous and male shapeshifters look monstrous, but the former was true. She was tall, curvy, and had that aura men just wanted to be around. That was a shame for them, since her interests were decidedly Sapphic.

Today, she was wearing a pair of shorts and a House Stark t-shirt with the bottom cut off to expose her midriff. Emma was wearing sandals and completely ignoring the fact that we were hiking through poor terrain with way too many bugs. She was also carrying a picnic basket like Little Red Riding Hood.

I, by contrast, was wearing a green fishing hat and a purple tie-dyed shirt over cargo pants. I had a thick backpack on that probably weighed more than I did (never go out hiking unless you are prepared for everything to go wrong) and a wooden staff in hand. The staff was mostly cosmetic since, weighing slightly over a hundred pounds, I still could lift about three or four times that much. It was one of the benefits of being a shapeshifter of Clan Cervid (weredeer, for occult laymen).

Compared to Emma, I was Plain Jane, rather than just the equally unfortunately named Jane Doe. My parents loved puns, you see. It's a weredeer thing, like the fact vampires have to count sesame seed buns and werewolves are vicious buttheads with a couple of exceptions. I was short, had freckles, only had curves when I used the right bra, and looked younger than my age. Things had gotten a little better since I'd turned nineteen, but I still felt like the ugly stepsister whenever Emma and I went out. I hated feeling that way too, since I knew it was wrong. Maybe I just needed some companionship to cheer me up. Yeah, that sort of thinking had never gotten me into trouble before.

"I killed the Earthmother's son," I said, spraying some environmentally friendly bug spray around me in response. "I honestly think Gaia has it out for me now."

I was referring, of course, to last year's event where I'd joined the ranks of those very rare mortals who'd slain a god. This particular god, whom I called the Big Bad Wolf for lack of a better name, had been a mean piece of work who'd tried to make my family a human sacrifice. It had successfully corrupted and murdered Emma's sister too. Since that time, I'd always felt vaguely uncomfortable in Bright Falls' woods that it had been the local lord of.

The thing was, though, shapeshifters needed to go out into nature. The urge to change during the full moon could be resisted, but almost no one did it. Hell, the only way to successfully resist it was to take regular trips out into the woods and get down with your wild self. That usually wasn't a problem in Bright Falls, but lately it was getting far more difficult with the sudden influx of tourists.

Supernaturals had been public for the better part of eleven years now and humanity was starting to soften its abject terror thanks to a sterling propaganda campaign by the vampires. Yes, the most dangerous and evil of us all were doing the best job at marketing themselves. It had benefited the local economy, though, as Bright Falls was only a couple of hours' drive from the Las Vegas of the Midwest in the undead-controlled New Detroit.

People who wanted to get up and close with the supernatural but didn't want to have their blood stolen or their wallets emptied had Bright Falls as an alternative. Someone somewhere had the bright—ha!—idea that shapeshifters were more family friendly and turned the town with the highest population of them in the country into a tourist trap. Outside of Michigan and five other states, it was legal to shoot us if you felt "threatened," but here the bigger danger was being cornered for a selfie.

"Don't be silly," Emma said, turning a corner in the path and finding an abandoned picnic area that looked like it hadn't been maintained in decades. "You're just upset we're in a new place and haven't yet found a spot we can run around in."

"Do you know what it's like to have a bunch of horny fourteen year olds stalk you from the bushes hoping to see some skin when you transform?"

Emma gave me a sideways look. The sort of look that said she probably had much more experience with it than I did. "We don't even get naked when we transform. That's a myth. Clothes go wherever the rest of us goes and comes back when we return to human form."

"Yeah, but tell them that," I said, flopping my backpack on the table. "This spot is as good as any."

It actually wasn't. This particular area was a patch of dead earth full of broken picnic tables surrounded by five-foot-tall grass and ancient Eastern white pine. There was a cliff about thirty feet tall that had cut the area in half. I saw the shower and bathroom area had collapsed into rubble too. Oh well, it wasn't like I was self-conscious about using the bathroom in deer form. There were just some things you had to get used to as shapeshifter.

"Are you sure?" Emma asked, looking around. "This doesn't look safe."

"We've literally faced down serial killers together," I said, sorting through my stuff.

"Yes, and I'd rather not do that ever again. Crowds of pawing tourists are not so bad compared to some of the things in Bright Falls' woods."

She was right. The Spirit World was closer to Bright Falls than in most spots on Earth, with all manner of creepy crawly things having been attracted by the Big Bad Wolf's death. That was in addition to all the spirits, ghosts, and monsters that had always been there. Just a few months ago, I'd had to put down a Wendigo who had been eating campers. It was the first human-like thing I'd had to kill.

"It wasn't so bad before your sister started giving tours," I half-joked. "Does she really want to bulldoze Shadow Pine Park and build another resort?"

"Yes," Emma said, sighing as she unpacked our lunch. Cherry pie, two thermoses of black coffee, three mushroom sandwiches (it was a deer thing), plus five or six plastic containers full of meat. The brunch of champions. "Alice thinks Bright Falls could be even better if we had a few less miles of virgin forest and a few more golf courses."

"I sense your inner eco-warrior has been stirred," I said, smiling.

"This is our home and we have to fight for it," Emma said, shaking a fist. She then spotted a small black-and-white animal nearby. "Ack, is that a skunk? Keep it away! Keep it away!"

The skunk then scurried away, thankfully not spraying us.

I tried not to giggle but failed. "You'd think she'd have more to do with all the publicity regarding the Old Wolf's trial."

Emma frowned.

"Sorry, sore subject?" I asked. "I know Marcus is your grandfather, but—"

"No," Emma said, sighing. "I'm glad he's going to jail. I just wish the trial would finish. I want to move on with my life."

Marcus O'Henry had been, until last year, the most powerful shapeshifter in North America. He'd been head of the Werewolf Clan and a man with about half a billion dollars to his name. He'd also been an abusive evil scumbag who'd tortured his children and grandchildren. It had been him who'd unleashed the Big Bad Wolf on the community.

"Alex will make sure he spends the rest of his life in jail," I said, confidant in the beautiful FBI agent I'd met.

"Have you and Agent Timmons talked lately?" Emma asked, picking up a piece of cherry pie and stabbing it with a fork.

"Hey, no dessert before the rest!" I said, mostly worried she'd want more pie than I was willing to share. "Yes, we text all the time."

Emma got a mischievous look in her face. "Have you exchanged nude photos yet?"

"Perv!" I said, appalled. "Where has my innocent best friend gone?"

"Maybe I'm in heat," Emma said.

"Or you're just a bitch," I said, smirking. "No, I haven't sent him anything like that. Not that I haven't been tempted. This long-distance thing hasn't exactly been easy."

That was understating things. I wasn't sure we were even

dating, which wasn't something you should have to ask about your boyfriend. Alex and I had had a moment together last year after taking down Marcus, a moment that could have been more if he wasn't so damned chivalrous. We'd only started getting flirty a few months ago and hadn't been able to see each other face-to-face since then. The perils of being an FBI special agent with a specialization in occult crimes.

Oh, and a wizard.

"Does he know you slept with his brother?" Emma asked, taking a big mouthful of cherry pie as she did so.

I turned bright red then stared at her. "No, no he doesn't."

Lucien Lyons and I had also had a thing. Unfortunately, said thing had died after we'd both gotten drunk one night and had amazing sex that I'd immediately regretted. Our friendship had suffered tremendously as a result. Lucien was, by the way, the gorgeous local crime lord and owner of a variety of vice-related businesses. He was also, as Emma had mentioned, Alex's foster brother.

Funny how these things work out, huh?

"You should definitely tell Alex before you sleep with him," Emma said, sagely. "It will not go well if he finds out after."

"Yes, because you are the sage of relationships, Oh Teen Wolf."

Emma giggled and I picked up my mushroom sandwich to take a bite when I heard two humans moving through the underbrush around us.

"Oh, that's not good," Emma said.

"Do you think it's more tourists?" I asked, chomping down and chewing.

"Or something worse."

That was another drawback of recent events. Marcus O'Henry wasn't exactly still in his cell. There had already been attempts on the lives of family members and Alex had texted me a couple of warnings. I was, after all, just as much responsible for his downfall as anyone else. It turned out even when you stripped a billionaire of all his visible assets, he still likely had a few million stuffed away here and there for a rainy day. There was also the possibility it was one of the region's many monsters too. You know, just in case I wasn't paranoid enough.

Moments later, a pair of heavily armed hikers stepped through the tall grass and weeds. That was not a good sign. The first one was a large white man with a cowboy hat, jeans, boots, and built like a linebacker. He had the same kind of build most male shapeshifters did, but something about his posture told me he was human. He was openly armed with a pair of holstered Berettas on his side as well as a knife on his side like an action-movie hero. He was carrying, of all things, a dowsing rod that I would have dismissed outright if not for the fact it radiated familiar magical energy that made me wonder if it had been created by someone I knew.

The second person was significantly more threatening, as she was outright carrying a futuristic rifle with laser sight, multiple clips, and a silencer on the barrel. She was an African-American woman about five foot six and built like Serena Williams. She was wearing camouflage fatigues with her hair pulled back in a ponytail. I felt the bullets inside their gun radiate out the "aura" of silver, and it smelled like their clothes had been doused in silver.

Oh crap, hunters. Not the kind that went after unintelligent animals, either.

"Howdy!" the man in the cowboy hat said, waving his dowsing rod around. "Nice to meet you."

The woman approached more cautiously.

Emma and I exchanged glances, both of us having come to the same conclusion we were in a life-or-death situation. Hunters were those humans who spent their lives going after supernaturals because we were unnatural abominations against God or whatever. Every shapeshifter child was warned about them growing up, though they'd become a legal issue after the Reveal. It was the reason virtually the entire shapeshifter population no longer lived in the states where varmint laws were still in effect.

Emma opened her mouth painfully before saying, "Hi."

I stared at them with undisguised hatred. "Move along, bigots."

"Excuse me?" The man said.

"That's Emma O'Henry, Larry, one of the daughters of the big werewolf family," the woman said.

"She's a werewolf?" the man asked, unable to believe it. "She doesn't look like it."

Emma said, "That's racist."

"You don't get to talk about racism," the woman said. "Racism is for people."

I stared at her. "My grandfather was an Odawa Indian. I'm pretty sure I know when people are out for genocide and murder. You know, what with plenty of people wanting it."

The woman glared. It was the kind of broken angry glare of someone who'd suffered terribly in their lives and needed someone to blame for it. "And what are you?"

"Weredeer," I said.

"Of course," the man called Larry said. "We have a werewolf practically cowering behind the least-dangerous shapeshifter of them all who's calling us a bunch of murderous bigots. I swear to God, I hate this job sometimes."

"I call a spade a spade," I said.

"Hey!" the woman said.

"That's an expression from Plutarch and literally means a shovel is a shovel. An FBI agent told us that," Emma said, coming out from behind me. "I'm also not cowering. You just smell awful!"

Yolanda and Larry exchanged a confused look at Emma's speech, though I wasn't sure if it was because of the first or second part.

"If you think weredeer are helpless then you don't know jack pal," I said, clutching my staff tightly. The item was hand-carved and allowed me to enhance my admittedly limited mystical talents greatly. I was ready to throw down and had the magic to do it.

*No you don't*, a voice spoke in my mind, but came from the direction of my back pocket where I could feel its owner's presence. It was the Merlin Gun, my all-purpose weapon against evil. It was an old-timey Beretta possessed by an angel. Not kidding. *They are not your enemies.*

"I'll be the judge of that," I said.

"Whom are you talking to?" the woman asked, looking equally ready for a fight.

"We're not here to fight," Larry said.

"We're not?" the woman said.

"Dial it down, Yolanda," Larry said, pointing the rod at us. "See? It's not registering anything. They're not what we're looking for."

Yolanda frowned and pointed her gun to the ground. Her actions weren't very reassuring.

"What? You have an evil-detecting rod?" I asked, snorting at the very idea.

"Basically, yeah," Larry said. "It was a gift from an FBI agent."

I paused then closed my eyes before opening them again. "Would this FBI agent, by chance, be Agent Timmons?"

The hunters exchanged a glance.

"Goddammit." Yolanda muttered. "Another group of his friends."

"Alex just became like ten percent less sexy," I muttered, remembering he'd been a hunter before he'd been an FBI agent. He'd just used magic and gone after demons and serial killers versus generic supernaturals. So of course he'd know other people who were in the same profession. I just had done my best to ignore that uncomfortable fact about him. Mages were in the middle-ground between supernaturals and regular humans. Sometimes, they were burned at the stake with the rest of us and other times they were the ones doing the burning.

*I brought you to this location*, the Merlin Gun spoke in my head. *A great transgression has been done. It must be punished.*

Oh crap. "Uh, Emma, I think I may have accidentally led us to something nasty in the woods."

Emma stared at me. "Again?"

"I don't do this on purpose!" I snapped.

Larry aimed his dowsing rod over the side of the cliff and it started jerking toward it in a comical fashion, dragging along the football-player-sized man. I found myself following him right up until the point he pointed just downward from it.

*It is there.*

Being a weredeer, I leapt down thirty feet and landed on my feet without injuring myself. I mentally made the *Six Million Dollar Woman* noise as I did so. The side of the cliff face was black rock of a kind I didn't recognize and covered in strange pictograms of red trees, a gold woman (I could only tell because it had little circle boobs on its stick figure body—men, they never change), and a bunch of other symbols I couldn't contextualize. Some of them had worn away, which helped obscure the symbols' overall meaning even further.

That was when I saw something sticking out from the ground,

underneath a pile of moss, that smelled all too human.

"Oh Goddess," I said, cleaning away the dirt and mud to reveal the bones inside. A whole pile of tiny skeletons sitting on top of one another without any of the care or love that a proper burial would have shown. All of them were newborns. I had no idea how many of them were there. It took me a second to take it all in before I ran over to one of the nearby trees and threw up.

# Chapter Two

Say what you will about humanity, but when they find out a bunch of babies have been murdered, they will usually react with the appropriate amount of shock and horror. A few hours after the discovery, Shadow Pine Park was full of every cop and state police officer in Bright Falls, plus the media.

I was forced to sit by the wooden table with Emma, drinking coffee as we were interrogated over and over again by authorities about just what we'd found and why. It helped that the authorities were ostensibly led by Clara O'Henry but even she wasn't going to be able to keep a lid on a crime this monumental.

Not that she'd want to, hopefully.

"How many were down there?" Emma asked, looking shell-shocked.

"I dunno, but a lot," I said, taking a deep breath. "Dozens at least."

"Do you think it was one of us?" Emma asked, her voice shaking a bit.

"No," I said, helpfully. "The bodies looked intact. A feral werewolf or other rabid predator shapeshifter would have torn them apart."

Emma looked at me. Her nose wrinkled in disgust and I realized that hadn't been the answer she was looking for. "You are terrible at this."

I took a sip of my sixth or so cup of coffee. "Yeah, I really am."

The two hunters were nearby, having disposed of their weapons nearby and were adopting the position of being just a pair of hikers. I could have exposed them to Clara and was tempted to, but the fact that they were, ostensibly, friends of Alex kept me from doing so. Still, I wanted to know how they knew him and what my not-really-but-maybe-someday boyfriend was doing with this.

"Maybe it was Satanists!" Emma said, speaking up as if the idea had just popped in her head. "Evil baby-sacrificing Satanists!"

"Really?" I looked at her sideways. "That's your working theory?"

"There's a lot more of them since demons turned out to be real," Emma said. "Not the atheists-who-like-to-wear-black-and-listen-to-metal kind either."

"Hey, metal is cool and a lot of it based on *The Lord of the Rings* and World War Two," I said defensively. "There's also nothing wrong with black."

Emma gave a half-smile that quickly faded. I didn't blame her for that. "Who could have done something like this, Jane? It's so… evil."

"I dunno," I said, going through various scenarios in my head. "I have a few theories, but nothing I want to think too hard upon."

In my study of ancient history, a course of a few dozen history books my magical tutor Kim Su said were "less wrong than most", there was a lot of messed-up stuff humans used to do. History was closer to a blood-filled soap opera than Disney's treatment of it with virtually every evil thing a person could do having been done somewhere sometime—and usually as part of an accepted cultural practice.

"Do I want to know the theories?" Emma asked.

"Maybe the children were unacceptable in some way," I said, frowning. "The skeletons didn't look damaged, so it was probable they were left to die of exposure. There's also a much, much more acceptable possibility."

"Which is?" Emma asked.

"It's a cemetery," I said. "Some time long ago, some rural folks took their babies who died at birth and put them here under the gravestone."

Emma blinked. "That would be much, much more acceptable."

Sheriff Clara O'Henry marched up to us, wearing a brown button-down shirt and black leather pants. A pair of mirror shades rested on her face, giving her a quiet authoritative look. She was a beautiful woman with short-cut hair and freckles mixed with a face like Naomi Watts. The fact she was considered the homely one of the sisters should tell you what the rest of the O'Henrys looked like. "The newborns were left to die of exposure."

I looked up to her. "Goddess dammit."

"Does the Goddess damn people?" Emma asked. "I thought she was all about peace, love, and Wicca."

"Wrong religion," I said, looking at her. "Deeristrianity is kind of an interface smoothie of Christianity, paganism, and magic."

"Thirty-two so far," Clara said. "Going back almost a century."

I blinked. "Okay, that's unsettling."

"Yeah, it means we're dealing with a long-lived organization like a cult—" Clara started to say.

"Or a monster," I said, frowning. "Something long-lived or immortal like a vampire."

"Or a demon," I added, remembering the Big Bad Wolf. "Maybe it was our old enemy we killed last year. It was pretty insane."

Clara grimaced. She'd briefly been the Big Bad Wolf's host and the experience had left her a changed woman. Not that I knew how, since she was still the ball-busting legalistic cop who harassed me about Lucien Lyons all the time but Emma assured me she was different. "As much as I'd like to think so, I doubt it. The Big Bad Wolf's cult ended in the fifties and it was obsessed with fertility. It wouldn't have harmed children."

I would have argued but I hadn't been mentally linked to the monster. "There's a lot of things that prey on children. Some of which live in Bright Falls."

"Fewer since you arrived," Clara said.

It was the closest thing to a compliment she'd ever given me before. "Is there anything you've seen the, uh, victims have in common?"

"What are you asking?" Clara looked down.

I closed my eyes. "Are they deformed? All girls? You know, the stuff evil patriarchal old men might think made them unacceptable? I'm thinking Craster from *Game of Thrones* here."

"Craster killed his male offspring," Emma pointed out.

"Shut up, Emma," I said.

"Sorry!" Emma winced.

I had another theory which wasn't going to be popular and that was the children didn't show any sign of being shifters. The

Pre-Reveal shapeshifter culture had been a lot more brutal and atavistic than any of my grandparents' generation had liked to admit. Marcus O'Henry would have gladly killed any human children of his lineage. The only problem with that theory was that there was no way to tell whether someone would become a shapeshifter until adolescence. There were five thousand shapeshifters in Bright Falls and twice as many humans who had shapeshifter ancestors.

"I don't watch anything but ESPN," Clara said simply. "I also don't read fantasy."

"Surely someone would have reported stolen children," Emma said. "I mean, we're not that kind of place."

"All of the children had fae blood and all of them died before the Reveal," Alex's voice spoke through the air.

My head turned to look about the dark-haired, classically handsome form of Agent Alexander Timmons. Alex was triracial, having said his grandmother was Chinese and his mother Hispanic. To me, he just looked awesome. He was wearing his usual black business suit and coat, which must have been sweltering in this heat unless he'd had it enchanted (a real possibility). He was carrying a staff like my own, which meant he was loaded for bear, as they were more blunt-force enhancers.

"How did you get here?" I asked, standing up. Last I heard, Alex was in Hawaii investigating wereshark attacks on surfers.

Alex walked over and gave me a hug. "Heimdall gave me a lift via the Rainbow Bridge."

"You know the Norse Gods?" I asked, wondering if it was possible. Alex was a spirit mage and they regularly visited the Spirit World's stranger places. The ones where gods, dreams, and imagination regularly collided.

"No, the comic book characters." Alex smiled, looking around. "Though I suppose they're more movie characters now."

"Did Loki look like Tom Hiddleston?" I asked, more curious than I should have been. "Just, you know, for clarity's sake?"

"Loki looks like whatever he wants to look like," Alex muttered. "But that's not important now."

Right. The dead children. God, I felt like an ass.

A deer's ass.

"What are you doing here, Alex?" Clara said, smiling.

I felt unconsciously jealous. "Well, we've found a big pile of bones, so why shouldn't an FBI agent be here?"

"I didn't call them, though," Clara said, crossing her arms. It was obvious she was torn between obvious gratitude for his presence and annoyance. "Also, how the hell do you know case details before I do?"

"The FBI is actually establishing a permanent regional office here and in New Detroit after the destruction of the Department of Supernatural Security. I've volunteered to take up residence here," Alex said, referring to events with the vampires.

Apparently, something had eaten the souls of all the bigoted murderous agents in Washington D.C. before re-animating them as monsters. Couldn't have happened to a nicer bunch of guys. It hadn't done much for supernatural-human relations, though, and was part of the reason varmint laws were still on the books despite shapeshifters having nothing to do with it.

"None of which is set to happen for months," Clara said, removing her sunglasses and staring.

Alex sighed. "Very well. Truth be told, I had a vision of the Lady of in the Lake telling me—"

"Stop it," Clara said, raising her hand. "Forget I asked."

"Probably for the best," Alex admitted, smiling. "As for how I recognized the bodies had fae blood, I know from experience. Prior to the Reveal, the mages of the Americas kept a watch on fae-born children, since they tended to inherit a greater propensity to the Art than most humans. I also know that, because of this, many monsters preyed on them. Including fae themselves."

Fae, or the Manitou as my grandfather called them, were those spirits who chose to merge with humans on a permanent basis. It was less like demonic possession and more like a synthesis. They passed down their genes to their human children, who merged with fae themselves. Unfortunately, they tended to grow as arrogant and ruthless as any humans with power. Combine it with the fact spirits were amoral at the best of times and plenty of them were real dickbags.

"Do you have any idea what caused this?" Clara asked the most pertinent question.

"Perhaps a Daughter of Baga Yaga or Lilith," Alex said, as if he was profiling a serial killer. White, male, may be related to Satan, mid-thirties, and you should probably check to see if he has cloven hooves.

"I take it these are real things?" Clara said. "Just because I live in Bright Falls doesn't mean I've memorized the Monstrous Manual."

I was stunned Clara had inadvertently revealed she was a geek. "Yeah, Lilith Fair aside, Lilith's daughters are actually pretty awful to women. Alex once told me they often get jobs in maternity wings to—"

"Stop," Clara said.

"Alex got the one he found."

"Stop," Clara said, shaking her head. "Consider yourself recruited, Alex; I want this thing found and killed."

"You mean arrested, right?" I asked.

"I know what I said," Clara said, walking off.

"Did you get sent here by the Lady of the Lake?" I asked.

"Yes," Alex said, watching Clara leave. "Kim Su asked me to come investigate. I sent Larry and Yolanda ahead. I'm as surprised as you that it led here, though. I was actually investigating something much more insidious."

"More insidious than mass infanticide?" I asked.

"Yes," Alex said, not missing a beat. "That doesn't mean I'm not here to help."

"Yeah, well maybe you shouldn't send hunters!" I said, angry that Alex had made time to come investigate another great evil but hadn't made time to visit in months.

"They're not like that," Alex said, taking a deep breath. "Larry and Yolanda only want to protect the innocent. They've both had very hard lives."

"Well, welcome to the rest of us," I said, growling. "What did werewolves kill their entire family?"

"Only Yolanda's," Alex said. "She only found out years later they were doing so to cover up the fact that they were kidnapping her son."

Ouch. Didn't I feel like a douchebag. "What happened to him?"

"Marcus O'Henry had him raised as a member of the werewolf clan here in Bright Falls. He left and eventually got himself shot in Louisiana. Not for being a werewolf either."

Now I felt outright shitty. "I'm sorry. That still doesn't give her permission to be High Queen of the Nasty to people just trying to have lunch."

Alex looked at me with sympathy in his eyes. "I'm sorry. It is good to see you again. I've missed you. I had nothing but the open road, bad coffee, and ill dreams to keep me company since I left Bright Falls."

I smiled. "Well, I'm glad to see you too. Maybe we can make up for our last failed first date."

"I'd like that very much," Alex said, giving as much of a smile as appropriate when you were a hundred feet from a mass grave. Which was to say, slightly pained. Then again, most people didn't have my "unique" ability to compartmentalize. "Are you still working at Pinehold?"

I grimaced. "Yeah, that didn't work out. I've been between jobs since the whole incident with the Big Bad Wolf."

I sustained myself by serving as a tour guide to all of the visitors to town I complained about constantly. As much as I hated giving out selfies, the fact was they were pretty easy to charge for since someone had put the bare bones of the story about the Big Bad Wolf on the Pinehold website. I wasn't fond of being referred to as a Native American witch since, well, I knew plenty of real Odawa who resented my inclusion, but that was racism for you. It was enough to keep the lights on, though, since Mom and Dad had entered witness protection.

"How's my brother?" Alex said, cheerfully asking about Lucien.

I stepped on Emma's foot.

Emma took the hint. "So what did you come here to investigate? You know, in case we have to Cthulhu-proof our houses or something."

Alex didn't respond as he turned to look at the woods where a man in a brilliant-white suit with a thick bushy beard and blue mirror sunglasses started tromping through with a seeming army of similarly white-clothes-wearing individuals behind him. There were men, women, and even children among them.

"Son of a bitch," Alex said.

"Hey!" Emma said. "Don't use that word! That's our word."

"Now is not the time, Emma," Alex said, clutching his staff

tightly.

The deputies and police moved to intercept the newcomers but they all took steps back and parted like the Red Sea for the man in front. He raised his hands and spoke with a Southern evangelist's flair. "We have here the sign of what the O'Henry family has wrought with its rampant destruction of these sacred woods! Evil has been brought to this town and it has cursed us all. This is why we must stop the development here and cast out the darkness."

"Who is the reverend?" I asked, wondering how the hell he'd gotten here and who he was. He wasn't a local. It was a quirk of the town that almost all of the clergy were women. I also didn't recognize any of his followers and Bright Falls citizens knew better than to wear white when tromping through the woods.

"Dr. John Winston Jones," Alex said, his look one of passionate hatred. It was a striking contrast to his usual calm and easygoing manner. "Quite possibly the most dangerous man in America."

# Chapter Three

"John Winston Jones," I said, blinking. "Wait, I know that name. Isn't he the butthead who does all those religious infomercials and internet banner ads?"

Emma looked at me. "I don't think someone Alex came here to fight would—"

"Yes," Alex interjected. "He's the leader of the Ultralogists."

"Oh, those guys," I said, snorting.

Ultralogy, despite the name, wasn't related to the similar-sounding religion based out of Los Angeles. It was a product of the Reveal with the selling point of being led by a wizard (apparently Jones) who promised to share the real secrets of the universe. Since the Reveal had shaken the faith of atheists and believers alike, it had proven pretty popular in certain circles. You too could know what happened when you died for the low price of $49.95, or $15.99 for the Kindle version.

Alex kept his gaze focused on Jones. "He's a doctor of psychology and a game theorist. Did a lot of consulting work for the FBI."

"Speaking as game, I dislike anyone theorizing on me," I said, smiling.

Alex smirked then frowned again. "I wouldn't joke. Jones is a far more powerful wizard than me."

Impressive, since I understood Alex was probably in the top twenty in the United States and top fifty worldwide.

"The FBI had a cult leader as a consultant?" I asked, watching him go into a speech for the various media outlets here that seemed to rush to give him airtime despite the fact that they had a mass murder to report on.

Alex gave a half-smile. "Before he founded the Ultralogists, Jones was heavily involved in a lot of the United States' more unsavory experiments with LSD and mind-control. MK Ultra and the Stargate Project—what the show was named after rather than the reverse."

"So he's a hundred-year-old kook who looks like a forty-year-old kook," I said, wondering if he was related to all this or if Bright Falls had two big magical problems now.

*The two problems will become related*, the Merlin Gun said. *The evildoer seeks the goddess.*

I thought back to it, *You think you could clarify that, a bit?*

*No.*

Of course. *Did anyone ever tell you that you are profoundly unhelpful?*

*Yes.*

Alex nodded. "He founded the Ultralogists after the Reveal. There was a lot more money to be made dispensing books about how the universe worked. That generally just covers up the fact that he's a major player behind the scenes. Mages who oppose his efforts to reshape society tend to die, and he knows how to harvest their power post-mortem. I have personal reasons for hating him too."

"So he's a bad guy," I asked, cutting to the heart of the matter. "Does any of his religion work?"

Alex paused before answering. "I'm hesitant to call any organized spiritual group a complete fraud if the members are sincere in their belief—"

"I'm not," I interrupted. "The difference between a cult and a religion isn't just the size."

"Then no, no it doesn't. The Ultralogy movement is just a tool for Jones to feed off of. I mean that in the literal sense. He drinks of their worship and devotion to power his magic. Believers suffer insomnia and weak wills at best, suicidal depression at worst. That's in addition to funding his lifestyle."

"Sounds like a great religion. Where do I sign up?" I asked.

Emma, I noted, looked disgusted. "Why does he want to come to Bright Falls? We don't want a cult here."

"To save the environment," Jones's voice carried over to us like a tune. "To stop the evil developers of O'Henry Construction and O'Henry Resorts and Hotels from destroying this pure natural resource."

"Deershit," I said, turning around to look at the man.

Now that I got a closer look, John Winston Jones looked even more creepy. A dull quartz crystal hung around his neck from a leather cord. His face seemed to have been through several facelifts, making him look like a man his thirties. There was a palpable aura of power from the man, magnetic in a way, but also slightly repulsive. I felt confused and dull-eyed whenever I looked at him, but felt my head clear when I looked away. He was a vampire, but not the blood-sucking kind. He was the kind who scooped up everything inside you and used it up. I hated guys like that.

Standing beside him was a tall woman about my age with long purple-dyed hair and bangs. She wasn't wearing any of the white the other members of the Ultralogists wore, but a black hoodie that read "Pandamonium" with a cuddly fat panda wrecking a table. She was also wearing ripped jeans and looked like the kind of girl who I might have been friends with during my younger, more rebellious days of last year. There was an aura of magic about her that seemed strong but diminished somehow. Both her hands were in her pockets and she was wearing a pair of extremely well-worn sneakers.

"Who are you?" Jones asked, looking at me sideways.

"Jane Doe, Shaman," I said proudly.

"Wow, your parents were cruel when they named you," Jones said, not inaccurately. "Also, look to the side."

"Why?" I said, blinking.

"Because when I look at you from one angle, I'm seeing Sherilyn Fenn and Winona Ryder, but when I look at you from another? Eh, not so hot."

"Wow," I said sarcastically. "I don't have validation from a random man off the street. However will I live with myself?"

I actually was sort of pissed, because I liked both actresses even if I questioned the resemblance.

"I try and define all people by how much they amuse me," Jones said, shrugging. "So unless your much-hotter friends want to talk, I'm going to go threaten Alex here."

"Hi," the girl beside him said.

Jones smiled and conjured a pack of gum. "Have some gum, Robyn."

Robyn looked uncomfortable but clearly picked up on the unspoken command and put it in her mouth.

"What do you want?" Alex asked, his voice low and threatening.

Jones spread out his arms and the light seemed to dim around us while glowing around him. "The reduction of Earth's population by two-thirds, a restoration of the environment, the death of all supernatural beings but mages, peace on Earth, and to find the Moonchild so I can rule the next Age of Magic through her."

"I meant here, in Bright Falls," Alex said.

"Oh," Jones said, blinking. The light around him returned to normal. "I want to stop the O'Henry family from building their next hotel here so I can underbid it and construct a spiritual retreat for the wealthy. I can also make over a billion dollars in yearly profit by selling the land's spiritual healing waters in bottle form."

"Our waters have spiritual healing properties?" I asked.

"Maybe!" Jones said cheerfully. He then pulled a bottle of water from his sleeves with town's titular waterfalls on the label before unscrewing the lid then taking a long drink. "Ah, taste the ley line convergence."

I shook my head. "So you're just a money-obsessed fraud."

"Oh no," Jones said, shaking his head. "I meant everything I said. It's just that it's amazing how much magic you can do with money. You can turn it into buildings, followers, airtime, and political power."

"Why do you want to kill all other supernaturals?" Emma asked, offended. "What did we ever do to you?"

"It's just the symmetry of the thing," Jones said before pointing at Alex. "Where is your master?"

Alex didn't miss a beat. "Why do you want to know where Kim Su is?"

"To kill her, obviously."

"I appreciate your honesty," Alex said.

"I don't!" I snapped, angry he was threatening my mentor. "Besides, you can't kill Kim Su. She's immortal. Like really immortal, not vampire immortal."

"I'll settle for chains, a mine shaft, and filling it with concrete," Jones said, still relentlessly cheerful. "I know she's taken a new student and is hoping to raise a new champion for whatever weird little agenda she's pursuing. Tell me, Alex, and you won't end up trapped in a television set forced to be a guest star on *Friends* for the rest of eternity."

Wow, forced to hang out with Courteney Cox, Lisa Kudrow, and Jennifer Aniston for all eternity. What a punishment. Oh wait, I remember the scripts. Yeah, that would be hell.

"Is that what you did to Laura?" Alex asked, barely keeping control of himself. "Banished her to some sitcom prison in the Spirit World?"

Wait, who was Laura?

"No, she's just dead," Jones said, his voice soft and yet still sarcastic. "I prophesized she would come to a bad end if she continued her investigation of our finances and she did. I understand the FBI found numerous financial irregularities, a drug habit, and affairs. Her own spouse and child were disgusted with her. Remember that when you consider crossing me."

Alex went very still. "How do I know I can trust you?"

Jones smiled. "You're just the black knight of Kim Su's pieces. I'm after the pawn she's made into a queen."

"I stole the Merlin Gun from her and it's never been returned," Alex said, shrugging as if the question was irrelevant. "She's replaced me as her student and I have no way of knowing where she is right now. I know you know that's the truth."

He was leaving out the part where we'd tried to return the Merlin Gun but she'd let us keep it, I was her student now, and while he didn't know where she was now, it was highly likely she was thirty miles away at her occult shop in the dirt mall by the Pinehold hotel.

"Don't get in my way, Alex," Jones said, pointing at him threateningly. "Destroying you would require a great deal of weregild to be paid to the gods you serve, but not so much I'm not willing to pay it. I could also target the people around you."

"Don't you just love when people talk about you like you aren't there?" I said, talking to Emma.

"Did you hear something?" Emma asked Alex.

"Ha-ha," I said. "That wasn't funny when my parents used to do it."

"Ciao!" Jones said, grabbing Robyn by the shoulder and dragging her back to the cameras.

"Wow, that guy was both intimidating and kind of dorky at the same time," I said, watching him depart. "Still, I wouldn't think of him as capable of carrying a movie as my archnemesis. *Weredeer II: The Search for More Morels* will have to look a bit further for its antagonist."

"Who is Laura?" Emma asked the question I didn't want to ask.

"Laura Lee. My partner," Alex said, taking a deep breath. He visibly deflated. "An excellent investigator and formidable mage in her own right. She was working against Ultralogy with three other agents. They were erased from existence. Not even their families remember them, only mages like me. Laura was my friend. I'd been hoping until now that she was just missing or being held prisoner. Now I know the truth."

Ouch. "You know, if you want, I can point the Merlin Gun and take him out. I'm pretty comfortable with making stupid decisions like that when they involve evil wizards."

"It wouldn't work," Alex said.

"It can kill just about anything," I said.

"Yes, but he can take over any of his followers," Alex said. "His spirit moves into their bodies and warps their flesh into a duplicate of his current body."

I blinked. "What, like in *The Matrix*?"

"Let's just say I have personal experience with this," Alex said, all but confessing he'd tried to take him out before. "There are some threats that the United States prison system is ill-equipped to hold."

Okay, that would be hard to deal with. "So he's going after our teacher and wants this land for some reason."

"Yes," Alex said, sighing. "However, he's always playing a much deeper game. She needs to be informed of this."

I had no doubt she referred to Kim Su. "I was going to ask her to help me with finding out who was responsible for the whole murder pit too."

"She might help," Alex said, frowning. "Kim Su has a soft spot for children, slaves, and runaways."

Kim Su was, at least according to her, the oldest mage in the world. She didn't look it, as the Earthmother had given her immortality when she was seventeen in the early days of what would become China. I liked her but I also noted she was in hiding from the plethora of enemies she'd made across the past few millennia. She was the oldest mage in the world rather than the strongest. I felt like telling her one of those enemies had traced her within a single county limit was not going to be news she appreciated, even if it was possible Dr. Jones was here for other reasons.

"Yeah," I said, frowning. "We're going to nail both Jim Jones and this child-killing son of a bitch."

Emma muttered under her breath. "It's like I'm a supporting player in *Wynonna Earp*."

"You're Waverly," I said without missing a beat.

Alex blinked. "You realize it's very possible the person responsible for this tragedy is probably long gone, correct? The youngest of them was killed over twenty years ago and the Reveal caused many of the most heinous supernatural to move to larger cities. Places where their crimes could be blamed on others."

"How far as you willing to go to get justice?" I asked, unwilling to imagine any circumstances that justified whoever created that pit of horrors getting away.

"As far as it takes," Alex said. "A creature that does that is a threat to the innocent."

"Damn straight," I said. "I'm the resident shaman in town and it's my job to put away the evil."

Of course, the reason I was the resident shaman in town was because I'd forced my mother to testify against Marcus O'Henry. Prior to the Reveal, she'd been the person who'd helped him with some truly heinous stuff like purging the Dragon Clan from Bright Falls. She'd also helped with some nastiness afterward, which was something I was less than pleased to find out about. Neither of my siblings had entirely forgiven me for doing it, which was damned ungrateful since I'd also saved their lives from the Big Bad Wolf.

"Good luck, Jane, and don't forget that Jones is a very dangerous man."

I paused, preparing to watch him walk away. Again. "You know, you don't have to talk to me exclusively about work."

Alex didn't move for a second. I was about to look away when he spoke. "You are in my dreams."

The two of us kissed. It was nice. Alex was older than me but someone I felt I could enjoy the company of. He was also weird and wonderful in a way that worked well with my own hundreds of quirks. Our lips lingered and while I had to stand up a bit to reach him, I didn't mind one bit. Then he was gone, having to go deal with another monster or serial killing nutjob while I was stuck here picking up the pieces.

Again.

"You should totally tell him about Lucien," Emma said, watching. "Because you two sucked face for like a minute."

"Shut up, Emma."

# CHAPTER FOUR

"Waverly?" Emma asked, following me down the dirt path of Shadow Pines Park to the parking lot. "Really?"

"What's wrong with that?" I asked cheerfully.

"You know," Emma grumbled. "You associate me with Wynonna's *sister*?"

Oh right, the fact Emma had crushed on me since about the time we'd hit puberty. That was awkward and not entirely for the obvious reasons. I was ninety-five percent into guys, but the primary problem was that she was my *best friend*. Thinking about her that way did not compute on a fundamental level. We were like Rizzoli and Isles or Rachel and Ivy from Kim Harrison's the Hollows. Okay, wait, that last one was a bad example.

"I hereby solemnly swear not to compare you to any of my blood relatives."

"Thank you," Emma said, putting her hand over heart. "I also promise, in return, never to speak of how hot your sister is."

"Ugh," I said, making a gagging gesture.

"Are you really going after both these guys?" Emma asked. "I mean, the head of a cult and the baby-killing cult or demon?"

"Why not?" I asked, wondering why it was even an issue.

"I don't know—is it your job?" Emma asked, sounding unsure even as she looked back toward the way we came. "It could be dangerous."

No shit, Sherlock. Of course it was dangerous. That was part of the reason I was doing it. "The Big Bad Wolf was dangerous."

"Yes, but it was going after our families," Emma said, causing me to deflate a little. "It killed my sister and threatened your brother."

"Now it's going after someone else's sister and brother," I said, not really getting her point.

"I see," Emma muttered under her breath. "Never mind, forget I said anything."

"Are you scared?" I asked. "It's okay if you are. I mean, not all of us are adrenaline-addicted supernatural bounty hunters."

"I'm not fawning over you, truly," Emma said. "But mostly I'm worried about you getting shot like Bambi's mother."

"Oh, the puns."

"More like a comparison."

We reached the bottom of the staircase that had two large hedges blocking our view of the parking lot and I turned to give her a hug. "I'll make sure no one turns me into venison. I've herd you."

"Get a room, you two," the voice of my other closest friend (sort of) called from the parking lot.

I grumbled and pulled away before walking out into the parking lot and seeing a four-person group I didn't expect to see together. It was Maria Gonzales, the aforementioned friend, who was standing there in a black sexy goth Catholic schoolgirl's uniform with a black wig on, despite it being her natural hair color. Maria was my other best friend, a wereraven, and my brother's girlfriend. They had an unconventional relationship I tried not to think about because, hey, brother, but mostly seemed to be built around a monogamous relationship that allowed them to sleep with other people.

Standing beside Maria was my older brother, Jeremy, who was a handsome (from a sisterly perspective) dark-haired man wearing a House Baratheon t-shirt underneath a leather jacket and ripped jeans. He'd gone through a bit of a growth spurt, which made him about a foot taller than me now.

Jeremy wasn't a weredeer despite being the child of two, because shapeshifting was always hit-or-miss when passed down. He was, however, a pretty good mechanic and had taken up a semi-honest job working for one of Lucien's legitimate businesses. The fact he still dealt drugs on the side made me want to smack the hell out of him even though his primary product was legal in Michigan.

The two other people present were Alice O'Henry and Jeanine Doe. They were dressed identically with red jackets and white pants meant to deliberately resemble fox-hunting costumes. Alice O'Henry was, in simple terms, so gorgeous you could probably describe her as looking like Nicole Kidman's more-attractive sister.

Jeanine had brown hair but, mimicking Alice, looked a great deal like her. That was probably genetics at work, since it turned out she was my half-sister by Emma's adopted father, Christopher—it's complicated—which meant she was also Alice's niece despite being unrelated to Emma. Still, the revelation made Emma's longstanding crush on her all the weirder.

The four of them were gathered in front of my car I'd dubbed the Millennium Falcon. It was a green 2001 Hummer my grandfather had owned and got roughly a mile to the gallon. Given I couldn't afford a new car on my own and it was damn near indestructible, I'd come to appreciate my vehicle a lot more than I'd used to even if it wasn't exactly eco- or finances-friendly. Lucien had, before I'd screwed up our relationship, also gotten the car enchanted with a few blessings that made it even harder for evil to get at me inside.

"Is this an intervention?" I asked, looking between everyone. "Because if it is, I'd like to state that Alice shouldn't be here. I have enough bitch in my life with Emma."

"Hey!" Emma said before pausing. "Oh, wait, that's actually funny. Also, racist against female werewolves."

"Only if you take it as a bad thing, which it is in Alice's case," I said. "She's our town's much prettier Cruella De Vil."

Alice smiled. "My dear, I would very much love to make a deer-skin rug out of you, but I suspect Jeanine would object."

"You would be right," Jeanine said, frowning.

"Also Emma," Alice said.

"Hey!" Emma said.

"You wouldn't object?" Alice said, raising her eyebrow.

I looked around the parking lot, noticing there was a surprising lack of people present for such a disaster. Then again, the vast majority of them were back up at the crime scene. Still, it was unusual to see Alice O'Henry present without her army of cronies. I supposed Jeanine was enough of one for her.

"Listen, guys, I've already got the makings of a really crap day starting, so if we could cut to the chase it would be nice," I said, unhappy to say the least. I would have loved to have my brother and sister show up on my doorstep normally. A year ago, I'd been incredibly close with Jeremy and friendly rivals with my sister. I'd barely talked to them since they'd almost been sacrificed, though, and didn't think there was anything good coming from this conversation with Alice's presence.

"Yes, you've created a real shit storm for us," Alice said, putting her hands on her hips. "You didn't think to call me or someone else before exposing our town's dirty laundry to the media?"

I stared at her. "You mean, I didn't think of calling someone other than the authorities when I found a bunch of dead newborns? No, I can't say I thought of that."

Alice stretched out her hands as if trying to resist the urge to strangle me. "This will be national news, Jane. We're making progress as a species to get recognition as having equal rights with regular humans and protection against bigots. This has the potential to set us back to the beginning. Witch-burnings, internment camps, and hunters with the full support of the government."

"Shapeshifters didn't kill those children," Emma said, blinking.

That wasn't something I was sure about yet. They hadn't done it because of instincts, but there were plenty of possibilities for shapeshifters wanting to leave fae-blooded children to die.

"It won't matter," Alice said, staring at her sister. "All that matters is the fact this was done on shapeshifter land."

I rolled my eyes, not remotely convinced by her argument. "And the fact that this probably affects your plan to build a hotel on the area isn't remotely affecting things. Hard to build a resort on the place where there was a murder pit, isn't it?"

Alice's face contorted and grew exaggerated canines as both her hands became covered in fur.

I pulled out the Merlin Gun, keeping it on the ground. "You don't want to know if my gun thinks you're an evildoer."

"Whoa!" Jeremy said, stepping in between us. "Dial it down, you two."

Alice growled at Jeremy, causing him to take a step back toward me.

"Please don't kill my aunt, Jane," Emma said.

"I'm not afraid of you," I said, putting my gun away. "My family has been here every bit as long as you and I've seen gods, demons, and worse. It will take more than money and threats to scare me. I'm not a deer afraid of wolves."

Alice pulled back her anger then looked around. "There's a

pecking order to this world, Jane. You should learn to respect where you are in it."

"Yeah, I'm at the top of it," I said, sighing. "But maybe you can tell me why the hell you're here with my siblings."

Jeanine had pulled away from Alice during her transformation, a look of fear and concern on her face I'd never seen before. My sister was a sorceress and shaman herself, but since taking the job as Alice's personal assistant, she'd become diminished, and that worried me. What had happened to the person I'd grown up with? The girl I'd used to steal the makeup from and envy? What had happened to Jeremy that he was defending her boss?

"Wow, you've really become Wild West Jane," Maria said cheerfully. "I like it."

Jeremy looked at Maria in exasperation.

"Oh, by the way, if you need me to feather Alice, I'm totally cool with that," Maria said, giving me two thumbs up.

Jeremy covered his face with his palm. "Oh God and Goddess."

"We're here to talk business," Jeanine said, intervening. "Nothing more. It was something we had scheduled for today even before we discovered the tragedy."

"Which we'll be fixing," Alice said, returning her features to normal. "I've put too much effort into the Shadow Pines Project to let some freakish West Coast hippie cult ruin it, Indian burial ground or not."

"Oh, you are not going to state that this was something done by the First Nations," I said, about ready to cast a hex on her.

Alice was about to say something nasty again.

Jeanine ended my focus on Alice with a single sentence. "Jane, we've decided to sell the Deerlightful Diner. We need you to sign off on it, though."

You could have knocked me over with a feather. "What? You can't sell Mom and Dad's business!"

Emma covered her mouth with her hands, horrified. "We still eat there every day!"

"Yeah and none of us are working there," Jeremy said, shaking his head. "It's not exactly a family business anymore and it's barely making enough money to stay open. We managed to get in touch with Mom and Dad through the FBI. They're okay with it."

Witness Protection wasn't nearly what it was supposed to be. Then again, there was the fact that you couldn't exactly move shapeshifters to states where it was legal to shoot them either, and we'd declined moving. "That business is a part of our lives and belonged to Grandpa Jacob before it belonged to us."

"We need the money, Jane," Jeremy said, looking over at Maria. "Some of us have plans, and you aren't exactly rolling in cash either. Alice has made a fair offer."

"More than fair," Jeanine said. "Enough that we can start focusing on moving our lives forward after last year's tragedy."

"You want to demolish the Deerlightful Diner so you can build another one of your crappy casinos, don't you?" I said, disgusted.

Alice rolled her eyes. "Bright Falls has the potential to be more than a dying city and pitstop on the way to New Detroit. A greasy spoon in the middle of downtown doesn't exactly contribute much to the city versus all the jobs new entertainment complexes can."

"Will anybody be able to afford to live in your new Bright Falls?" I asked, disgusted.

"Don't be a child, Jane," Jeanine said, a lifetime of disdain crammed into five words.

"If you think I'm going to hand over our family—"

That was when I was knocked to my knees by an ear-piercing screech that shattered several car windows around the parking lot. Every other shapeshifter in the group, save Maria, also fell to their knees, as the enhanced hearing of both wolves as well as deer made it a crippling attack. Maria and my brother covered their ears but still managed to stand on their own two feet.

Looking up into the sky, I had to blink several times in order to make sure I wasn't seeing an illusion since a Volkswagen-sized eagle was coming down toward us. It was the size of a J.R.R Tolkien member of that race, except there was something sickly wrong with it. A black disgusting tar was covering his wings and body, oozing and twisting around it like it had just come from bathing in an oil slick. The creature's torso also surprised me too because it was feline and golden underneath the patches of oil. It took me a second to process the descending wholly organic stealth bomber was a frigging griffon.

Despite what you might think about this making me a hypocrite,

I didn't actually believe griffons existed until this moment. I mean, just about anything human beings could conceive existed in the Spirit World, but that was made of human dreams as much as the reverse, so that didn't count. Things like car-sized eagle-lions were not things that existed in this world for obvious reasons.

By the time my mind adjusted to the fact I was in the face of the impossible, I saw it was diving toward Alice O'Henry and my siblings.

"Son of a pus bucket," I said, grabbing Alice and turning into a deer in one single motion, bounding away from the Falcon in my new form. Alice was on my back, weighing more than I expected, and I hoped I'd made the right choice in rescuing the griffon's target.

To my mixture of fear and relief, the griffon didn't smash into the Falcon or go after my siblings but shifted position to go after a new pair of targets: us. Alice cursed at me in a mixture of three different languages before I came to a stop across the road. Turning back into a human, I barely managed to avoid having my head taken off as both Alice and I fell to the ground.

The griffon let forth another ear-splitting howl before flying over near us, landing with a *thump,* and assuming a leonine attack position.

I pulled out the Merlin Gun, dropping my staff, and aimed at my attacker. "Ten points from Gryffindor!"

Oh God and Goddess, that was terrible. Still, I fired, twice.

It barely reacted, gnashing at me and advancing.

*Uh, why isn't it dead?* I asked my gun.

*It is an animal. It is not evil.*

*Oh come on!* I snapped.

*I don't make the rules.*

*Who does?* I snapped.

*God.*

Ask a stupid question and get a stupid answer. Still, the Merlin Gun was still a real gun with a clip of enchanted steel-jacketed silver bullets. I took aim, steadied myself, and fired repeatedly at the creature's face. Because it was a creature of magic, it didn't die, but the creature did cover its face with its wings in pain.

Alice, who had spent most of her life in boardrooms rather than learning to fight like a "proper" werewolf, ruined her suit trying to climb to her feet but didn't shift immediately. I suspected giant eagles were a new one for her too. The griffon then pulled its wings away and lifted up its claws to attack us both, only to have a six-foot-long wolf land on the griffon's back before tearing into it with her claws.

Emma!

The attack continued with Maria flying up above in a hybrid of crow and woman form to throw glowing feathers onto its back. The griffon thrashed and roared even as the black goop covering it seemed to grow thicker, seeping into its wounds and causing the creature immense pain. The griffon's cries grew erratic then it flopped over, thrashing like a wounded animal.

*The spellbinding is poorly done and killing it*, the Merlin Gun said.

"Can it be helped?" I spoke aloud, having only two bullets left.

*It can be put down. I will help you do that.*

"So you'll help me mercy kill a griffon, but not kill it when it's trying to kill someone?"

*When that someone is evil, yes.*

"You suck."

Emma leapt off the wounded griffon's back as I aimed the Merlin Gun and felt its power charge. I fired a single bullet into the creature's heart. The creature glowed for a second as all of the black sludge burned off its body before it fell over dead. It was a majestic creature, one I felt bad about being unable to help.

"Someone sent that thing to kill Alice?" I asked.

*Yes.*

"Who are you talking to?" Alice asked, covered in mud and looking embarrassed.

"Mr. None of Your Damned Business," I said, walking over to look at the creature. "Well, I'm not a detective or anything, but I think it's very likely the work of Dr. Jones."

*Probably*, the Merlin Gun said.

Alice's face shifted as she stared at me then the creature. "That filthy mage thinks he can kill me? I'll tear his cult down around his ears."

"Uh…" I started to say. "I don't think it's a good thing to go after this guy. He's hella powerful."

"Shut up!" Alice growled, looking down at her ruined outfit. "I owe you a debt and it will be repaid, but don't test me."

"A debt enough not to buy the Deerlightful?" I asked.

"No," Alice said, walking over to my siblings, who'd watched the whole thing from the sidelines. Both looked ashamed, and I wondered if they felt like they should have contributed. Jeanine had abandoned her shaman training for business school while Jeremy didn't have any powers. I couldn't help but feel disappointment in both of them, not for not helping, but for the fact that they were allied with someone like Alice in the first place.

And for money!

Emma and Maria both assumed their human forms.

"Need any more help?" Maria asked. "I mean, aside from killing this giant bird-lion?"

I looked over at it. "Well, I'm not getting rid of its body. You should call the forestry service or something."

I couldn't imagine that would help out Alice's plans to develop the area. I imagined the media would be on the discovery of a "new" species like a griffon every bit as much as the murder pit. I hoped no one identified me as the person who killed the only probable griffon on Earth at this time. That would totally ruin me with the tourists.

"Gotcha," Maria said, walking over and putting her hand on my shoulder. "You know, Jeremy didn't want to do this. He just wants to get out of drug dealing and live a normal life. Buy a house and so on."

"Yeah, right," I said, not believing that was in my brother's plans at all. "If you'll excuse me, Maria, I have a mage to go see."

Emma just watched her aunt leave and I wondered what she'd thought about all this. Alice hadn't even bothered to thank her.

What a bitch.

# CHAPTER FIVE

It wasn't a very long drive from Shadow Pines Park to Kim Su's strip mall. It was not the sort of place you expected an archmage to hide. Then again, that would be sort of the point of hiding wouldn't it? If she had a big Isengard-style tower in the middle of Michigan it wouldn't exactly be that hard for people like Dr. Jones to find her.

Still, I couldn't help but a feel a bit disappointed every time I drove up to "Kim Su's The Tower – For All Your Occult and Scented Candle Needs" right next to the liquor store and Lowcost Buy. The entire place was covered in magical glyphs and runes so no one but friendlies would be able to see it, but didn't have the kind of verve you'd associate with the world's biggest do-gooder. The fact she was hiding and had been for the better part of the past few decades also hurt my respect for her.

Parking the Millennium Falcon across the street from her, I looked over at Emma. "So what do you think I should bring up first when I talk to her: the murder pit, the Ultralogists, or the fact that Mrs. Potter is trying to shut down the Deerlightful?"

Emma frowned. "You don't think it's a good idea to sell out?"

I stared at her. "Emma, how could you even think that?"

Emma blinked at me. "Because I know you've got a bunch of bills you're barely able to pay off. You haven't been able to go to Bright Community and Technical since taking up classes with Kim Su, either."

"Learning how to be a wizard is more important than learning how to be a writer," I said, making a somewhat painful admission. "There will be chances for that latter."

"Will there?" Emma asked. "Also, have you even learned how to do any magic?"

"We're still studying the theory of magic," I said, sounding a bit more defensive than I wanted to. "Apparently it involves a lot of theory."

"What can you do?" Emma asked.

"I can read objects!"

"You could do that before!" Emma said, looking over at me and shaking her head.

She was right, sort of anyway. Fighting the kelpie of Darkwater Lake, I'd discovered accidentally that I could share my object readings with someone else in contact with the object. It saved my life, but it also showed me that I hadn't really explored what I could do. With Kim's help, I was getting better at shifting between different impressions in an object, and changing perspectives while in the vision. Still, it was arguably little progression versus being able to throw fireballs or turning people into newts.

I decided to switch subjects. "Seriously, Emma, you can't tell me you think I should sell out to your aunt. The Deerlightful is part of my heritage."

"I'm thinking about practicality," Emma said, reminding me she was an O'Henry. "I get a piece of everything Alice makes with O'Henry developments. Even if most of it is tied up in trusts and lawyers, I can give you my section of whatever she makes from all this and encourage Alice to give enough so that your family is taken care of until your parents come home."

I rolled my eyes. "I don't need or want your charity. I don't want my parents coming home to having no business to run either."

"Will they even want to run it after this?" Emma said, unknowingly twisting the knife. "I mean, when the trial finally happens, it's going to drag a lot of nastiness through the mud. Things like human sacrifice—"

"Stop," I said, raising my hand. "Collaborate and something-something, Ice is back with a brand new blah-blah. I get what you're saying. I just don't agree."

Emma said, unbuckling her seatbelt, "It's just four walls and a kitchen is all I'm saying."

"It's more than that," I said, remembering growing up there. "Emma, you don't think like normal people."

"Define 'normal,'" Emma snorted.

"You thought *Pound Puppies* was a cartoon about a concentration camp."

"It is! Think about it from their perspective."

"Regardless of whether that's right or wrong, that's not thinking like normal people."

"Normal is overrated," Emma said. "I'm a lesbian werewolf and proud of it."

"There's nothing abnormal about either of those," I said, unbuckling my seatbelt. "I mean, yeah, there's some question about whether you need to tell a date you've maybe got heartworm, but you're taking medicine for that."

Emma glared. "Buck off."

"Hehe," I said, deliberately enunciating my laugh. "It's funny because we're both being racist to each other."

Emma smirked. "We both have mixed ancestries in more ways than one."

"America as it should be."

Heading into Kim Su's shop with Emma following me, I saw a single long chamber full of tables and shelves containing magical items. Unlike Harry Potter's version of them, they all looked like normal objects, but they'd had special meaning to their owners that allowed mages to use them as material for their spells. Teddy bears that kept away evil spirits, lucky rabbits' feet that were actually lucky (just not for the rabbit), playing card decks whose owners never lost, and so on. There were books of and about magic, but those were all hit or miss. Magic came from the will of the user rather than any mystical language and you could get as much oomph from saying, "El Blasto this guyo!" as an Enochian phrase.

Kim Su was sitting behind the glass counter to the left of the room. She had her feet up on the counter and was reading a newspaper. Despite being the oldest human alive, at least as far as I knew, she didn't look all that much older than me. Indeed, she looked like a Chinese girl who'd just started college with blue jeans and a Yoda t-shirt. She didn't acknowledge my presence and just turned the page to the comics section.

Walking up beside her and pulling over a stool to sit across from her, I said, "So where to begin—"

"There's a murder pit, the Ultralogists are in the city looking for me with their chess-obsessed leader, and your restaurant is for sale."

"It is not for sale," I corrected her. "How did you know any of that?"

"I used my palantir," Kim Su said.

I stared at her. "You forget, I know Alex and he owns an honest-to-God lightsaber. I don't know if you're kidding."

"Not kidding but cheating," Kim Su said, handing me her newspaper.

I picked up the newspaper and stared at the date. "This is tomorrow's newspaper."

"Yep," Kim Su said. "The clock tower is going to be destroyed by a lightning bolt at midnight, so if you want to get back to your time, you'll have to hit eighty-eight miles per hour perfectly."

I stared at her. "You know, it's funny when I make the pop-culture references. Not so much you."

"That's because you don't get my Jack Benny and Sun Wukong references."

Emma didn't respond to our conversation and, instead, wandered around the shop looking for new knick-knacks to fill her collection out. Despite having no talent for magic, my bestie loved how enchanted objects felt to her shapeshifter senses. Mostly she bought small but useless things like a sweater that was always snug and warm or a chocolate bar that renewed every night if you didn't eat all of it.

I leaned in on the counter and looked at her. "Well, obviously, I'm going to need your help in solving the problem."

"That's too bad," Kim Su said, taking back the newspaper. "Because this is really not my scene."

"Oh come on, Alex said you have a soft spot for children!"

"I do," Kim Su said, frowning. "But there's nothing that can be done for these fallen ones."

"Prevent their killer from striking again."

Kim Su's eyes turned to me and I got a sense of just how old she was. While she never talked about it, she occasionally dropped hints about just how much rape and murder she'd witnessed across the millennia. Enough to break a thousand mages, let alone one, but she'd kept on trucking regardless. "Are you familiar with the story of Abraham and Isaac?"

"From the Bible?" I asked, wondering about this sudden change in topic.

Kim Su's gaze narrowed. "No, the two guys who tend bar down at Applebees. Yes, of course from the Bible!"

I raised my hands. "Okay, okay. Yeah, I know the story. God asked Abe to sacrifice his son, Abe tried to, and God said, 'Just kidding. Lol. Take a goat instead.' Not my favorite passage in the book."

Kim blinked a couple of times. "Not quite how I remember the story, but essentially, yes."

"I always felt God was being a bit terri-bad there."

Kim frowned. "The common interpretation was that God was testing Abraham's capacity for obedience and trust in his deity."

"Isn't that right?"

"It is if you're trying to apply it to twenty-first-century values. The truth is there were another lesson people my age would pick up on."

"Which was?" I asked, genuinely surprised even if I wasn't a big fan of theology. I mean, I knew millions of gods and spirits existed, so the issue of faith was kind of a nonstarter with me. I mean, hell, my gun was an angel.

*Don't mention Hell in the same sentence as me,* The Merlin Gun projected to me.

*What if I said, 'and my gun helped me shoot up Hell'?* I suggested back to it.

*That is acceptable.*

"The passage can also be interpreted as the more straightforward: don't sacrifice your children," Kim Su explained.

I looked at her sideways. "Did that really need to be said?"

"Unfortunately, yes," Kim Su said, sighing as she picked up a bottle of whiskey from behind the counter. "The cult of Moloch, more a series of practices than a god, was one of the most popular religions at the time. It managed to last right up until Carthage when the Romans exterminated it. The Romans were no strangers to infanticide themselves, but even they thought the group was sick. The Romans and Jews were pretty much the only people at the time who thought baby sacrifice was a bad idea. Strange bedfellows."

"So this could be related to Moloch?" I asked, blinking.

"I knew it was Satanists!" Emma called from the back of the shop.

"No," Kim Su said. "I eventually destroyed the last of the spirits tied to the cult with the Merlin Gun in 1945. However, those babies out in Shadow Pine Forest were laid out before an altar. I don't think whoever was doing it expected them to die, though. Someone was meant to pick them up, but that person or persons weren't there anymore."

I blinked. "Wait, someone was dumb enough to leave children exposed and never pick up on the fact that they were dying?"

Kim shrugged and went back to reading her paper. "I cannot say more."

"Can't or won't?" I asked.

"Can't," Kim Su said, pointing to the television set behind the counter. *The Vanilla Ice Project* is on. He flips houses now, you know."

I reached over and mock strangled her. "Kim, this is serious."

"So is this!" Kim Su said, lifting up her remote. "I have every confidence you can handle this, Jane. Hunt a demon for a man and you'll be hunting them for a lifetime. Teach a man to hunt demons and it's not your problem."

"That is *terrible* advice," I said, appalled.

Kim Su's voice lowered as she stared forward. "All I can tell you, Jane, is that the situation with the fae-blooded has been resolved."

"Resolved," I said, at first skeptical then angry. "How exactly does that resolve a century or so of child murder? Because I'm hoping it involved a flamethrower."

Kim Su went back to watching her TV show. "I can't say any more about it, Jane. I gave my word."

That was the end of it. I wasn't being sarcastic either. One thing you learned when dealing with older supernaturals was that they all put really big stock in their word. It wasn't about personal honor or anything so easily discarded either. It was a simple matter of, when you could alter reality with your mind, you tended to not need much from or fear anyone but another magic-user. The only way such encounters could progress was if the other party could trust the other's promise.

"Well, dammit," I said.

"Don't worry, Jane," Kim Su said, briefly looking back from Robert Van Winkle's show. "I meant it when you said you'll be able to handle this. He'll probably start killing innocent people to lure me out, but I can handle that."

"That's a little cliché," I said, thinking about all the various shows I'd seen people doing that on.

Kim Su didn't bother to look away from the TV as she circled a personal ad that contained a chess move as well as a loose description of a young female in her late teens who was presumably the intended victim. Apparently, this was Dr. Jones's plan to lure her out. Keep killing people until she came to the rescue. The sad fact was that I wasn't sure it would work as she was a big-picture sort of gal and greatly attached to her own life. You needed to be if you were willing to live past your first hundred years, let alone a thousand.

"John Winston Jones isn't exactly a fountain of originality," Kim Su said, frowning. "He couldn't even come up with his own religion. It's just a shapeless combination philosophy of a bunch of other people's ideas. Like Jeet Kune Do except sucking instead of being awesome. Mmm, Bruce Lee."

I hesitated in my next question. "Do you need help with him?"

"He's a pussycat compared to his master, but is too dangerous to directly attack, especially with his followers serving as walking batteries. Worse comes to worst, I'll leave Bright Falls and lure him away so he won't be a threat to the people here."

"Alex says he's immortal."

"Everyone is immortal and everyone isn't." Kim Su shrugged. "I'm more concerned that Alex is going to try to do something stupidly heroic."

I rolled my eyes. "Oh yes, it would be terrible for him to stop the bad guy from murdering people."

"I know, right? You'd think he'd have learned by now," Kim Su said, probably joking. She turned back to me. "Okay, I've seen this episode. How are you and Alex doing anyway? Have you told him you slept with his brother yet?"

I blinked. "Wait, what? Who told you about that!"

"Sorry!" Emma called from the comic book aisle. "She tricked me into telling her."

"Asking is not tricking, dear," Kim Su said, turning around to face me.

"She's the deer!" Emma said.

"Oh, Goddess," I said, covering my face.

"I don't see what's to be ashamed of," Kim Su said, smirking. She then adopted a dramatic and exaggerated speech pattern. "Weredeer are creatures of wild untamed passions, the succubi of shapeshifters, prone to uncontrollable torrid love affairs as well as luring men to their doom!"

I stared at her then raised one eyebrow. "Uh-huh."

"It's all true," Kim Su said, smirking. "Go read the myth of the Deer Woman in any book about Native American mythology. Besides, female Cervid should only hook up with men during mating season and raise their children alone if American. In Europe, you would be part of a stag lord's harem. Which would be a good basis for a story where you led a bloody revolt!"

"Stop being a hind," I said, rolling my eyes.

Kim Su sighed. "You see? That's why I don't interact much with shapeshifters anymore. You've all gone soft. Werewolves should be wild and vicious predators who smolder with generic rage! Not…"

Emma opened a jar on a shelf that contained a butterfly, causing it to fly up above her head as she batted it several times.

"I like Emma just the way she is," I said, smiling. "Well, if you're not going to help, then I'll shop around for some goodies to help me with my investigation. Alex is going to need my help and while I believe you that it's been resolved, the Merlin Gun says there's been a terrible atrocity that needs avenging."

"The Merlin Gun thinks Velcro is a terrible atrocity that needs avenging," Kim Su said, her sarcasm even more biting than mine. "Don't always believe it."

I didn't but it was hard to think there could be any circumstances that could justify what I'd seen. Those bones would haunt my nightmares for decades to come. "By the way, while your prices are pretty reasonable, uh—"

"You can't pay for anything," Kim Su said.

"Err, no," I said, blanching. "I could, however, get you a nice discount at the Deerlightful on some delicious cherry pie. If I don't eat it all bringing it to you, at least."

Kim Su shook her head. "Take what you need, Jane. I'll add it to your tab. Just beware it's not a good idea to be in debt to a wizard. Even one as affable as me."

"For you are subtle and quick to anger. Gotcha."

Kim Su snorted. "I much prefer Galadriel to Gandalf. She should have taken the ring and laid waste to the countryside. Would have made a more interesting story."

I was about to respond when the front door of Kim Su's shop opened. I turned to look at who had arrived, half expecting Alex, since only certain people could see her store, but was instead stunned by the appearance of the purple-haired girl from earlier. Robyn. One of Dr. Jones's cultists had found us.

Crap.

"Uh, hi," Robyn said, looking around. "This is going to sound crazy but is one of you Jane Doe the shaman? I need her help."

# Chapter Six

The sight of one of Dr. Jones's cronies in Kim Su's shop made me immediately reach for my gun, hidden in the back of my pants underneath my t-shirt. I wasn't going to let that crazy cult leader get anywhere near my mentor. As soon as my fingers touched the Merlin Gun, though, I heard its voice in my head. *She is not evil.*

Oh, cool, it was rare that the Merlin Gun gave a straight answer like that.

It continued speaking in my head, She is lustful, vain, materialistic, and rude. In other words, she is a typical twenty year old of this time period.

*Grading on the curve, huh?* I asked.

*No,*Raguel responded.

"I'm Jane the shaman," I said.

The woman named Robyn looked at me then Kim Su then at Jane. "No, seriously."

I glared. "I really am."

Robyn raised an eyebrow. "Is this one of those magically young sort of things? You know, where you look like a teenager but are actually ancient?"

"Don't you hate those?" Kim Su said, turning around on her stool. "I mean, who would want to look like a young adult for millennia? I mean, you'd get no respect from anyone and have to constantly assert yourself."

"No," I said, taking a deep breath. "I am a shaman and I am nineteen."

"She's the shaman because her mom got sent to jail," Emma said cheerfully.

I shot her a glare.

"To testify!" Emma corrected rapidly. "Not to jail. It just feels like she's in jail because she's in Witness Protection and she would have gone to jail unless—"

"Stop helping, Emma," I said, sighing.

"Wow," Robyn said, blinking. "Well, that makes things easier a bit. This is going to sound strange—"

"It probably won't," I said, interrupting. "I live in a world of incredibly surreal and supernatural things."

Emma lifted up a golf club. "Like this driver is blessed to kill demons! It's not just a joke in *Dogma* anymore!"

Robyn looked over at Emma. "And she is?"

"Emma O'Henry, werewolf slayer of darkness!" Emma said proudly. "I have wounded and bitten many an unholy thing! Like six!"

"Uh-huh," Robyn said, clearly taking Emma's posturing as seriously as it deserved.

"Jane Doe," I said, introducing myself.

"Really?" Robyn asked, looking at me. "Did your parents hate you?"

"I wonder sometimes," I said. "Yet, their last name was Doe, so it was a temptation they could not resist. I also have aunts and a great-grandmother named that."

"You poor thing," Robyn said, walking toward me and putting her hand over her heart. "I am Robyn Taylor. I am…weird."

"Weird," I said.

"I know things," Robyn said, shrugging. "I can sense where things are. I can even know whenever someone is lying. Which is always, by the way. I have a lot of luck, both good and bad. However, I can't do magic and I'm not a vampire or a shapechanger. My best ability is also kind of creepy."

"Your best ability?" Kim Su asked.

"You are—?" Robyn asked, looking at her.

"Amelia Earhart," Kim Su said.

Robyn blinked. "Wow, the parents in this town are cruel. Yeah, well, my best ability is something I can never use ethically. Let me show you."

Kim Su ducked behind the counter.

I was about to tell Robyn she didn't need to demonstrate anything when everything around her seemed to dim. The air smelled of the woods and I instantly relaxed as Robyn became the single sexiest thing I'd seen in my entire life. It was a full-on *Wayne's World*, "Dreamweaver" playing in the background love-at-first-sight moment. I wanted to wrap my arms around her, kiss her, and ask where she'd been all my life.

Then it was over.

I shook my head and blinked rapidly, noticing Emma was now wrapping her arms around Robyn and nuzzling her. Robyn tried to pull herself free, gently at first, before pushing her away.

"Oops, sorry," Emma said.

"What the hell was that?" I asked, coughing a bit and trying to get the sensation out of my head.

"My Gift," Robyn said, sighing. "It usually only affects straight guys like that."

Emma looked away. "Well, it's a power that works on most men and some women, I'd guess."

"Ah," Robyn said, grimacing. "Sorry about that."

"You have the power of *magical roofies*?" I asked, appalled.

"Pretty much," Robyn said, sticking her tongue out in disgust. "I can outright control people when I kiss them or touch them during that state."

"That sounds both awesome and very evil," I said, thinking through the implications.

"Yeah," Robyn said, sighing. "Thankfully it's voluntary now that I've reached adulthood. It was killer on my love life before."

"You're like Poison Ivy from *Batman*!" Emma said, staring. "That is incredible!"

"Did you miss everything I just said?" Robyn asked.

"No," Emma said, pausing. "I was thinking of us buying a house together, though. I'm going to go get some fresh air."

"Probably a good idea," Robyn said.

Emma ran out of the front door and starting breathing the strip mall air in and out.

"Dryadkin," Kim Su said, popping up from behind the counter with a set of polarized sunglasses and a pair of nose plugs in. "Probably first generation."

"What now?" Robyn asked.

Kim Su's voice was slightly altered by her nose plugs to be more nasal. "A specific form of fairy-kin, i.e. the son or daughter of a Dryad. They possess supernatural beauty, charisma, and the ability to talk to plants or help them grow."

"I do have luck growing a certain kind of plant," Robyn said, rubbing her chin. "It's for personal use only, though. I also talk to my plants."

"Well, lots of people do that," I said, unsure what to make of her.

"Well, they talk back," Robyn said, chuckling. "That settles one reason I'm here. I was hoping to find some insight into what I was. I certainly wasn't getting it with the Church of the Emptied Bank Account."

"So you're not one of the Ultralogy cult?" I asked.

"Oh, hell no." Robyn snorted, putting her right hand one her hip. "I'm an atheist. I don't go in for any of that religious mumbo jumbo."

The Merlin Gun growled.

*Down, Raguel,* I thought, using the Merlin Gun's actual name. He'd shared it with me during the Wendigo hunt. *Please don't change your opinion of shooting her now that we've started to become friends.*

*Ignorance is not a sin by itself.*

*What, really?* I asked. *I thought it would be up there. Like fixing your door on a Saturday.*

*Ignorance is to be corrected, a sin punished,* Raguel replied.

*Wow, I wonder what you think of me,* I said.

*I judge you through your works, not piety. You are…acceptable.*

Aww, that was kind of sweet, and also terrifying since I thought the Merlin Gun was inhabited by a crazy fundamentalist nut job.

*I hear you, you know,* Raguel said.

Open mouth, insert hoof. "So, Robyn, not that I don't like meeting new people, but how did you find me?"

"Yes, that would be a very good thing to know," Kim Su said, spraying the air with an antiseptic deodorizer.

"Oh, the FBI guy," Robyn said, as if it was unimportant. "As soon as Dr. Jones made it clear he was an enemy, I knew I had to talk with him. He directed me to you."

"He did, did he?" I said, my voice even. "Did you *Charm Person* him too?"

"Yeah, but it didn't work," Robyn said, frowning. "I thought it might be because he was unattracted to women, but the annoyance in his eyes told me it wasn't that. Some guys just have better self-control than others, or any at all, really."

I tried not to feel an irrational dislike for her drugging my possible-future boyfriend and failed. Mostly because it was an entirely rational dislike. "Did Dr. Jones or any of his minions follow you?"

"Minions?" Robyn asked, smirking. "Yeah, that's a good name for them. Some of the church's higher-ups aren't so bad. David Jones, the doctor's son, is a good guy even if I don't understand how he can follows a religion he knows is a scam. The others are all under their leader's spell. As for how I managed to escape, I slipped away in the forest during one of the good doctor's speeches. I asked the trees to hide me and they did, at least until I got here. Who builds a strip mall in the middle of the woods?"

"People who like to shop in privacy," I said, annoyed.

Kim Su picked a ring out of the jewelry display in the counter before placing it on the top. "Put this ring on. It'll hide you from him."

"And if I don't?" Robyn said, clearly not trusting jewelry from strangers.

"Then Dr. Jones will probably track you down, brainwash you, or kill you then reanimate you as a zombie so he can still have access to whatever information he's kept you alive," Kim Su said.

Robyn looked between us then took the ring and put it on. "So you know him?"

"Alex does," Kim Su said. "He painted a vivid picture."

"No offense but why hasn't he mind controlled you and what does he want?"

Robyn paused. "I need you to promise to help me if I tell you."

"Okay, I promise."

Kim Su smacked her face. "Gods and goddesses, Jane!"

"What?" I asked.

Oh right, the whole 'promises are not made to be broken' thing.

"I ran away from home about two years ago, trying to find out who I was and what I was. I went to a lot of magicians and fake magicians looking for answers. I even hooked up with a vampire for a bit. Eventually, all roads led to the Ultralogy and Dr. Jones had more answers than most."

"Really?" I asked.

Robyn frowned, looking angry. "Yeah, I should have known he was just using me, but when you've been everywhere from single motherhood to doing things you don't want to do for money, even cult leaders look benevolent."

"You're a single mother?" I asked, surprised by that.

"Not anymore," Robyn said, staring. "I left Sparrow with my parents. My adoptive parents. They live in Bright Falls and will do a better job than I ever could."

I was surprised by the revelation she was from around here. Bright Falls wasn't exactly Mayberry, but it wasn't that large of a community either. I would have thought I'd know someone who was part Dryad. Also, she had no right to comment on my parents' cruelty if she named her kid Sparrow.

"What I didn't realize Dr. Jones was more interested in what I was rather than who I was," Robyn said, sounding sick with herself. "He's looking for something related to my family, something called the Grove."

I remembered Bright Falls was built on a convergence of dimensions that made it a hot spot for all manner of weird and spooky things. "Is that anything related to the Lodge?"

"Same zip code, different street," Kim Su said.

I looked at her. "Anything you want to share, Amelia?"

"Nope," Kim Su said, smiling. "Though she'll have to buy something if she wants to hang around much longer."

The revelation Jones wasn't here just for bottled water and Kim Su didn't surprise me in the slightest. I remembered how Jeremy, Maria, and the late Victoria O'Henry had gathered together at one of the "sacred" spots in my town. They'd made a pact with the Big Bad Wolf and reaped great magical rewards for it (though I'd never found out what my brother had gotten). I didn't know what Dr. Jones planned to get from such a place but the thought of him draining such a place dry or making a divine pact terrified me. Even if whatever spirits lived in the Grove weren't deranged like the Big Bad Wolf, they could alter reality or strengthen a wizard's powers tremendously if they got something suitably valuable in return.

Like human sacrifices.

Crap.

Suddenly, everything was starting to fall into place.

*Perhaps*, Raguel said. *Either way, Jones must not be allowed to find the Grove.*

For once, the Merlin Gun and I were in complete agreement. "Okay, I'm following you so far, but I don't know what you get out of this."

"I know what I am now," Robyn said, looking at Kim Su. "Something for which you have no idea how grateful I am. While I have no idea who my biological parents are, I have some suspicions. Also some clues which I hope will lead me to them."

"You do?" I asked, getting a bad feeling about this.

"Yeah," Robyn said, sucking in her breath. "I think those kids in that pit were my siblings."

No one said a word for almost a minute. Albeit, Kim Su didn't seem remotely surprised by this revelation and had gone back to watching reality TV.

"Yeah." I finally broke the silence. "That would fit with a lot of what we know. You realize who your parents are might not be a good thing, right?"

"I had good parents," Robyn said. "Andy and Wilma found me in the woods and they raised me as their own. Like a gift from Heaven or Superman without his rocket, as they used to say. I'm not looking for a mother and father to love me. I got plenty of that."

"Then why?" I asked.

"So I can kill their asses," Robyn said, pointing at me. "Which you promised to help me with. No backsies."

Kim Su gave me a sideways glance as if to say 'I told you so.' I wondered if Alex knew about Robyn's murderous intentions before directing her my way.

*Alex was a flawed wielder of the Merlin Gun and one I often conflicted with.*

*How's that?* I asked. *I would have thought you two would get along like salt on a lick.*

*He was too compassionate. You do not have that problem.*

I didn't have a response to that.

*You could try, "You're welcome."*

I didn't respond to him but looked at Robyn, instead thinking about all the dead children her parents had left in the woods. "Yeah, I'll help you kill them."

*See? You are righteous*, Raguel said.

*Shut up*, I said, hating myself. *I do not like this. I just think it's necessary.*

*Good. I would be worried otherwise.*

Man, I really wished I had an angel more like Roma Downey than Christopher Walken. Hell, I would even have settled for Misha Collins right about now. Actually, I would generally take Misha Collins over just about any other angel. Mmm, Castiel.

*The actual shield of God is a woman.*

*Don't ruin my fantasies, Raguel.*

"Thank you," Robyn said, releasing a breath I hadn't even realized she'd been holding. "I also have a way to help find where my parents are."

"How's that?" I asked.

Robyn reached into her pocket and pulled out a tiny piece of bone. "This should help."

"Please tell me that didn't come from the murder pit."

"I won't tell you," Robyn said, staring at it. "However, combining it with my blood should make a pretty good spell for tracking them down."

Robyn had a point there. Unfortunately, that was straight-up necromancy. "Kim, err, Amelia, I don't suppose—"

"No," Kim Su said simply. "Besides, you're the weredeer who can read objects."

Oh, right.

This was going to suck.

# Chapter Seven

I looked at the piece of bone and imagined experiencing the newborn's fear and sadness as it died. Would it even have those emotions? Would it know it was going to die? How long would it take? I couldn't help but feel terrified at the prospect of experiencing that set of emotions. However, it might be my only clue to knowing who was responsible for their death.

It's why I felt like a coward when I tried to opt out. "It's got to be over twenty years old. There's no way there's any kind of impression left."

Kim Su ruined that thought of mine. "You've been practicing to master your Gift for over a year now. You'll be able to look that far in the past if you want."

I glared at her. "Thanks. Really."

"Much like the gods, I believe suffering builds character," Kim Su said, changing the channel on her television to *Wheel of Fortune*. "Also, I'm a sadistic bastard."

Kim Su had me there. Taking the piece of bone from Robyn, I sighed. "All right, I'll do it."

"Thank you," Robyn said, her voice almost pleading.

I looked at her sideways. "You really want to get revenge on your biological parents that much?"

Robyn's expression was a mixture of emotions, all of them bad. "Most adopted kids want to know why they were given up. I know the people involved not only didn't want me, they wanted to kill me. I now know there's an entire family of siblings I had who will never get to experience half the things I do. So, yeah, I want to kill them."

Kim Su muttered something noncommittal.

"I get that," I said, closing my eyes. "Ala-ca-deer, reveal to me what I fear."

"Is that really a spell?" Robyn asked.

"It is if I make it one," I said.

Then the vision hit me. Like a truck. I always had hated the expression "caught like a deer in the headlights" and not just for the obvious reason that I sympathized with the deer rather than the driver. Deer had an instinctual response of going still when threatened. It was so you could be stealthy and avoid getting yourself killed by cougars or other predators but, like skunks spraying their opponents, it was less than useless with cars. I couldn't help but think of all of those poor deer hoping they wouldn't be seen and unwittingly having led themselves to their doom—which is how I felt about the next few moments of my life.

The first part of my vision was almost overwhelming by itself. It was the raw, painful experience of being a newborn. The sensory overload of being surrounded by a new and terrifying world where you couldn't do a damn thing by yourself. This bone fragment belonged to someone who didn't have a name. A girl who would never get a name. She'd never love, laugh, or experience all of nature's joys. I was tempted to ask Raguel or Kim Su what happened to babies when they died, but I didn't want to know—I just wanted to believe she'd be all right.

*Nina*, I thought. *You should have been a Nina.*

Strangely, the act of naming seemed to ease my pain and I mentally named all of the thirty-six or so children found. That was when I sensed the rest of the world around the newborn child and saw the spiritual reflection of Shadow Pine Park. Except it wasn't a park yet and I saw it in its raw virgin state. A place of giant owls, wolves, elk, and other spirits who resented the presence of man in their home.

Manitou.

Fairies.

That was when I felt a woman's arms holding me and I was overwhelmed with a sense of raw bliss. The figure was a being of sunlight and the Earth, as close to the two things humanity most often associated with the divine. She was almost incandescently beautiful and if Robyn was like "Dream Weaver", then the being I assumed to be her mother was like a religious experience. Certainly her presence calmed the figure I was experiencing life through. I almost cried then, overwhelmed with her beauty, until I reached out to feel her mind. What I felt was apathy.

The spirit was honoring a compact to lay the child at the black altar. Nothing more. The Dryad had no love toward its offspring and barely acknowledged it. It did not think like a human being; it did not even think like an animal, but instead as an intelligent tree. What it did enjoy was the gifts it was given for the children it offered.

Things its fairy slaves could not provide it like mirrors, gold, ribbons, and other trinkets. These were given in exchange for children from the act of sex in a human form. They were taken by the Brotherhood of the Tree and raised to be magicians in its eternal war against….what? I could not say. The Dryad, which had no name, didn't care about such things. Once it laid down the babe at the base of the cliff face, it gave no further thought to its child. Then it forgot she had ever existed.

My vision ended.

I stared at the piece of bone. "Yeah, Robyn, we're going to track down and kill this psycho."

Robyn deflated. "That bad, huh?"

"Yeah," I said, closing my eyes. "You could make an argument it's just acting out its nature, but—"

"But?" Robyn asked.

"Its nature sucks," I said. "As empathic as a storm."

"Or a tree," Kim Su said.

How much did she know and how much was she keeping to herself? There was no way of finding out, since Kim Su was the high queen of keeping things close to her chest. "I'm not sure killing this thing is going to bring you any peace, though."

"It might keep her from killing more newborns," Robyn pointed out. That was specious logic, but I understood her point. "Either way, I have to confront her. Did you see any sign of my father?"

"No," I said, frowning. "I did hear of something called the Brotherhood of the Tree, though. Any idea what that is?"

"Yep," Kim Su said, looking at the television. "Oh come on, it's clearly *Star Trek: Discovery*. You don't need to buy a vowel."

"She's not just a teenage store clerk, is she?" Robyn said, looking at her.

"Nope," I said, sighing. "But that's not my place to tell. You're not going to help us any further, are you?"

"You're wrong," Kim Su said, not turning back to look at us. "If you want to find the Dryad then you have to get something to narrow the search more. I'm not going to help you with that, but I will direct you to one who can."

"Why do I feel like I'm following a trail of breadcrumbs to a gingerbread house where a witch will eat me?" I asked.

"Because you know me so well," Kim Su said.

"I always hated that story," Robyn said, looking out to see Emma staring through the window and pawing at it with her hand. "A pair of thieves and homewreckers murder an old lady to steal her stuff. Also, I think you should let your dog back in."

I waved Emma in. "Got any granola, Kim Su? We should keep treats on hand when she comes back in."

"Werewolves used to have dignity," Kim Su muttered before sighing. "You should go to Lucien's. He knows something about the Brotherhood of the Tree. He also has access to wizards who can make for you an object that'll help you find the Dryad."

"Lucien's," I said, biting my lower lip. "Great. That's just great."

"Ex-boyfriend?" Robyn asked, coming up behind me and smiling. She was almost six feet in height to my five-foot-four stature. She reminded me a bit of how a female weredeer was supposed to look. Deer women were a leggy breed, and I was the runt of the herd.

"What? No!" I snapped, a little too defensively. "There was a thing, but it was nothing. It's doubly nothing which is still nothing because that's how math works."

"Yeah," Robyn said, nodding. "I know exactly how that feels."

Emma trotted on in. "Okay, the smell is mostly gone. So where are we going?"

"Her boyfriend's," Robyn said.

"Alex's?" Emma said.

"No, some Lucien guy," Robyn said. "Who is Lucien?"

"Alex's brother," Kim Su said, enjoying stirring the pot.

"Oh, you dog!" Robyn said, more amused than anything else. "That is not going to end well."

"No kidding," I muttered. "Also, Emma is the dog."

Emma glared at me and growled.

Kim Su handed me a granola bar, which I passed to Emma. Emma unwrapped it and ate it, growling between bites.

"Delicious salty nut goodness," Emma said, crunching and swallowing the last of it. "I'd be a vegan if not for all of the deliciousness of meat."

"Lucien is the owner of the town's Red Light District, you know, until Alice turns the rest of the town into one," I said, trying to figure out how to best explain him. "He's also a weredragon."

"Dragon, not weredragon," Kim Su corrected. "Though, technically, you could call him a werecrocodile. They're the origins of the dragon myth, though."

"He's also a drug dealer!" Emma said, cheerfully. "Except he's not actually a bad guy since when he's not committing crime he helps kill monsters!"

"Sounds awesome," Robyn said, putting her arms around Emma and me. "So let's get going."

I didn't want to go to Lucien's, despite the fact I still considered him my friend. I disapproved of everything from his lifestyle to the way he did business, but he'd saved my life on a number of occasions. I also knew he cared about me. Wanted me for more than the night we'd spent together. If I hadn't known any better, I would have said I'd broken his heart when I'd said it was a mistake.

But you couldn't break the heart of the Devil.

Right?

I also wasn't sure what sort of reception we'd receive once we got there. Lucien and I hadn't had much contact with each other aside from several angry text messages. I regretted that as well, since I did consider him a friend. A stupidly sexy, beautiful friend who had been really talented in…okay, Jane, that was not helping.

"Thanks for all the help," I said, looking at Kim Su. "I'll try not to get you involved any further."

"My students keep saying that, but they never follow through," Kim Su said. "Robyn, there's also something you should know."

"Yeah?" Robyn asked. "Some ancient secret of Dryadkindom?"

"That's not a word," Kim Su said. "No, it's that you should be aware this kind of fight is one that begets other fights down the road. You might find a much more peaceful life by just going in the opposite direction of this town and never looking back."

Robyn paused. "That was the plan. Except, somehow, I ended up coming back. This town sucks you in like a black hole."

"You have no idea," Kim Su said. "Don't come back, Robyn, until you've figured out whether you're coming or you're going."

Wow, that wasn't rude.

Piling into the Millennium Falcon, we took to the road and headed toward the Outlands. They were the bad part of town that was now becoming the *other* bad part of town, thanks to Alice O'Henry's influence.

Eleven years ago, when the O'Henry family had massacred the Drake family in the last battle of the old shapeshifter wars, the Outlands had become an abandoned shantytown. A place where all of the unemployed humans who'd formerly worked for the family had lived or worked.

That wasn't the Outlands today, as all of those buildings had been torn down to be replaced by casinos, strip clubs, nightclubs, and other entertainment industry. For once, vice-ification had worked out as Lucien employed virtually the entire portion of the town the O'Henrys didn't. He milked every dollar possible from the local tourists and poured it back into the economy.

The place was always under construction and new buildings were constantly replacing the old as the place expanded, changed, and shifted. It had started as a place that was sleazy with a bit of grit on top but now had an increasing amount of New Detroit glitz with theme hotels and even an entertainment arena that was going to be showing Black Chorus, the all-vampire band in a few weeks.

I was ambivalent about the changes the town was going through. It had been a dying community as I'd grown up but it had also been a place I'd felt was safe. That turned out be an illusion, though, and I couldn't help but wonder if the monsters had gotten worse or simply changed form.

"I can't believe how much the town has changed since I was last here," Robyn said, looking out of the back driver's-side window. "Two years ago, Bright Falls was the sort of town that outlawed dancing."

"Yeah, well Kevin Bacon took care of that problem," I said, sighing. There was a lot more traffic than I expected. "Now a bigger issue is who is addicted to what drug or whether to go into prostitution or stripping."

"You don't have to choose," Robyn said cheerfully. "I also recommend having a blood-tasting option if you want to make some real cash."

"Yikes," I said.

"Eh, it's not so bad," Robyn said, shrugging. "If you know the right places and people. I would still be doing it if not for deciding that a bunch of cult leaders were more trustworthy than the vampire I used to hang with."

"What happened there?" Emma said, looking somewhat uncomfortable with our new companion's presence.

"Gerald and I got separated," Robyn said. "He tried to do the right thing and it bit him in the ass. The vampires in New Detroit exiled him then divided up his stuff, which apparently included me."

I paused, thinking about the one vampire who lived in Bright Falls: Gerald. He was a doctor who worked for Lucien. "Wow, small world."

"Hmm?" Robyn asked.

"So, Robyn, do you intend to stay in Bright Falls after this?" Emma asked, sounding more than a little suspicious. "You know, I mean after your vengeance and everything."

"Why?" Robyn asked. "You afraid I'm going to steal away the girl you love?"

"No!" Emma said. "I mean, she's totally straight...ish. Wait, goddammit. I'm not referring to you, Jane."

"You betrayed me!" I said, lightly mocking her feelings in hopes she'd find someone else. There had been a couple of girlfriends since she'd come out to me, but nothing that had lasted. Which was a shame, since Emma deserved happiness more than anyone else I knew. "How will I live with this knowledge? All is lost."

"I hate you so much." Emma covered her face with her hands in a manner that reminded me of a dog and her paws.

"Ha-ha," Robyn said, smirking. "I swear, I don't know what being able to pick up people's secrets has to do with being a tree spirit, but I am so glad being a Dryadkin came with the powers it did."

"A lot of powers don't make sense," I said, looking around for the

Lyons Den. Lucien was actually a Drake but he went by his mother's name even though Marcus O'Henry was in jail and presumably helpless. "For example, I'm a white-tailed deer despite the fact white-tailed deer are an American animal while my weredeer power comes from my European heritage. My Odawa grandfather was a weredeer, but he wasn't a Native American weredeer lineage."

Crickets might as well have been chirping in the car.

"Yeah, that's not really the same," Robyn said. "To answer your question, Emma, I haven't decided yet. I wanted to travel around the world and see the sights. It turns out you need money for that, and I saw a lot more in New Detroit than I ever expected to. Even so, I don't think I could go back to my parents."

"They wouldn't take you back?" I asked, expecting some sort of horrible backstory like she was homeschooled to believe in a murderous Sky Father who hated fairies.

*That is malicious slander,* Raguel said.

*I didn't refer to yours, necessarily!* I snapped. *Yours is totally forgiving and compassionate to people who actually haven't done anything.*

*Thank you.*

"No," Robyn said, shrugging. "They're just boring."

The Lyons Den came up soon after, the Taj Mahal of goth nightclubs.

A place that sang with its own rhythm.

# CHAPTER EIGHT

The Lyons' Den was not the sort of place you expected to see in an even formerly small town like Bright Falls, Michigan. What had originally been a bank had transformed, physically, into a literal frigging cathedral that had been turned into one of the most popular nightclubs in the country. People came from Hollywood to New York to spend time there with celebrities diverting from New Detroit to enjoy the place.

That wasn't because Lucien Lyons owned the place or had even paid for it. It was because it was a little slice of hell on Earth—the fun parts at least. Last year, the Big Bad Wolf had literally merged part of the club with one of Hell's dimensions and turned it into a lodestone to the Spirit World. Any sane person would have sealed it off with every ward imaginable and a sign that said, "DO NOT ENTER OR YOU WILL FRIGGING DIE."

Not Lucien.

Lucien had taken advantage of the brief infestation of Beelzebub and harnessed the magical energies in order to shape the building to his liking. The sensual, forbidden, and corrupt oozed out of the brick work while the music seamed to permeate one's soul. Supposedly, you could consume an entire platter full of drugs within its walls and suffer no ill effects while also indulging all manner of hidden vices. The two buildings beside the cathedral were often rented out for conferences of vampires, warlocks, and corporations to. It was why Lucien was the second-richest man in the city.

*He plays with fire*, the Raguel said. *Hell plays a long game.*

*No kidding*, I thought back to him. *It's why I'm not with him.*

*Would you be with him if he wasn't?*

*I don't know*, I said, honestly. *It'd be a lot harder choice, though.*

Lucien had a quality his brother lacked: he never made any

attempt to put the mission before other relationships. He was a lot of fun, and while Alex was too, I never had any doubt I would see Lucien again. He was a good friend, but he wanted more than that, and now we were neither friends nor lovers. Goddess, why I had slept with him?

*Because you were inebriated and found him attractive*, Raguel said.

*I wasn't talking to you.*

"Okay," Robyn said, looking at the Lyon's Den. "I am one hundred percent sure I would remember a cathedral-turned-nightclub with lines around the block. There's no way in hell this was constructed in just two years."

"As Golden Earring would say, 'Step into the Twilight Zone,'" I said, shrugging. "Mind you, it's still a city where the majority of tourists are looking for hiking and fishing versus enjoying our retro-goth hot spot."

"Yeah, across the tracks we have more Country Bears than Pleasure Island," Emma said.

I looked for a parking space, failing miserably. "A word to the wise, Emma. People would take you more seriously if Disney wasn't your go-to pop culture reference."

Emma crossed her arms and stared. "*Beauty and the Beast* is my favorite movie and I make no apologies for it."

Robyn was still fascinated by the Lyons Den, staring at it sideways through the window. "Honestly, I never liked *Beauty and the Beast* all that much. I never could get why Belle didn't go for Gaston. I mean, yeah, he was an asshole, but dude was ripped. The Beast just didn't do anything for me."

I pondered that. "I feel like you may have missed the point of that movie."

"What, the Beast being rich? No, I got that," Robyn said, finally turning away. "I hope the toilets in the castle didn't talk. That would have been gross."

I decided to pull into the V.I.P parking lot since it was otherwise a five-block walk. "Okay, now you've just made the movie weird."

Driving up to the parking-lot booth, I tried to figure out a way to convince them to get in when I didn't have a spare couple of thousand dollars to buy a ticket.

"Welcome, Ms. Doe," the parking lot attendant said, opening the boom barrier for us.

Okay, that was easy.

"Thanks," I said, pulling in and surveying the large number of sports cars and limousines present. "Emma, do you have a lifetime membership here or something?"

"Pfft!" Emma snorted. "I'm rich but not that rich. I have to go through three lawyers and a magical ritual to get at any of my money. Remember, I still clean rooms at Pinehold."

"Shouldn't you be going to business school or something?" Robyn said, showing herself to be innocently insensitive.

"That assumes I want to be a businesswoman," Emma said, surprising me. "My father is a lawyer, my mother is a lawyer, my aunt is a hotel magnate—"

"And a madam," I said.

"And a peddler in flesh," Emma said, frowning. "My other aunt is the sheriff. She's considered the disappointment in the family, by the way. My brother is going to Yale, the first recognized therianthrope to do so—"

"Couldn't get into Harvard, huh?" I said, smirking.

Emma glared at me. "I don't know if that's who I want to be."

I found a parking spot after surveying the entirety of the V.I.P center. I was surprised to find it was marked "DOE FAMILY ONLY". Pulling in, I said, "You can be whoever you want to be, Emma. I'll support you no matter what."

"Well, she's rich, so maybe that's true," Robyn said, crossing her arms. "For the rest of us, we don't have the option of hanging around doing nothing like a fuzzy Kardashian."

"I do stuff," Emma said, looking disappointed. "I want to be useful."

I glared at Robyn with my rearview mirror. "What exactly did you do, Poison Oaky?"

"Survived," Robyn said, grimacing. "I was raised in the middle of Shadow Pine Park with my mother, my father, and a partridge in a pear tree. I was homeschooled and about the only people I ever got to associate with were the other woodland folk. I was about ready to go insane by the time I was eighteen. I think I still had imaginary friends by the time I was fourteen."

"Maybe they weren't so imaginary," Emma said.

"Don't gaslight me, Lassie."

Emma blinked confused. "I'm not, really! Just there's all sorts of invisible supernatural beings and we really—"

I interrupted with a question that probably shouldn't have been asked. "You left your kid in that sort of environment?"

"I have four years until he's kindergarten age," Robyn said, showing no shame. "My parents weren't bad people. The opposite, really, but they were afraid."

"Afraid of what?" I asked.

"I think what might happen to a supernaturally beautiful little girl in a town full of perverts and weirdoes," Robyn said, unbuckling her seatbelt. "Marcus O'Henry was still in charge of the town back then and he made sure every kid fit into his plans. It's not like I could hide that I was something strange back then. My hair was green during the spring, blonde in the summer, brown in the fall, and white in the winter."

I opened the door and stepped out of the car as everyone else did. "Your hair was tied to the seasons and you had trouble telling you were tree related?"

"It's not exactly like there's a bunch of Dryad horror movies," Robyn said. "I did what I thought was best for my kid and myself. Do you think you're ready to have a kid?"

"Buck no!" I said, aping Emma's earlier comment. "Goddess, no. Nope. No. No sir. Not even close."

"I rest my case," Robyn said, stretching her arms out. "It's why I'm extra cautious on birth control now unless I'm with someone pregnancy is impossible to happen with. The fact that Dryads are fertility spirits is a real case of being blessed with suck now that I think about it."

Emma started sniffing the air.

"So what are your plans?" Robyn asked.

I looked at her. "Not sure anymore. I'm trying to study to be a shaman, but that's not really a job that pays the bills until I learn how to know what stocks will pay out dividends. I'm also pretty sure that's insider trading now."

"Stupid government always getting in the way of supernaturals making themselves rich." Robyn smirked. She was uncomfortably close and I took a step back.

Emma, meanwhile, was sniffing the side of the only other car that didn't look like it cost more than my parents' house. It was a white van that, normally, would have been the model of inconspicuous. "Larry and Yolanda are here."

I blinked. "What?"

Emma growled at the car. "I smell the verbena, gun oil, and sweat."

I walked closer and got a whiff. "Yep. Dammit. Someone should tell those people one size does not fit all with getaway vehicles."

"Larry and Yolanda?" Robyn asked.

"Hunters," I said, frowning. "Friends of Alex."

"So you're a pair of shapechangers who are friends with an FBI agent wizard who is friends with hunters. You're also friends with a drug-dealing dragon wizard," Robyn said.

"That's about the size of it, yeah," I said.

"Just wondering if I need to make a chart or worry about someone chopping me up to make a pyre for you two."

"No, we have gasoline for our witch burnings now," I said. "Besides, Bright Falls is more like the crazy pagan town in *The Wicker Man* rather than the kind of place that does witch burnings. Like ten percent of the town is weird in one way or another."

Probably because there were so few places where that was an asset rather than a disadvantage. Whoever had chosen America to be the new supernatural homeland had seriously erred. The vampires, I supposed. The United States was the most religious Western nation on Earth as well as one of the most militant countries in the world.

As much as I loved my country tis of me, sweet land of deerbity, it was not the sort of place you wanted to reveal supernatural beings had been secretly living among you to. The fact that most supernaturals were religious and militant in their own way didn't make it easier. Me? I would have chosen Canada to be our Promised Land.

*You still live in America despite its harsh laws. A home is not chosen; it chooses you.*

*Shush you,* I replied to the Merlin Gun. *We are not bonding.*

"Never saw *The Wicker Man*, not a big fan of Nicholas Cage."

I immediately lowered my opinion of Robyn. I'd been referring to the classic Hammer film with Christopher Lee. "Well, let's just go to the backdoor. On an awkwardness scale of one to ten, this should only be about an eight and a half."

The doorway into the back of the Lyons Den was a pair of metal doors with two stocky men dressed like Secret Servicemen guarding it. There was also a security camera hanging over it that scanned everyone who might come through.

"Anything else anyone wants to add before we go see Puff the Magic Drug Dealer?"

Emma came up behind me. "I wanted to be a veterinarian, but animals are scared of me."

I opened my mouth to say something snarky and play it off as a joke, but looking back, I could see how devastated the confession had made her. Emma had always loved animals but they'd never loved her back.

"Their loss," I said, approaching the backdoor. "Yo, shaman business. Let me on in."

They both stepped in front of the door. Ah, dammit, and things were going so well too.

That was when I heard a voice over the intercom beside the door, one I hadn't even seen because the two bulky guards standing in front of it. It was feminine but harsh and full of more venom than a cobra. "You have a lot of nerve coming here, Jane Doe. I'm coming right out."

I covered my face with my hand. "Oh joy, Deana is coming to meet us. This is going to go over like a ton of bricks."

"Why do I get the impression you're not that popular around here?" Robyn said, taking a seat behind me. "Reserved parking space aside."

"Because I'm not," I said, sighing. "Deana Parvati is Lucien's second in command. She's an Elemental."

"Is that a thing?" Robyn asked.

"Yeah," I said. "It's like being a wizard except you can throw around your element a lot easier than any magician, but not much else. Also, she's Emma's ex-girlfriend."

Robyn did a double-take between us. "Just so I'm clear, we're going into a nightclub the size of a hotel that is powered by evil magic—"

"You picked up on that, huh?" I asked.

"To talk to a pair of gangsters that both of you have dated."

I snorted. "Well, when you phrase it like that, you make it sound foolish."

Seconds later, the door opened to reveal a beautiful Indian woman with light-brown skin, black hair tied into a ponytail, and piercing dark eyes. Her wardrobe was gorgeous with a button-down shirt tied around her waist to expose amazingly perfect abs and tight, short skirt that was probably criminal in a few places. Deana had a half-dozen bracelets on each of her arms, earrings, and a belly-button ring that all radiated supernatural energy.

"Hey Deana," I said, looking at her. "I'd say long time no see, but it's been like a couple of months and I don't actually like you. Really I sort of hate you, but kind of tolerated you because you were Lucien's friend or, well, actually aren't you like his slave or something? Because you swore allegiance to him so he wouldn't kill you or something like that, right?"

Deana's eyes narrowed at me.

Emma covered her face with her hands.

Robyn sniggered.

"No judgment," I said, raising my hand. "But you were mean to Emma, so I don't like you. Let me in, I need to talk to Lucien."

Deana paused. "You know, I am genuinely confused on how to respond. I was going to yell at you for putting Lucien into a months-long funk. However, now I have the benefit of being able to use your incredibly rude doe-eyed rants as an excuse to keep you out. Thus thwarting whatever dangerous little excursion you're going to involve my boss, whom I love, in."

"It's to solve who was responsible for that child murder pit in Shadow Pines," I said, realizing I may have overplayed my hand.

Then again, I really hated her.

"I hate kids," Deana said, waving. "Goodbye."

"Please, Deana, this is important!" Emma said, clasping her hands together.

"Insult her," Deana said.

"What?" Emma asked.

"I liked you, Emma, but you have some severe issues with your friend. If you want to meet with the boss, insult Jane. Not something stupid, either, but the kind of hurtful thing only someone who really knows someone else can say."

"Wow, this is better than my soaps," Robyn said, putting her hands on her hips. "Anyone got any popcorn?"

"Do it, Emma," I said, taking a deep breath. "I'm a big girl, I can take it."

"Are you sure?" Emma said, looking sheepish.

I rolled my eyes. "Positive."

"Okay, uh," Emma took a deep breath. "Remember when you got your new bra and pants size and you thought it was because you were coming into your gorgeous weredeer powers? I actually think that's just because you were really athletic and put on a few pou—"

"You are dead to me," I said, narrowing my eyes.

"It's a good look! Super-lean isn't great!" Emma said, panicking.

I opened my mouth in (mock) horror.

Deana burst out laughing. "Oh, I'd forgotten how amusing you two were. Also, you've seemingly added a new member to your all-girl comedy troop. Come on in, the boss is waiting."

"He is?" I asked.

Deana nodded. "Oh yeah, he told me to let you in. The hunters said they were supposed to meet with you before they gave him their plans to kill the cultists in town."

# CHAPTER NINE

The interior of the Lyons Den was built to look like a deconsecrated church with stone balconies, stone gargoyles, stained-glass windows, and so on—it overlooked a massive cross-shaped dance floor with shimmering lights as well as fog machines. There was a massive bar on every level with a remixed version of "Bela Lugosi's Dead" by The Bauhaus laying in the background.

It was packed to the rim with beautiful people dressed in black and white, with every day being Halloween here. Quite a few of them looked a lot more attractive than the people in the lines outside, and I could feel the energy of the place making everyone feel sexy as well as dangerous. It was a mild glamour, but part of the experience you paid for in order to experience Lucien's world.

*To use the power of Hell as makeup and cologne,* Raguel grumbled. *That is akin to using an atomic bomb to remove vermin.*

*Overkill but effective?* I suggested.

*Yes.*

"Wow," Robyn said, walking up behind us. "This is not like any goth nightclub I've ever been in. Those are mostly just people's basements with some fake cobwebs."

"It's a place of power," Deana said, her voice cold and businesslike. Somehow I could still hear her over the din outside, though. "The boss feeds on the sexual and illicit energies generated here. It makes him a more powerful sorcerer."

"Which he uses to, what, make an even bigger nightclub?" I asked. "Read what stocks are going to be good tomorrow? Forge iron daggers to raise his Smithing score?"

Deana didn't respond.

"I'm right, aren't I?" I asked.

"Not about the iron daggers," Deana said, looking like she was more annoyed she had no idea what I was talking about than the quip itself. "The boss has been somewhat aimless since achieving his revenge against the O'Henry family."

Robyn looked at Emma. "Is this another thing I should have known about?"

"No, he doesn't want to kill me!" Emma said cheerfully. "Just my family!"

Robyn shook her head and picked up a bottle of tequila as well as a glass from a barely dressed waiter passing us by.

"Don't rob our hosts," I said, not even bothering to turn to look when I heard it.

"I'm part plant, I need watering," Robyn said, pouring herself a drink.

She had me there.

Our group arrived at pair of luxurious wooden doors where a pair of French maids who didn't breathe opened for us. Beyond, there was a massive apartment I took to be Lucien's with an oversized flat-screen television filling an entire wall, massive drapes blocking out the sun, marble floors, a huge fireplace (that was just a wall computer screen showing flames), and an enormous pair of black leather couches in front of a canopy bed that was three times the size of a normal one.

Lucien was sitting on one of the couches, lounging between two barely dressed punk women with more piercings and tattoos than an issue of *Revolver* magazine. One of them I recognized as Marish, a local musician who turned into a cougar (in the eats-deer, not-attractive-older-woman sense) while the other was her blue-haired and equally feline band mate Felicia.

Lucien Lyons was the only man I ever knew to be as supernaturally attractive as the Gifted women of Bright Falls. He had shining shoulder-length silver Targaryen-style white hair, skin that was almost alabaster, a lean, sculpted frame, and cheekbones you could cut your hand on. He also didn't mind showing it off, either, wearing no shirt and a pair of leather pants. He had a tattoo of an ankh on his right pec as well as a dragon eating its own tail on his stomach.

Almost as an afterthought, I looked over to the second couch where Larry and Yolanda were standing. The two hunters had changed into "normal" clothes, which made them stand out like a pair of sore thumbs in the surreal stylized death-metal-video world in which Lucien lived. Yolanda looked especially comfortable, probably because she was surrounded by supernaturals as much as Lucien's Alice Cooper lifestyle. Well, the fictional Alice Cooper, not the one who was a reverend in real life.

"I have brought the shaman and her friends, boss," Deana said, acting like he was a prince more than the local crime boss. Then again, Lucien had a palace, army, and owned a small kingdom. He was as good a match for it as anyone I knew. It's just he was more Mordred by way of Stuart Townsend than Arthur.

Lucien didn't look at me, instead stretching out his hand and summoning Robyn's tequila bottle to him telekinetically.

"Hey, I stole that fair and square!" Robyn said, looking sideways at his abs. "Okay, hold on, I forgot what I was talking about."

"He has that effect on people," Emma said. "I mean, I don't get it-get it, but he is pretty to look at."

Lucien took a long drink of the tequila bottle then looked at his shapechanger companions. "Out, girls, this is a private meeting."

Both women shrugged then got up, grabbing their jackets and walking past me. It was clear that their relationship wasn't particularly deep, if not outright professional.

"Bye Felicia," I said, waving at the blue-haired girl as she departed.

Felicia gave me the bird with both middle fingers as she left.

Classy. It was good to see that Lucien's taste remained consistent.

*You just insulted yourself,* Raguel said.

Dammit, I did, didn't I?

Lucien put a pair of sunglasses on over his moon-colored eyes. He looked right at me then Deana then everyone else in my part. "Jane, must you antagonize everyone you meet?"

"Lucien, you know me. Yes. Yes, I must."

"Hell, I've known her an hour and I know that," Robyn said before laughing.

I ignored Robyn. "Yeah, well, Lucien, we need your help. I need your help. Alex needs your help. The whole town needs your help and you're going to give it."

Lucien took another swig of tequila. "Yeah, there's a lot of that going around today. I'm not sure if I'm feeling any of it."

"We were here first," Yolanda said, her voice capturing the sort of anger only a woman thoroughly unimpressed with Lucien could manage. It was something I'd never heard of from anyone who'd met him.

"This is not a first-come, first-serve situation, hunters," I snapped at them. "This is a ranked-by-authority-comes-first one. Who is the shaman of Bright Falls? Defender from all things dark and oogie-boogie?"

Emma leaned up and whispered in my ear, "They'd take you a lot more seriously if you didn't use words like 'oogie-boogie'."

"No, we wouldn't," Deana said, having overheard Emma despite her whispering.

"Your mother is the shaman of the town," Lucien said, staring at me. "You're the self-appointed shaman of the city."

"And I am the one people are gonna call when they call…. Spiritbusters?" I said, wondering if that actually worked as a line.

No, it didn't, did it? Oh well, they couldn't all be winners.

Lucien propped his elbow on the arm of his couch then put his head in his palm, looking at me with a bored expression on his face. I could tell he was trying to cover up what he was feeling but I couldn't say exactly what that was. "Larry and Yolanda want my help in killing an evil wizard visiting the town with his bunch of cultists. He's apparently immortal, so that makes it a bit tricky. Are you going to back up their claims my FBI rules-abiding brother has become a man interested in contract murder?"

It was a trick question, of course, so I just told the truth. "I think your brother has always cared about the spirit of the law more than he's cared about the letter."

"So he'd be up for us just blowing up the Lumberjack Motel with all of them inside?" Deana said.

*Just a reminder, Deana is evil. She is a murderer many times over as well as a thief and liar. You could slay her with my power.*

*I'll keep that in mind*, I said, not at all interested in killing Lucien's major domo. *However, it'll take more than her calling me fat to get me to kill her.*

*You're a perfectly healthy weight for your size. Just because you've put on a few—*

*Do not say another word!* I mentally shouted. *Cherry pie with whipped cream is delicious and pure! It was worth it and I will slay all who say otherwise!*

The angel older than modern man backed down and said no more.

*Good*, I thought. *Now let me handle this.*

"That's not why I'm here," I said, closing my eyes. "I think Dr. Jones is dangerous and looking after something horrible but I'm here to get your help in stopping the thing that killed all those kids in Shadow Pine Park."

"The Brotherhood of the Tree and the Dryad," Lucien said.

"Yeah!" I said before pausing as his words registered with me. "Wait, what?"

"You knew?" Yolanda stood up, growling. "You knew about this thing!"

"Stand down." Deana conjured a trio of icicles in the air that floated as if ready to impale her.

I pulled out my gun and aimed it at her. "Step the hell away."

The icicles turned to me as Emma transformed into a half-woman, half-wolf creature that stood a foot taller than Deana and almost two feet taller than me. It lacked all of Emma's mercy and in a second, I suspected it would knock Deana's head clean off.

That was when the doors opened again and Dr. Gerald Pasteur, the town's only vampire, walked in with a Chinese girl in a goth-cheerleader outfit. Gerald was, in his own way, shockingly beautiful, and probably the third handsomest man I'd ever seen off of TV. He had black hair, luminescent skin, and wore a white doctor's coat even outside of his office.

The girl caused me to blink, as it took me a second to recognize Elena Chang from my high-school years. She'd been in one of our class of two hundred and I couldn't say I knew her very well, but I did know her. Her eyes were predatory now, and cold, while her skin had the slightly papery texture regular humans didn't notice on vampires but shapechangers did. Elena had been transformed into the town's second vampire.

"Hi, everybody!" Gerald said, smiling. It was the first time I'd seen him happy in the roughly one year I'd known the undead doctor.

While I was distracted, Deana almost took my head off with her icicles, only for Emma to push her to the ground and wrap her jaws around her neck.

"Doh ahead, mock mah day," Emma said, her words jumbled by the circumstance.

"Please don't kill Deana," Lucien said, standing up. "I promise you, she'll be punished for her actions. No one attacks a guest under my roof."

I stared at Lucien. "Guest?"

It was a poor way to refer to us after all we'd been through.

"Friend," Lucien said, his enunciation of the word full of bitterness and spite. "A life-long friend whom I will never betray."

Ouch. Those were some familiar words being parroted back at me. I'd said them after we'd slept together. Was Lucien still not over it? I mean, Jesus and Brigid, he'd certainly not stayed celibate, if the band girls hanging off of him were any indication. It had just been the one time after all. Well, technically twice. Well, okay, it had been all night, but that didn't mean anything. Yeesh.

"Gerald?" Robyn asked, looking up at the vampire.

"Robyn?" Gerald said, stunned.

"Who is she?" Robyn asked, looking surprised. "Your new girlfriend."

"I am his creation!" Elena said. "Also lover! Who are you?"

"His baby mama," Robyn said, snorting. "You will never transfer the curse to someone else, eh, Gerald?"

Gerald looked away, guilty. "Oh dear."

Elena opened her mouth in shock. "His *what*?"

Lucien stood up. "Jane, we should talk in private."

"Your psycho henchwench just tried to stab me with icicles!" I snapped at him, wondering if this was going to degenerate further.

Lucien said, "Her magic can't hurt you."

"What?" Deana said, her neck still in Emma's mouth. "It can't?"

"No," Lucien said. "I enchanted you, Jane, so you're immune to her powers. It was a while back."

"You enchanted me without my permission?" I said, appalled. That was a gross violation of my personal space even if it was for my supposed good.

Deana tried to speak, only for Emma to put a paw over her chest.

"You are all now under my protection," Lucien said, addressing the walls of his cathedral. "Let a terrible vengeance fall upon anyone who harms anyone else. Everybody got that?"

"Got it," I said, glad someone had stepped up before I'd had to kill people. "Emma, down."

Emma opened her jaw and stepped off Deana. "Don't try to hurt Jane again."

Deana held her neck. "This is why we didn't go anywhere."

"Yeah, amazing how trying to hurt my friends makes me think you're awful," Emma said, her voice contemptuous rather than hurt.

To her credit, Deana looked ashamed, and for once I thought she registered just how much she'd screwed up. I turned to look at Gerald and Robyn, expecting some sort of disaster in the making. Instead, I saw Robyn and Gerald hugging as the former introduced herself to Elena followed by the latter returning the same.

It seemed that I wouldn't have to shoot anyone after all. "Okay, Lucien, I'll trust your people not to do anything stupid."

"Just make sure yours don't start anything. Mine know how to take orders," Lucien said, walking to a door on the left I was certain hadn't been there before.

Seeing as the person I needed to interrogate was leaving the room, I hopped to it and moved to follow him. "Try not to kill each other while I'm gone, guys. Actually, no, there is no try. Do not. I mean that."

"Have fun!" Robyn waved, looking at Gerald and his new progeny with a sour expression on her face.

"Will do!" I said, waving back.

*You have my permission to shoot the vampire*, Raguel said.

*Hush you*, I said. *Just tell me I can't shoot Lucien. I don't want to know what he's been up to this entire time.*

Raguel took a moment to reply. *I generally restrict the final judgment to those who have murdered the innocent, raped, or tortured. Lucien has not committed these sins the way his soldiers have.*

"That's not as reassuring as you might think," I muttered aloud.

*He stands on a precipice with one side solid ground and the other a dark abyss few climb out of. As long as he punishes those who do evil under his command and does not succumb to temptation, he is not worthy of death or damnation. Two hands hold him back.*

"I prefer when you speak in short, easily understood sentences."

*So do I.*

I reached the door where Lucien was waiting for me. He held the door and I passed before him, entering into a beautiful wooden conference room bigger than my parents' house. It had a massive conference table in the center of it and a huge circular skylight that showed storm clouds gathering overhead. The place looked more like a movie set than a place of business and I could easily imagine the Illuminati (which didn't exist—as far as I knew) or the Vampire Nation's leaders gathering around to discuss ruling the world.

"Talking to your guardian angel?" Lucien asked, shutting the door behind us. It faded away seconds later, leaving us alone. I wasn't worried about my safety with Lucien, but it was a rather tacky thing to do when my friends were alone with his minions outside. Lucien removed his sunglasses and put them in his pants pocket. I was surprised they fit.

"More like the guardian pain in my ass," I said, turning around and finding myself face-first in his chest.

Oh my.

I looked up into his eyes. "Listen, Lucien, this is a really complicated situation so I'm going to have to call in every favor you want to—"

"Shh," Lucien said.

I quieted. Mostly. "Uh…"

He then leaned down and kissed me.

# CHAPTER TEN

Lucien's tongue met mine and his hands pressed against the soft of my back, sending waves of pleasure throughout my body. Part of the appeal of supernaturals, wizards in particular, was they could control the responses of their partner's bodies. It was something I'd found out with Lucien and had been left with a somewhat giddy feeling about ever since. I returned his kiss despite my best efforts and moved my hands up and down his chest before he moved his hands to my shirt.

"No, dammit," I said, pulling away. "Bad Jane!"

Lucien grumbled and pulled away, crossing his arms. "Spoilsport."

"I told you last time was a mistake!" I snapped, taking a deep breath.

"I remember," Lucien said, leaning up against the wall. He was channeling his inner James Dean and managing to look annoyed as well as cool at the same time. "It was the most surprising breakup I've had, I've got to tell you."

Breakup? Oh, that was rich.

"We weren't dating!" I said, appalled. "I mean, yeah, we'd go to movies and hang out.

Maybe have dinner every now and then as well as talk about stuff but...oh my Goddess, we were dating."

Lucien threw his hands out in the air. "For almost two months."

Oh Goddess, that changed everything.

And nothing.

"You didn't pick up on the fact I hadn't had sex with you in all that time or even kissed you?" I said, futilely looking for an excuse. Yeah, that was great, be upset at the guy for being a gentleman. But seriously? He had to have been clued in! Right?

*Men are genetically designed to be stupid in this area*

*No kidding, Raguel,* I responded.

*Not that women are any better.*

*Where the hell did you get that kind of sass?* I asked.

*I can't imagine,* Raguel said. *Though please don't suggest it's from Hell.*

*Sorry,* I apologized. But don't distract me. *This is a cataclysm of epic proportions.*

*I'm sure.*

"I just thought you were religious," Lucien shrugged. "I liked you, you liked me, so I was willing to take it slow for once."

"Deer religion does not work that way!" I snapped, ignoring the rest of his statement for the very valid reason it made me look bad. "We're totally sex positive. I think."

"You think?" Lucien asked, distracted at last from my screw-up.

"I didn't get to find out much from my mom before she got sent away!" I said. "Also, my gun is an angel. That really screws with my whole Neo-Pagan beliefs."

"Pfft," Lucien muttered. "To think I gave up sex with other women for almost six months."

That diluted most of my sympathy. "Oh you poor baby, you."

Lucien laughed. "I picked up on the fact that you weren't interested when you didn't talk to me for a few months."

"You didn't call either," I said, still trying to weakly defend myself.

Lucien narrowed his eyes as they turned a serpentine yellow with slits. "People call me, I don't call them."

I cocked my head to one side. "Does this Bad Boy Sex God thing usually work for you?"

Lucien's eyes returned to normal. "Up until recently, I had almost a perfect track record."

"Word of advice, it doesn't work for all women."

"I don't need it to work for all women," Lucien said, looking to one side. "In any case, I just figured you had someone else in mind."

"Well, I do," I said, taking a deep breath and recovering my dignity.

Goddess, he was hot. No, focus! Important stuff to think about like…like… something to do with tree cults?

"Just tell me it's not Alex," Lucien said, jokingly.

I grimaced and looked guilty.

"Oh Lord," Lucien muttered, covering his face. "Really, Jane?"

"Hey, I didn't ask you to sleep with me!" I said.

"Yes, you did. Three times."

I paused, thinking back on that night. "Stop confusing the issue with facts."

"I care about two people in the world, Jane—you and my brother. Sometimes my foster mother, and even then that's iffy."

"A rift there?" I asked, never having heard Lucien talk much about his foster mother. I mostly knew about her from Alex and the portrayal he gave of her was *Star Trek*'s Khan in a dress.

"Diane asked me to choose between her and Alex during one of our fights. I chose Alex."

Yikes.

"I'm sorry," I said, taking a deep breath. "As you know, I can sympathize with that kind of rift."

"Yeah, well, it's just another sign of the fucked-up nature of God's creation."

Lucien had, in his own words, seen too much of the world in order to disbelieve in God. Unfortunately, this had made him sullen and angry at the universe rather than comforted. It was probably why he could make deals with demons and not be tainted, since his distaste for the divine was born from too much love for his fellow man rather than too little.

Alex was the opposite as he was filled with a fury against the existence of evil and a priestly reverence for the universe, but I honestly didn't think he held any particular one thing above another. As far as Alex was concerned, everyone was a child of the divine and everything was a part of it, so it was all worth adoration. He didn't even hate evil people, at least as far as I knew, but just wanted to stop them injuring themselves by injuring others. I felt that was an overly complicated viewpoint myself.

*The tarnished knight versus the shining one. However will you choose?*

*Do not get involved in my love life or I will mess you up!*

*Hehehe.* Perhaps the first time I'd ever heard the Merlin Gun laugh.

I'd chosen, too. Sort of. "Listen, I like your brother and I'd never do anything to hurt him."

"Except sleep with his brother."

I felt my face. "Just, uh, keep it to yourself, would you?"

Lucien stared at me. "Now you want me to lie for you?"

I sighed. "I'll...probably tell him, I mean I will, it's just...listen, this isn't important now."

Lucien walked over and put his hand on my cheek. "Jane, you are a beautiful, fascinating woman who easily blows away most of the girls who come here to party. If you don't want what I have, that's unfortunate, but I'm a big boy. I'll live. Just don't hurt Alex. He's had to deal with sultry femme fatales like you before."

I smacked him across the abdomen. It was like smacking a brick wall. "I'm sorry I hurt you, Lucien."

"I hurt others, I don't get hurt."

"Deershit."

Lucien shrugged. "So what can I do to help you with the dual punches of human sacrifice and the evangelical temple of holy infomercials?"

"They're related, I think," I said, trying to put it all in my head. "There's something called the Grove, a dryad living there, the dead children were left for something called the Brotherhood of the Tree, and Ultralogist guy is after whatever is there. He also wants to kill Kim Su, who he knows is in town."

Lucien listened to me, nodding his head as I spoke. "Okay, I got it and know how everything relates."

I blinked. "Really?"

"Really," Lucien said.

"Because it's only been a few hours into this and it usually takes me a couple of days to figure out who was responsible for everything. This is like them catching the killer before the first commercial break."

"Life doesn't work like television, Jane."

"I've yet to find that to be true."

Lucien smiled. "The Brotherhood of the Tree is a religious sect that used to live in Bright Falls. They were driven out of England by Queen Elizabeth under the belief that they were secret Catholics."

"What did they worship?" I asked.

"They were druids," Lucien said. "Semi-Christian druids."

"Semi-Christian? How could a bunch of pagans be

semi-Christian?" I asked, only noticing the hypocrisy after the words came out of my mouth.

Lucien shrugged. "It'd been a while since the Romans and Saint Patrick smacked them down. Some religious syncretism was inevitable even in a persecuted secret sect. Besides, I get the impression they were able to wrap their head around the idea of a god becoming a human sacrifice better than most. You know, if you believe in that sort of thing."

*Hey, Raguel, want to weigh in on that cosmic mystery?* I asked, not really expecting an answer.

*Michael has forbidden us from conversing about religion with mortals or each other. It never ends well.*

*Huh*, I said, thinking about that. *He is wise.*

*Indeed.*

I paused. "So you're telling me Bright Falls had a *sect of druids* a couple of hundred years ago and I've never heard of them?"

"You probably have," Lucien said. "After all, you worship a bunch of Celtic deities along with the Christian God. Eventually, the Brotherhood of the Tree all became shapechangers and their beliefs disappeared into the local folklore."

I paused. "Okay, I'm feeling really stupid in this conversation. I still feel like I should know this."

"Well, I learned it from your mother."

I blinked, trying to wrap my head around this latest series of revelations. "When the hell did you talk to my mother?"

"I talk to her every other week," Lucien said, staring. "We are both working on making sure Marcus Henry spends the next four hundred lifetimes behind bars, after all."

I hadn't spoken to my mother since she'd gone underground. "I don't even know where she is."

"You can ask the FBI to talk to her," Lucien said. "I know your siblings did."

I lowered my head. "I don't even know what I would say. Did you know Jeanine and Jeremy want to sell the Deerlightful?"

"Yeah," Lucien said, shrugging. "I'm Alice's real estate partner, so I got a heads-up. Want me to buy it for you?"

"What?" I said, thrown off for the third time today. "No, I'm not going to let you do that! We've slept together! That'd be awful! Like kinda-sorta prostitution!"

Lucien rolled his eyes and threw out his arm. "I don't even know what you're talking about. This is why I'm not friends with any of my exes."

Were we exes? I hadn't even known we were dating until a few minutes ago. "Well, we are friends. Also, I'm the shaman of the city and you're a magic-user in it, so I'm the boss of you."

Lucien looked at me sideways, amused. "All right, sure you are."

"Do you know how the dryad fits into all of this?"

"Accent on the *'the'* in Dryad," Lucien said, frowning. "It's not just a tree spirit. It's the avatar of their god."

I took a second to parse that. "The druids summoned a god into a tree?"

It actually wasn't an entirely uncommon mystical practice. After all, I was walking around with the Beretta of Murderangelry.

*I can be any type of gun. Not just a Beretta.*

It was funny how that was the part he objected to.

Lucien nodded. "Yeah. The Dryad is an avatar of Danu that the Druids summoned into an Elder Oak, a living manifestation of the Earthmother in reality. Every spring, they would send a young man to join with her and sire a new child. It brought fertility and junk to the surrounding lands while also birthing children of exceptional beauty as well as magical power."

Wow, Robyn was a demigoddess. But who was doing the siring now? I'm pretty sure the young men of the town (as well as most of the old) would be up for it, but it's not something I'd ever heard advertised. Jeremy would have been unable to keep from bragging.

I took a deep breath. "Speaking as someone who worships the Earth, I'm not sure how it fits with my beliefs that she's just going to abandon her kids to die."

Lucien walked over to the conference room table and sat on it. "Nature is cruel, but I don't think she means to be. Avatars don't think like human beings, even if they can think more like us than their divine counterparts. It's possible she never noticed her children weren't being picked up after the Brotherhood was wiped out?"

"I thought you said the Brotherhood as absorbed into my people," I said, wondering if Kim Su had been there.

"The Brotherhood of the Tree, at least according to your mother, eventually split on religious lines. The shapechangers wanted to hide from the encroaching settlers after the War of 1812. The fairy-blooded-but-still-human wizards wanted to protect their Odawa allies and use their magic to fight the White Man."

"We know how that fight went," I muttered.

Kim Su had made references to the attempts to help the First Nations survive the encroachment of quote-unquote "civilization" but hadn't mentioned she'd been to Bright Falls before. It would explain why she was sworn to secrecy, though, if a sect had been hiding out here. Those oaths would bind her even centuries later.

Lucien nodded. "The White Man had wizards too. Many made pacts with demons and spread pestilence as well as famine among the locals. In the end the Brotherhood of the Tree was destroyed and the shapechangers were all that was left."

"And what, we just forgot about the goddess in our woods?" I asked.

"No," Lucien said, frowning. "I can't tell you more. Maybe you should call your mother, though."

"Maybe I should," I said, taking a deep breath. "It's sounding more and more like this is just a horrible accident."

"Perhaps," Lucien said, frowning. "There are still some serious questions. Questions which need to be answered."

"Yeah, who was siring the kids across the past century and a half and also why no one seemed to notice there was a goddess in our backyard."

"Also what John Jones wants with his very own incarnate goddess."

I hadn't even thought of that.

Then I cursed myself. "Oh, *fuck*."

"What?" Lucien said.

I felt my face. "I've promised to help Robyn kill the Earthmother."

# Chapter Eleven

"You...what?" Lucien said, staring at me with genuine astonishment on his face.

"I thought Robin's mom was a baby-killing murderer!" I said, pausing. "So of course I promised to kill her!"

*Just because it is a god does not make it immune to justice*, Raguel said.

"Hush you!" I snapped at the gun.

Lucien took a deep breath. "Jane, you can't kill the Earthmother's avatar."

The Earthmother, Danu, Gaia, Jord, and many other names existed as the spiritual embodiment of the world. She was a figure who, as Lucien pointed out, wasn't really good but she wasn't really evil either. The Earthmother gave life and took it in equal measure.

It was difficult to say if the spirit of our planet existed before sentient life had awoken her spirit or because of it, but hating her for apathy was like hating a storm. If there was an avatar in Bright Falls, it went a long way as to explaining why there were so many supernaturals drawn to the area.

"I know!" I snapped, panicking. "Wait, what would happen?"

"I have no idea, and it would be a very bad idea to find out," Lucien said. "You've already killed the avatar's child with the Sky."

Right, the Big Bad Wolf was supposedly the daughter of the Earth. It made more sense now that I knew his mother had been living a few miles down the road. It also explained why there were things like the White Stag and other powerful spirits living in the region. Not only was the Dryad sleeping with local mortals, but also similarly powerful spirits of nature. We had a whole Bright Falls pantheon and mythology here.

I felt my face. "What happens if I break my promise?"

Lucien grimaced. "You'll be branded an oathbreaker among the spirits as well as your fellow mages."

"How bad is that?" I asked.

"Bad," Lucien said. "Regular people can get away with breaking a promise, but supernaturals and especially wizards are creatures of their word. There's some leeway if it was made in haste but it sounds like you made a binding contract."

"Son of a hind," I hissed. "I feel like Cú Chulainn. He was sworn never to refuse hospitality or eat dog meat then had a roast dog offered to him by his enemies."

"What happened to him?" Lucien asked.

"He died," I said. I slapped my forehead and muttered several curses. "Lucien, you didn't really honor your promise to avenge your family."

Lucien stood up.

Oh right, he took his honor seriously. I mean, even more seriously than the fact that a promise was a promise among supernaturals. "I mean, you didn't kill my mother and she was involved in killing your family."

"My promise was to avenge my family," Lucien said, speaking very carefully. "I killed the Darkwater PMC mercenaries who were involved in the purge of the Dragon Clan, exposed your mother's crimes, and have Marcus O'Henry set up to spend the rest of his life behind bars. I think that's fulfilling the entirety of my oath."

He sounded like he was trying to justify it to himself. Truth be told, I knew Lucien wanted my mother dead, so it made me curious how they'd started chatting about local folklore. I wasn't about to debate the issue with him, though. "Yeah, you are the oath-fulfilling guy who glows with honor. Worf and Ned Stark bow before you."

"Thank you," Lucien said, rubbing the bridge of his nose. "In any case, I may have a plan."

"You do?" I said, hopeful.

"Nope," Lucien said, putting his arm around me. "You're going to have to kill Mother Nature."

I slapped him again across the abs then shook my hand to numb the pain. "Well, maybe my visions will provide an answer."

I half-jokingly closed my eyes and tried to use my powers for a vision of the future. As much as my ability to read objects had improved over the past year, my power to perform divinations was still almost completely random. Except this time I saw something terrible.

The first part of my vision saw Lucien shot to death by a sniper in the very room I was standing in now. He lay on the ground, bleeding from a massive hole in his chest from an Anti-Material Rifle—the kind used to blow holes in tanks. I saw the magic run wild in the Lyons Den, tearing apart the place as a tough-looking orange-haired woman in tactical gear stood over his corpse. She then shot herself in the head.

I saw Alex standing over a group of dead Ultralogists, some of who were shapechangers and others vampires while he was covered in sweat as well as wounded. The corpse of a dragon, not Lucien, was behind him even as he fell to his knees. That was when a twelve-year-old girl walked up to him and pulled out a gun, aiming at his head. Alex was unwilling to defend himself and she gunned him down.

Finally, I saw the sight of Robyn wearing a beautiful incandescent blue dress that was almost see-through with a cleavage-exposing v down her front. It was entirely not her style, nor was the fact she was wearing her hair up in a stylized beehive. I saw her speak with a voice of pure music before a great tree to audiences of millions. In the shadows behind her, I saw fish hooks and strings used to puppeteer her every move by Dr. Jones. I saw the Ultralogists spread to Congress, the US Senate, and beyond until shapechangers and vampires were outlawed. A million and a half people died in the resulting purge and civil war.

I saw Bright Falls rebuilt as the Mecca or Jerusalem of the Ultralogist faith only to be hit by an EF5 tornado that killed a third of the town. The Earthmother had grown tired of their blasphemies against her children and chose to end the civilization like she'd done with Pompei and the Minoans.

Then nothing.

"Whoa," I said, collapsing on my knees.

"Are you all right?" Lucien said, leaning down beside me.

"Total *Dead Zone* moment," I said, blinking rapidly. "The book, not the TV show."

"I stopped reading Stephen King after *The Dark Tower* finished," Lucien said, helping me up.

I looked up toward the skylight and saw the slightest outline of a woman aiming a rifle down at Lucien. She was standing up and holding the modified weapon in her hands rather than on a tripod, which from my little knowledge of guns marked her as a supernatural since normal people could handle that kind of recoil.

"Get down!" I said, shouting and pushing Lucien to one side.

If I'd been a normal person, I would have just gotten us both killed since the unusually close sniper tore a hole in the concrete behind us, but I was just fast enough with my enhanced deer-like reflexes to move us both out of the way.

"Stone, bring her to me!" Lucien shouted.

I didn't know who he was talking about until the ceiling underneath our attacker collapsed and the sniper proceeded to fall about twenty feet onto the conference table. Lucien stretched out his hand and, like a Jedi Knight, summoned her rifle toward him, breaking it across his knee. The thing looked like someone had carved a bunch of runes into the side as well as summoned a spirit into it like an inverse Merlin Gun. It burned with hatred for Lucien but I could feel its magic fade away with its shattering.

I turned my head to look at the attacker, seeing the woman from my dreams. She was wearing body armor, gray-and-white camouflage pants, plus a pair of nightvision goggles that made no sense in the daytime but glowed with mystical power. There were a number of weapons across her armor, including a long sheath attached to her belt. The woman underneath had a claw-shaped scar on her cheek, and a resemblance to Clara O'Henry that momentarily put me off. Then she drew a katana and charged at us. What the hell?

"*Deus Vult!*" The woman shouted with a thick Michigan accent that, well, everyone in Bright Falls spoke with.

Lucien wasn't about to let his assassin stab him to death, so he transformed. Unlike what you saw in movies, it wasn't a case of arms stretching or skin shedding, but more like slides in a film reel. One second, Lucien Lyons was a hot man in his mid-twenties, the next he was a twenty-foot-long fire-breathing crocodile.

I pulled back as Lucien unleashed a hell storm of flame the woman cut through with her sword. The weapon caused the flames to part around her and it was just luck that prevented me from being incinerated by the redirected flames. Transforming into a deer, I loped away from the fight to get a better look at what was going on.

*The woman has killed the innocent. You have my permission to slay her.* The Merlin Gun's voice was oddly ambivalent. Usually he was all about slaughtering whomever I pointed him at.

"I decide who pulls the trigger!" I snapped.

*As you wish.*

Lucien being, you know, a frigging dragon did not normally need my help in fighting. However, the woman slashed at him and forced him back even as she managed to avoid his claws as well as tail. When he failed to bite her head clean off, the woman pulled out a small chain bracelet from her pocket then hurled it at Lucien. The chain expanded and wrapped around him until he was trapped. Lucien tried changing back into his human form but the chain shrank around him. That was when the woman walked over with her katana and lifted it above her head.

Right before I smashed into her in deer form and sent her flying through the air. "EPIC SUPER DEER ATTACK!"

The woman on the ground pulled out a handgun and aimed it at me. "This isn't any of your business, Doe!"

She knew who I was? I would have thought about that more, but I was too focused on not getting shot. Looking at the woman, I clutched the Merlin Gun and remembered how that had given me a vision of the War in Heaven. Or a war in Heaven. I'm not quite sure what was true and what was metaphor in that. Either way, it was some of the most messed-up stuff I'd ever seen in my life. I'd learned how to share that sort of imagery with others.

"Ah!" the woman screamed, dropping her gun and clutching the sides of her head.

That allowed me to run up to her and pull out my enchanted Taser, another gift from Alex, and give her three electrical shocks that put her down.

*You used images of the fight with Hell.*

*Yeah*, I said, sighing. *Sorry.*

*No, I approve.*

Of course he did. I pulled out every weapon the woman had, grabbed a pair of zip ties she had on her person, and put them on her wrists as well as legs before going to Lucien's side. I didn't know much about breaking curses, but it turned out I just had pull on the chain in order to get it to return to its original tiny form.

"I'm going to kill that bitch," Lucien growled, climbing to his feet and walking over to my prisoner.

"Hold on, we need to know who she is first!" I said, looking up to the broken skylight. "Lady Boba Fett just attacked you with a sword!"

"I know who she is," Lucien said, picking up her pistol off the ground and aiming it at her head.

"Well, she's my prisoner and I just saved your life, so don't kill her unless I say so," I said, despite the argument not really making any sense.

To my surprise, Lucien seemed to accept it. "She's Sergeant Anne O'Henry, a.k.a Preacher. The former head of Darkwater PMC."

"*Anne* O'Henry?" I asked, having never heard of her. "Is she another of Marcus's daughters?"

"Marcus took advantage of the old laws that allowed him to have sex with any female werewolf or their human relatives," Lucien said, his voice disgusted. "He has a lot of sons and daughters other than the ones in the main line."

Yikes.

I looked between the two. "Wait, I thought you killed all of the Darkwater PMC. I mean, except for Deana."

"I thought I did," Lucien muttered. "It seems I was mistaken."

"You killed my friends and comrades," Anne said, growling. "You're a sick piece of work and you deserve to die."

Lucien stared at her, his eyes reptilian as his mouth belched fire between each word. "You murdered my family, you murdered my clan, and you murdered my people. You are the monster!"

Anne's eyes widened as she stared at him. "You're a Dragon Clan member."

"I am the last." Lucien spat fire on the ground where it sizzled before going out. His mouth basically worked like napalm when he was furious. "I spent a decade thinking about the Nazis who hunted down and exterminated my kind. I trained, studied, and prepared for the day I'd destroy you. My only regret when I found your drunken band of psychopaths? That I made it too fucking quick."

Anne didn't respond but I could tell there was more to the story.

"Don't you think you should wait until Deana is told about this to kill her?" I asked. "I mean, she is your friend."

"Deana is not my friend," Lucien said, sighing. "She's my vassal. There's a big difference."

"Deana is alive," Anne said, staring. "Why?"

Lucien gave her a disgusted look. "Not that it's any of your damned business but I killed the people involved in the murder of my family. You recruited Deana after their deaths. She begged for her life and I was tempted to kill her but I said she'd have a chance to make amends for what she'd done as a soldier."

"You're a drug lord," Anne said, growling. "What do you know about making amends?"

"More than you could possibly imagine," Lucien said, his voice almost a hiss. "I came to this town and saw its poverty, its addictions, its gun running, its sex trafficking, and worse. I took it over by killing the irredeemable while giving the others a second chance. I used the illegal businesses in this town to build a chance for the people dying out because they'd been forced into a position of no hope. I think for them because they couldn't resist the temptations and am building them a kingdom here. Once this damned land deal is done, Bright Falls will be saved."

"Is that what you tell yourself to justify all this?" Anne said, apparently unconcerned that she was at our mercy. "I can feel the black magic permeating the walls."

"Lady, you're the one who broke in here to murder Lucien. Yeah, he's kind of an antihero, but he's helping us solve the murder of those children discovered today. He's also trying to help us stop an evil cult," I said, pulling out the Merlin Gun and aiming it at her. "While that speech may sound way too much like he's the kingpin, he's also my friend. So this is going to tell me whether you deserve to die or not."

*She has not killed anyone for five years.*

*Why?* I asked.

*Regret. Lucien's rampage caused her to feel the fear that she had inflicted upon others. That led to her asking questions she did not want to ask. Questions that led her to want to find some other way to live than killing.*

"So she found Jesus?" I asked aloud.

*Something like that.*

"What is that thing?" Anne said, looking at it. "Why did it show me...that?"

I shrugged. "Your curiosity is not my problem. The gun says you haven't been killing people for a while. Why did you come after Lucien?"

Anne looked at him then me. "Someone sent me his information a week ago. It was a chance to avenge my soldiers. I thought he was hired by our latest employers to take us down. I didn't know he was involved in the...incident here."

"The incident!?" Lucien snapped. "Is that what you call killing—"

"Dragons," Anne snapped. "Dragons heavily involved in organized crime that killed a lot of my men. Thirty-six people died during that attack, six of them noncombatants. We didn't know civilians would be there. My father misled us. Even so, a lot of died. We were unprepared for what we faced."

Lucien's stare was contemptuous, but this wasn't the first time he'd been confronted with the fact his clan hadn't exactly been innocent victims.

"You don't know who sent you this info?" I asked, thinking of the griffon who'd attacked earlier.

"No," Anne said. "All I remembered is meeting with an intermediary. He was sickly smelling, rotting even, with oil on his hands as well as his face."

That didn't describe Dr. Jones at all.

"I see," I said, thinking we might have a new player in the game. "Thank you."

"Yeah, thanks," Lucien said, lowering his gun.

He then lifted it up again and fired.

# Chapter Twelve

"Son of a bitch!" Anne shouted, her ear bleeding from where Lucien had shot the edge off. It looked like pure agony, though I suspected it was more for the fact he'd made sure to make a deafening boom next to a person who had enhanced hearing.

I felt my ears as they rang. "You know I have enhanced hearing too, right?"

"Sorry," Lucien said, shrugging. "I just wanted to make this as painful as possible without killing her. I could have gone for a gut shot if you wanted."

"No," I snapped, looking at him. "Wait, you're not killing her?"

"I heard about the griffon attack from Alice," Lucien said, his eyes narrowed. "One is happenstance, twice is coincidence, and three is enemy action."

"It's only two attacks so far," I said.

"I'm more paranoid than Ian Fleming," Lucien said, looking like he was unsure of his next words. "Right now, Preacher is the only clue we have as to who is coming after you, Jane. I'm not going to execute her just to satisfy a debt that has already been paid."

"Then what?" I asked, suspecting he wasn't just going to let her go.

Lucien snorted. "She broke into my place of business, armed like a video-game character, and tried to kill me. There are benefits to coming out in the Reveal. I'm going to hand her over to the cops."

Anne shot a death glare at Lucien as she struggled in her bonds.

"Clara O'Henry is the sheriff," I said.

"She's also the only honest one in the family aside from Emma," Lucien said. "If they're willing to bargain for her, I'm willing to negotiate. The Shadow Pine development project is my way of recovering all of the Dragon Clan properties the O'Henry family stole. Covering this up would do well to get me more of what I want."

It all came back to the purge of the Dragon Clan from Bright Falls. Once, the Drake family had been every bit as rich and powerful in the city as the O'Henrys. The O'Henrys had owned most of the properties in the town while the Drake had owned the lumber mill as well as forests. The town's present depression was in large part because of the latter getting shut down, though it also meant we were surrounded by pretty forests too.

"I will not be used as leverage against my family," Anne hissed, her canines elongating as her eyes turned to a wolf's. Seconds later, she snapped from her bonds and transformed into a wolf.

Lucien threw her chain at her, where it wrapped around legs like set of boas before wrapping her up the same way he'd been.

Anne reverted to human form, still bound. "Well, this is ironic."

"I'd prefer karmic," I said, staring at her. "Lucien, promise you won't kill or torture her."

"I don't torture people," Lucien said, a slight edge to his voice. "My vengeance is swift and final."

"Except to the survivors," Anne muttered under her breath.

"Yes," Lucien said, his voice dangerous. "Then it is a pain one lives with every day."

Right, well that was taken care of. "I have a sample of a Dryad's descendant's blood and bone. Kim Su said you could maybe help with that as well."

Lucien shook his head. "I'm good at black magic and curses but not necromancy. There's only one wizard in town who is good at that."

"Great." I muttered, suspecting I was going to have to track down another evil wizard. "Who is that?"

"Alex." Lucien surprised me. "He's the only wizard I know who can do both healing and death magic. Blame it on his spectacularly crap childhood."

"Ah," I said, taking a deep breath. "Yeah, well, I suppose it's as good a reason to see him as any."

"Do you need a reason to see him?" Lucien asked.

I was a little scared to, actually, especially after kissing Lucien again. "No, I don't."

Lucien nodded. "You know, if you want my opinion, I think you'd do better with me than him."

"I don't," I said, my voice low.

Lucien gave a half-smile.

"Oh for crying out loud," Anne muttered, struggling to no avail in her chains.

"Goodbye Anne," I said, walking past her.

"Before you go," Anne said, stopping me with her words, "I need to know something."

"Yeah?" I said, staring at the wall that didn't have a door. "Hey, Lucien, could you provide me with an egress?"

"P.T. Barnum's favorite monster. Sure," Lucien said, waving his hand.

A door appeared in the wall where there previously had not been one.

Anne looked like she was struggling to say something. "Where did you get that image you put in my mind? It was…so lifelike."

"Oh, that's because there's an angel in my gun," I said, shrugging. "It's his memories."

Anne stared at me like I'd just told her the moon was made of green cheese then proved it.

"What?" I said.

*Some people react a bit differently to the discovery that their beliefs are no longer a matter of faith.*

"I can tell when people are lying, but you're not lying," Anne said, shaking her head. "There really is an angel in that gun. I can feel its power from here."

"Why were you called Preacher?" I asked, trying to wrap my head around her confusion. "Presuming you had it as your call sign before you found Wolf Jesus."

"Just Jesus," Anne corrected.

I shrugged. "Hey, I've found Stag Jesus. Lewis found Lion Jesus. There's Lamb Jesus…"

Anne closed her eyes. "Please stop."

"Okay." I wasn't trying to make fun of her faith. Quite the opposite. Even if religion wasn't my (medicine) bag, I was kind of doing the rounds as a spiritual leader anyway.

"My mother was Russian and very religious," Anne said,

frowning. "She rejected the ways of the shapechanger faith and raised me in Orthodox Christianity. I didn't believe in anything but what I could see or touch. Even when I found out spirits were real, I just assumed they were psychic background noise to humanity's subconscious. It's been hard adjusting to the fact it's so much more."

"Huh," I said, pausing as I considered her words. "Well, sucks to be you."

Anne continued staring at me. Perhaps trying to figure out how the hell I had a gun that killed demons. It had to be burning her that she'd gone through this entire struggle and I was walking around with a miracle gun.

*All life is a miracle*, Raguel said. *My status is no more or less than mankind's.*

*Yeah, yeah*, I said. *I'm still a polytheist rather than a monotheist.*

*Justice, not religion, is my purview.*

*And thank God for that*, I replied.

*I'm not sure how to respond to that statement.*

I waved at Anne, realizing she was awaiting some sort of answer from me. "Uhm, yeah, go sin no more."

Lucien gave a half-smile. "Yeah, Jane, I don't think you quite have the chops to pull that off."

"Their loss," I said, really wishing I had some coffee and cherry pie now. "Thanks again, Lucien."

"It's nice having someone to keep me from killing people," Lucien said, giving a Boy Scout's salute. "May your gods go with you."

"Yeah, and may I not have to murder one," I said, growling. "I swear, this never happens to Harry Dresden."

Heading through the door, I found myself once more in Lucien's apartment and was surprised to discover it wasn't filled with the dead bodies of my friends and acquaintances. Instead, I found them all gathered on the couches and chatting away merrily. Robyn was telling a story of her time in Vegas and had the entire group enraptured. A part of me believed it was just her powers at work but another thought she was just that charismatic.

*So how am I going to convince her she's a demigod?* I asked Raguel.

*The truth should work.*

Yeah, I bet that worked. I can just imagine grabbing young Prince

Arthur the kitchen boy and telling him he's actually the king.

*He was Sir Kay's squire, a perfectly respectable position.*

*Wait, Arthur was real?* I asked. I shouldn't have been since Kim Su talked about having been there but I also heard she'd been the Rat Pack's manager at one point.

*Arthaeus and his knights were real, though popular mythology has warped their legend. They were a rough-and-tumble band of Anglos, not shining French-inspired chevaliers. Lancelot didn't exist. Gawain was Arthur's right hand and Jennifer's object of adoration.*

*Jennifer?* I asked.

*Guinivere was actually pronounced Gwen-if-fer,* Raguel said.

*Huh, you learn something new every day,* I said. *Anything else?*

*Tristan and Isolde never met any of them. There was a romance that brought down the realm, but there was also an army of demon worshippers.*

That was surprising. *I don't remember that in my* Le Morte De Arthur.

*I hate that book. It accused Arthur of infanticide. But yes, Morgana was on Arthur's side and Merlin was a woman. Kim Su was also the Lady of the Lake.*

I blinked then spoke aloud. "So literally nothing I know about King Arthur is true. Also I owe Kim Su a Coke because I didn't believe her when she claimed that."

*There was a sword.*

Grateful as I was for the distraction, I was pleased when Robyn waved to me. "Yo, Hartbreaker, I'm glad to see you. Did you get what you wanted?"

"Not quite," I said, looking at her. "I did get most of the information we needed, though. We have one more stop to make before we go hunting for your parents, though. Deana, you may want to go talk to Lucien."

Deana shot me a glare that told me the two of us were unlikely to ever become friends, mostly because she kept getting humiliated or almost killed every time we met, but that preceded her getting up and walking to the door.

I wasn't sure how I was going to tell Robyn not only was she a demigod but her mother probably hadn't meant anything by leaving her to die. No, she was just supposed to be raised by a now-extinct cult of druids. The fact Robyn was an atheist would either make the whole conversation much easier or all but impossible. Then again, it was also an option just to leave explaining things to Alex once I told him the whole story, and that looked a lot more appealing right about now.

*So you're passing the buck?*

I paused a second before doing a double-take. "Did you actually just make a joke?"

*No, of course not.*

I pulled out my cellphone and looked through Alex's messages. We'd texted almost the entirety of the past few months. Despite the fact he was seven years older than me and in the FBI, Alex was an enormous goof. I'd even stopped caring about all the various deer puns my family had infected him with. We'd discussed everything from favorite sci-fi movies to video games to how we felt about our families. Well, I discussed my family and Alex mostly listened, I was pretty sure I knew how he felt about his family.

I smiled at the photos of his cases he sent me. I also remembered Halloween of last year when I'd managed to dress up like Elektra and not look ridiculous while he'd gone as Matt Murdock. We'd driven to New Detroit and gotten completely drunk. It was one of our five or six "actual" dates. Even long distance, Alex was one of my closest friends and someone that brightened my day.

"Monogamy sucks," I muttered. Dialing in his number, I waited for him to answer.

"Hello," Alex's voice spoke on the phone.

"So." I paused. "It turns out the purple-haired girl, Robyn Taylor, is actually a demigoddess daughter of a dryad avatar of the Earthmother. We're being attacked by griffons and assassin wolf girls. There's an ancient brotherhood of druids, which is sexist because women should be druids too, and I had a vision of the end of the world. That's what's going to happen if Culty McCultyPpants gets his hands on the Dryad and Robyn. Oh, Lucien says hi."

Alex paused. "Hmm, okay, that makes sense."

"Really?"

"Not in the slightest," Alex said simply. "Are you in any immediate peril?"

"Not really," I said, patting the pocket I kept the Merlin Gun in. "I did learn some fascinating factoids about King Arthur's court, though. Did you know Kim Su was Merlin?"

"Yes, I did," Alex said. "The Merlin Gun was originally Caliburn."

"Who?"

"Excalibur when it's not French."

I blinked. "Wow, you gave me Excalibur? What's wrong with you?"

*Get out*, I said to the Merlin Gun. *Why didn't you tell me you were originally Excalibur?*

*You never asked*, he replied.

"Let's just say Raguel and I had a difference of opinion on how to handle the problem of evil," Alex said, matching me reference-for-reference. "Actually, I'm curious if you could come over to the Lumberjack Inn if you have the time. You should probably bring your goddess friend, Yolanda, and Larry too if you can."

"Do I have to bring the hunters?" I said, looking over at them. "Because, you know, I'm terrified they're going to kill us."

"We're not trying to kill you!" Yolanda said, apparently able to hear our entire conversation. "I've only killed a few innocent supernaturals."

Everyone looked at her.

"By accident!" Yolanda said. "Honest!"

"Why do you want us to go to the crappy part of town?" I asked, knowing exactly where the Lumberjack Inn was. It was where flannel shirts and maple syrup went to die. "I mean, the uncool crappy part of town versus the part we're presently in with the goth nightclubs and casinos."

"It's kind of a long story."

"Hey, I just described my insane day in a decidedly unhelpful manner."

Alex chuckled. "Very well. Dr. Jones is dead and the police think I did it."

"See, you need to be less helpful. That was way too coherent."

# CHAPTER THIRTEEN

Alex, unfortunately, had to hang up soon after, but it put a burr on my butt and sent me straight to the car. The fact he wasn't calling from a jail cell was a good thing even if I wasn't sure what the situation was. I mean, he'd been arrested for the crime he was planning on doing. Assuming he was under arrest at all. Still, I took off with the Millennium Falcon and barely waited to get Robyn and Emma, along with the two people I wanted least involved in this.

Yolanda sat in the passenger's seat beside me while Larry sat behind her, next to Emma, and Robyn. It was a good thing the Hummer had a lot of room even though I was worried about the fact our hunter friends had put a bunch of tote bags full of weapons in the trunk area. I was really going to have to talk to Alex about the company he was keeping.

"So do you think Alex killed him?" Emma asked, speaking politely.

"Probably not," I said, watching rain pour down on my windshield. Bright Falls was one of the rainiest cities in Michigan and I often wondered if we had a bunch of mischievous spirits trying to ruin everyone's day. Then I remembered it was probably more likely the fact Detroit got one hundred and thirty-five days of rain every year and we were a couple of hours' drive away. "If Alex wanted to kill Dr. Jones then he'd do it when he couldn't reincarnate. Otherwise, some innocent is going to get their body hijacked."

"Excuse me?" Robyn said.

"Alex says your cult leader buddy is Voldemort," Emma explained. "We have to destroy his horcruxes first or something."

"Who?" Robyn said, clearly having no idea who that was. Wow, homeschooling in the woods had to be brutal. "A what now?"

"Oh you poor thing," Emma said, reaching over and patting her arm.

"Actually, it's the opposite of destroying a horcrux," Larry said, surprising me by speaking with us. I would have thought him incapable of talking with us monsters. "We need to find a magical object capable of housing Dr. Jones's soul and imprisoning it post-death. That way he can't reincarnate and return to menace the world. Lucien was our best hope for that, but he claims he doesn't have anything strong enough. It's not his kind of magic either."

"Yeah, Lucien doesn't do death magic," I said, frowning. "He said Alex himself is a better fit for it."

"Whoosh!" Robyn made a hand over her head gesture. It immediately en-deered her to me.

Pun intended.

"Yeah, well, we're going to kill Dr. John Jones," I said, my voice cold. "More permanently than he already has been. You have a problem with that?"

"Not in the slightest," Robyn said. "The guy is a total creep. He's one of those cult leaders who consider female followers a privilege rather than a responsibility."

"I'm sorry," I said, taking a deep breath. "Did he—"

"No," Robyn said, her voice losing its usual effervescence. "I was one of the few people he didn't make a move on. Given how it affected some of them, I almost wish he had made a move. It would have spared them some trouble. It's why I don't do religion."

"I used to do religion, but then my husband was eaten by my son," Yolanda said, her voice cold. "I thought the entire world was being overrun with monsters right up until I found a wizard healed a little girl of cancer. He was invoking the power of the Force."

No points for guessing which wizard that was.

"I'm so glad you got something to challenge your evil murderous worldview," I said, less than impressed. "How many innocents did you kill before?"

"Five," Yolanda said. "The rest were a collection of murderers, rapists, and worse."

"Was Alex the wizard?" Emma asked.

Apparently she thought there were multiple wizards who were

priests of pop culture mythology. Alex had once blessed a broken car with the power of Optimus Prime and it started running better than ever.

*That shouldn't have worked*, Raguel said.

*No kidding*, I responded.

"Yes," Yolanda said, not changing her tone. "He was hunting us."

I did a double-take. "What?"

Yolanda let out a gallows laugh. "He thought we were serial killers."

"Weren't you?" I asked.

"How many monsters have you slain?" Larry asked from the back.

I didn't have an answer for that. "Yeah, well, I try to kill things because of what they do rather than what they are."

"Power doesn't corrupt," Yolanda said, frowning. "Power reveals corruption. That was what Alex said to us."

"I think that's from *Dune*. Wait, no, that was power attracts the corrupt." I said, remembering the latter books that involved sex ninjas and Duncan Idaho defeating them with the power of his penis. Yeah, that was weird.

"Knowledge is power, power corrupts, therefore knowledge corrupts," Robyn said. "Which is why everyone in America should remain as stupid as possible."

"We're doing a good job of that," Emma muttered.

Yes, she voted for the other guy last election.

"Oh shush, you," I said, snorting. "By the way, you're a goddess."

"Huh?" Robyn said.

"Demigoddess like Hercules and Gilgamesh," I said, shrugging. "I was trying to figure out a way to break it to you gently, but we're kind of on a time schedule here. I don't know what that means exactly, but I suppose you can open shopping malls and officiate weddings."

"Maybe she can perform exorcisms," Emma suggested. "The Power of Robyn compels you."

"Don't be like Alex," I said, amused more than annoyed. "I remember him discussing the Gospel of Batman."

"No, that would be Robin," Robyn said. "The letters i-n ending versus y-n. In any case, I don't believe in gods so that's just silly."

"Do you believe in spirits?" I asked.

"No," Robyn said, crossing her arms.

"Yet you believe in magic and fairies," I said, trying to get her beliefs straight.

"Yes," Robyn said. "Also aliens. That's in addition to all the supernaturals I can see and talk to."

This was going to be harder than I thought. Also, who the hell believed in aliens? That was *ridiculous*. "So, Yolanda, Alex found your trail of murdered supernaturals and was going to kill you but decided it was better to spare your life."

"Yes," Yolanda said, looking out the window. "Since that time he's been directing us to the worst of the supernaturals he can find that the FBI can't touch."

"Wow, that's all sorts of awful," Robyn said, pausing. "Except, well, the vampires really are murdering hundreds of people every year and covering it up so no, forget I said anything."

*I told him to eliminate them both*, Raguel said. *I considered them too consumed with hatred to ever be anything more.*

*And now?* I asked.

*Everyone is entitled to be wrong once. I've only been wrong three times so far.*

*In all of eternity?* I asked.

*Yes.*

"Well, I'm going to take a big risk in trusting you," I said, taking a deep breath. "Because this is an all-hands-on-deck emergency if we have to bust Alex out."

"Are we?" Robyn asked. "Can't he just brain-zap people in letting him go? That's what Dr. Jones does."

Larry surprised me by speaking first. "Alex can't do that kind of magic. Near as I can tell, what you can do is determined by your personality. Mind-control requires someone who views people as objects and has the willingness to warp someone's soul, as what we believe and decide is our fundamental nature."

"Well I can do it if he can't," Robyn said. "As long as they're at least semi-attracted to girls."

"If they're not?" Emma asked.

"I'll try harder," Robyn said.

I tried not to imagine kissing Robyn but did anyway, which I chalked up to her nature-given sexiness powers. Yeah, that was it.

"Well, I'm willing to help you, Deer-Girl, but I'm going to need something in return," Yolanda said, her voice taking on a cold and downcast voice. "A favor."

"Yeah, sure, anything, I promise," I said, pausing at a stoplight and not paying too much attention.

Emma and Robyn stared at me, which I saw in my rearview mirror.

I blinked before banging my head against the steering wheel. "Idiot!"

Yolanda looked confused. "Is something wrong?"

"Please don't ask me to kill the Pope," I said.

"I...won't?" Yolanda said, now even more confused.

Larry laughed in the back.

"Just how many promises did you break before realizing they were important?" Emma asked, shaking her head.

"I plead the fifth," I said, sighing. "The important thing is that I don't start breaking them now."

"Eh, promises are made to be broken," Robyn said, stretching her arms about and putting them behind her head. "What's the worst that could happen?"

"A giant deer god eats me," I said, making a note how I'd started dealing with much bigger spirits than I ever used to. "Call it an alien if it helps."

"She's killed a couple of god aliens before," Emma said, stretching out her hand before closing four of her fingers. "Pinky swear."

Robyn looked between us and I wondered if she was going to unbuckle her seatbelt and make a dash out the door. "I'll take your word for it."

"That's why promises are important," I said, sighing. "It's also why spirits don't deal with humans very often. We're a race of lying liars who lie."

Not that they were much better. They could tell you the absolute truth and deceive you. They could also just lie and it would be up to the human to prove it. They were much like politicians in that respect.

The Millennium Falcon pulled into Southtown roughly around

this time. Southtown was the aforementioned "uncool crappy part of town." It was about fifteen different diners that served food that could only be eaten with maple syrup, six hardware stores, a few tractor supplies, and numerous cheap hotels that all had trees as the theme.

It would be the kind of solid working-class environment you could raise your kids in if not for the fact that it was also a place utterly soaked in drugs, penny-ante prostitution, and the human population of the town that considered the shapechanger population to be interlopers. You know, despite the shapechangers and their relatives having been here for three hundred years. Still, because of the Deerlightful's present state of danger, I was feeling charitable.

"You know, this is why we need to fight against Alice and Dr. Jones," I said, looking around at the various hundred pickup trucks and jeeps that seemed to be the only cars available.

"So our town can look like a flannel convention?" Emma asked, looking around. "Which, admittedly, it already does."

"No," I said, completely changing subjects. "To keep the heart and soul of Bright Falls from greedy developers and people who would kill the local forest goddesses so they can fulfill promises made in haste."

"I didn't ask you to kill any forest goddesses," Yolanda said, more confused now than ever.

"Not you," Robyn said, rolling her eyes. Clearly she was a lot more on the ball than I'd hoped her to be.

"This is America, goshdarnit," I said, not wanting to invoke any specific gods. "It's my job as the shaman to protect the environment and the people who make their living from it! The people who made this country great!"

That was when a jeep full of drunk teenage boys all wearing shirts with the Confederate flag on it passed by, yelling sexual epithets at us.

Yolanda turned and looked at me.

I watched them drive away, not stopping for the red light. "Michigan fought for the Union."

"Please don't go John Mellancamp on us, Jane," Emma said.

I grumbled. "I just want my parents' damn diner. Is that so wrong?"

"Are you as lost as I am?" Yolanda said, looking back at Larry.

"I haven't a clue about half of what she's saying," Larry said, chuckling.

"Good, then it's not just me," Yolanda said.

Robyn frowned. "Listen, Jane, if you don't want me to kill my baby-murdering parents then that's your business."

"No, I'm totally against baby murder," I said, clenching my teeth. "It's just a lot more complicated than that."

"I've had a baby," Robyn said, her voice firm. "It's really not. I could have left my child to die but I didn't, because I'm not a monster. My mother did, multiple times, and that's why she has to be destroyed. If she didn't want to have me, she shouldn't have, but she did and that's a promise. At least not to throw me away along with my siblings like garbage."

It was hard to argue with that logic. "I'll tell you everything I've learned after we take care of this business with Alex and you can decide."

"So is Gerald Pasteur the vampire really your baby's father?" Larry asked, curious. I was glad for the interruption. "Dhampir children have special needs."

"No," Robyn said. "Gerald just helped me raise him for a few months. Sparrow is as human as I am, which is apparently not as human as I thought."

"And Gerald is what, then?" I asked, actually curious. "Just your ex-boyfriend?"

"Yeah," Robyn said, sighing. "Sort of. He was one of the few people who ever treated me as something worthwhile."

"Vampires only possess, they never love," Larry said.

"And I suppose you know this from experience?" Robyn asked.

"Yes," Larry said, crossing his arms. "It's not me trying to say all of them are evil. It's just that when you gain the power to control men's minds and live forever, it's impossible to keep seeing people as equals. Love is something that needs to be between equals."

"That's a very sweet sentiment coming from someone who used to murder people because they're magical," Emma said.

"Thank you," Larry said, not missing a beat. "Though for me, it was because when I lost what I loved, the only thing I could fill it with was hate. Yolanda knows what it's like to be hollowed out like that."

By the way Larry was speaking, it was clear his feelings for Yolanda were more than just professional. I wondered if he'd gotten into hunting just because she was into it. Then again, maybe I was misreading the situation completely. They could be married for all I knew and I could be imagining a great unrequited love on his part.

I doubted that. Hunters tended to be single men and women or passed down from parent to child. There was something about the profession that required a lone-wolf mentality. I hadn't actually met any other hunters before now but it wasn't like *TIME* hadn't published plenty of articles about monsters as well as the people who slayed them.

The Lumberjack Inn wasn't difficult to find, as it had a twenty-five-foot-tall Paul Bunyan statue in front of it that probably cost more than the hotel itself. It was originally an okay place to stay according to my dad, but the years hadn't been kind to it and was now more the kind of place that charged by the hour. That didn't seem to be the case now since it was packed with cars and vans marked with the Ultralogy sigil (a blue tree and a white deer in front of it—which offended me on multiple levels). There were also a number of police cars, including the sheriff's own, that made me think Alex was in deep trouble.

"Yo, supernatural hitmen," Robyn said, as we pulled into the parking lot of the gas station across the street.

"You mean us?" Yolanda said.

"Yeah," Robyn said, taking a deep breath. "Just so we're clear, I'm like super-important to these guys, so please kill anyone who tries to kidnap me. Cool?"

Yolanda glared back at her.

"Will do," Larry said. "Scout's honor."

I took a deep breath. "You stay here, Robyn. Emma and I will go across the street to see about Alex."

"We will?" Emma asked. "But what if we need to break out Alex like Robyn said?"

"Then they'll hear gunfire."

*This is why I like you*, Raguel said before letting forth an deep, booming laugh.

# CHAPTER FOURTEEN

I decided to take my walking stick with me despite the fact that it felt like all of the magic I'd poured into it had dribbled out. It was supposed to have stored spells in glyphs I'd copied from a book. Spells that would let me hurl wind and fire at my enemies. Now it felt like a stick I'd bought from the hardware store. That was disappointing. Still, one should never underestimate the intimidation value of people thinking you were a wizard.

Walking over to the Lumberjack Inn with Emma, I couldn't help but have my attention go to all the construction going on over the railway tracks. The Deerlightful wasn't in Southtown, being part of North Row (wow, our tiny town had a lot of districts), but it wasn't that far from our present location.

"I feel like Biff Tannen has bought our town and is turning it into that bad timeline from *Back to the Future Part II*."

"Wouldn't that make Lucien into Biff?" Emma asked.

"Hush you," I said, frowning. "I was referring to your sister."

"I know you were, but my family isn't the Mr. Potters of the town," Emma said, looking both ways with me before we crossed the street. "That was just my grandfather. Alice wants Bright Falls to be a safe haven for shapechangers around the country. A place we can live in peace away from all the people who'd want to do us harm."

"You'll forgive me if I missed the part about blackjack and hookers in building the Promised Land."

"Yeah, she's not exactly Moses either," Emma grumbled. "However, we have to take what we can get."

"What does the rest of your family think of all this?" I asked, thinking about talking to some of the other O'Henrys. It was a long shot, but I needed to come up with a serious plan to save the

Deerlightful.

"My parents are ambivalent. They've been numb since Victoria's death. Brad is looking forward to whatever job he gets when the Shadow Pine Project is done. Clara doesn't want the town to grow. It was bad enough with all of the crime she had to deal with before, but she's had to double the size of the police force," Emma said, speaking of her family as if they were a collection of strangers. As far as I knew, she was only close to her Clara while her parents kept her trained like one of Pavlov's dogs. Alice would probably sell her to a rich couple in search of an exotic pet.

I stared at her as we reached the other side of the street. "Isn't it the mayor's job to decide how big the police force is?"

"He just does whatever my family tells him to do." Emma wrinkled her brow. "I suppose, technically, we are the Mr. Potters of the town."

I snorted. "Listen, I want this town to prosper, I'm just worried it's not actually going to improve things but make the one percent of the town's population even wealthier while the remaining ninety-nine percent get even poorer. A lot of small businesses are getting bought up or closed down. Mine in particular."

"Those businesses were getting closed down anyway," Emma said, showing she was still an O'Henry. "Besides, aside from the Outlands, Bright Falls' biggest appeal is its environment. They're not going to tear down everything green and ruin the very reason people might come here to our future tourist trap of a town."

"There's a difference between a golf course and a forest, Emma," I said, sighing. "You know as well as I do. Eventually, we'll all be running on O'Henry land or getting shot at by hunters."

"Yeah, well, the Lorax isn't doing us any good either," Emma muttered. "Did you really care before this started to affect you?"

She had a point there. Any further questions I might have asked were blunted by the arrival of Alex and Sheriff O'Henry. Alex wasn't wearing handcuffs or showing any signs of restraint. Indeed, he was wearing his FBI uniform and I could see the bulge under his jacket indicating he was still armed too. Not that owning a gun made Alex dangerous. Unlike me, he did have access to all sorts of nasty killing spells and supernatural martial arts—ones he hated using.

Clara looked amused and was wearing the stereotypical sheriff's hat that always looked better on a park ranger than a member of law enforcement. Indeed, her expression went beyond amused to the genuinely happy. It was an odd expression for someone who had uncovered a mass grave of newborns earlier that day.

"Hello, you two," Alex said, walking over and giving me a hug before a short kiss on the lips.

I blinked, feeling immensely guilty about kissing Lucien. "Oh, hey! Glad you're not arrested for murder!"

Emma elbowed me in the side. Perhaps it wasn't a great idea to announce that to the world.

"Yes," I said, glad she did that. "Because that would be bad."

Alex gave a pained smile. "Yes, it would seem while certain parties believe I did kill Dr. Jones, they don't seem too interested in pursuing the subject now."

"The evidence is very flimsy," Clara said, giving a wink. "It would be imprudent to throw any kind of wild accusations at parties unknown just yet. You can be sure we'll be on this murder case, no matter how many years it takes. I will say, though, our suspect list is leaning toward an out-of-towner we don't know. Race unknown. Sex unknown. Possibly male, possibly not."

"Subject is hatless," I said, staring at her sideways. "What am I missing here?"

Clearly, Clara wasn't taking the murder of the evil cult leader quite as seriously as she should. Wait, maybe she was taking it exactly as seriously as she should.

Clara gave me a thumbs-up, then Alex, before walking back to the crime scene.

"She thinks I killed Dr. Jones and is happy about it," Alex said, sighing. "Clara believes he's involved in the infant murders despite the lack of evidence."

"Yeah, well, he wasn't. Just to be clear, you were planning on killing him, right?" I asked, making sure I'd gotten everything correct.

"Yes, but not this way," Alex said, looking over at the room with the yellow police tape. "His spirit will move on from where he was killed and possess one of his followers. All it will do is lead to another innocent death and interrupt his operations for a little while."

"See, I told you," I said, looking at Emma.

Emma shrugged. "I didn't disagree with you in the first place."

"So who did do it?" I asked, frowning. "Assuming you can put your magnificent FBI wizard abilities to good use."

"I have not the slightest idea," Alex said, shrugging his shoulders. "This place is one of the most spiritually dead places I've visited, which is probably why Dr. Jones chose it for his temporary base. I was hoping to get your help here, Jane."

"Deputy Doe here to help," I said, giving the Girl Scouts' salute.

"You shouldn't say that or Clara will recruit you," Alex said.

"She's offered," I said, more tempted than I'd like to admit. "How have you been? Any attacks by griffons or werewolf mercenaries?"

"I can't say that I have," Alex said, blinking at my statement. "I did solve a thirty-year-old murder but that turned out to be unrelated to this case."

"Well, here's what's gone on in my past few hours." I clasped my hands together. I neglected the part where I made out with Lucien.

Alex blinked after I finished. "Well, you've had a more productive day than I have."

"Yeah, I know it sounds a little strange…" I muttered, trailing off.

"Strange? Hardly," Alex said, smiling. "I talked with Carl Sagan's ghost once. We smoked pot and discussed the nature of the universe as an accidental place versus a deterministic one as well as whether the nature of the latter would require intelligence. We also discussed how the Klingons looked in *Star Trek: Discovery*."

"Who won?" I asked.

"Science," Alex said. "I admit, I'm not sure how he won the part about disproving ghosts existed, though."

"Well, clearly he's an expert on the subject," I said. "So yeah, Robyn's a demigoddess and I'm neck-deep in promises."

"One of which is to kill a god," Alex said, nodding. "Do you want me to talk to her?"

"Please," I said, sighing. "I need a break to cleanse my brain."

"Temporarily dead or not, Dr. Jones is at least off the board for a bit," Alex said, sighing. "That does give us a bit of breathing room to plan our next move."

"Good," I said, waving my staff. "I'd hate to have to use this on some of the cultists over there."

"Your staff is actually empty," Alex said, acknowledging what I'd hoped he'd miss.

"Yeah," I said, grimacing. "I think I screwed up my rune carving since it was three a.m. on a Friday night. I hadn't been asleep for three days thanks to trying to pass my two-year-degree final exams."

"If I may?" Alex stretched out his hand.

I handed it over. "Don't bust it. I worked hard on this."

"I'll treat it as my own." Alex pulled out a large pocket knife that he used to adjust one of the runes on it. "Glyph magic isn't like other sorcery, since it invokes spirits to allow effects to be done regardless of the skill of the magic user. Yours was leaking do to the wrongly inscribed moon seal. You still need to charge it, though, which the runes serve as batteries for."

"Yeah, I know that," I said. Taking my staff back, I closed my eyes and filled it with mystical energy. After a few seconds, it hummed with power. "There, full."

Alex blinked a few times and opened his mouth to say something before stopping himself.

"Something wrong?" I asked, wondering why the usually blunt FBI agent was holding back this once.

"Just noting it would have taken me a week to do that," Alex said, showing the barest hint of envy.

"Huh," I said, looking at the staff. "I guess I was conceived by the midiclorians."

"I actually know what Lucas was going for with those and I still think it was a dumb idea," Alex said, looking on at me in amazement. "Your potential is off the charts, Jane. Stronger than any other natural wizard I've encountered."

"Yeah, I just wish I could utilize that potential," I said, grumbling. Emma's earlier digs about me not having any 'boom-boom' magic were accurate even if I was ten thousand Duracell batteries. I couldn't resist asking how I compared, though. "How long would it take Lucien and Kim Su to charge up ye ol' walking stick?"

"About a month and two weeks probably," Alex said, giving me a surprisingly precise answer. "Magic is like music," I muttered, "an art rather than an exact science. Some people have a natural talent they can cultivate and other people are just tone deaf to it."

"Well thank you for tooting my horn," I paused. "Okay, that sounded dirty."

Emma giggled, having been notably quiet during this conversation. It took me a second to realize she was trying to be supportive.

Alex smirked. "I'll buy you lunch after we take a look at Dr. Jones's body. I'll also fix up Yolanda and Larry's dowsing rod with samples of Robyn's hair and that piece of bone she brought. I can turn it from a generic evil finding device to a specific Dryad-finding device. I'll need your help to do it, though. I don't have the *oomph* you do."

"You have plenty of oomph but I'll gladly do it," I said, looking across the street at the Falcon. "How did you become friends with those two, anyway?"

"You mean how do I maintain friendships with people who hunt the supernatural while being the supernatural myself?"

"No, you're ninety percent human. I mean how did you meet them period? *Why* be friends with them?"

Alex paused and looked at my waistband where I'd hidden the Merlin Gun under my shirt in a leather band I'd sewn into most of my pants. His demeanor shifted and I knew he was about to share something personal. Despite having the typical attitude of Cloud Cookoo Land's king, Alex had a tragic past. There were things he'd not opened up to me about he kept from everyone else. He'd been abused as a child, killed his abusive father (and innocent sister) during his power's awakening, and spent time in a mental institution run by quacks. That was before he'd become a hunter and FBI agent.

Finally, he spoke. "I used to be a person who devoted himself to killing. Trying to eradicate evil and quench the fury in my chest from all the things I'd suffered at my father's and the asylum's hands. Feeding my bloodlust only made it worse, though. I destroyed two dozen supernaturals and as many evil humans across two years with the Merlin Gun. Rapists, serial killers, human traffickers. The worst of the worst on both sides. I was so successful, the FBI nicknamed me the Huntsman and covered up my crimes. They eventually tracked me down, though, but not to arrest me. They wanted me to take a more legal route to fighting evil. To assist them in coordinating anti-supernatural operations along with other hunters. An offer I accepted. It was during my second mission when I saw that same fury I felt in Yolanda and, to a lesser extent, in Larry. I wanted to give them the same opportunity I was pursuing. A chance to be better than the anger."

I blinked, processing that. "Did you ever kill an innocent as a hunter?"

"No," Alex said, sighing. "The Merlin Gun prevented that. I killed people who might have abandoned the path of evil, though. People who were victims before they became victimizers. People I was starting to resemble. Enough that I grew utterly sick of that and wanted to serve as a protector instead of a punisher."

"Lucien is like you in that," I said, sighing. "Did you inspire him to do that?"

Alex paused. "No, I was the one who helped him go on his mission of vengeance."

*He is the most successful hunter of the modern era,* Raguel said. *It is a shame he decided to give it up.*

*You used him,* I said, disgusted with my weapon.

*As he did me.*

Emma looked deep in thought. "Wait, how did you get a degree in psychology when you were being the Punisher?"

I looked at her. "That's what's bothering you?"

"Yeah," Emma said. "I mean, the numbers just don't add up."

"I had Hermione's Time Turner," Alex said, smiling.

Emma paused before leaning in as if to whisper. "I know you're joking but I really hope you're telling the truth. Which is possible, because you're you."

"Quite a few of the monsters were in groups," Alex said, trying to downplay he'd been Van Helsing on steroids when the world had descended into chaos following the Reveal. "I also took a lot of online courses. Lucien was with me on a lot of those missions too. He blamed me for abandoning him when I decided to join the FBI, and he wasn't wrong for it."

"Did you drive a black Impala while listening to hair bands?" I asked. Man, I loved *Supernatural* to an absurd degree.

"No, Jane."

"Aww," I said, surprisingly okay with the idea Alex was a hunter.

It was massively hypocritical on my part, but I knew he wasn't the kind of guy to ever hunt my people just for what they were.

*It was massively hypocritical on your part since you are a hunter.*

*You shut your damned mouth! If you had one!*

*Divine mouth if I had one.*

Stupid grammar angel.

"To answer your earlier question, yeah, I'd love to get lunch with you," I said, smiling. "I'm about tuckered out from people trying to kill me and I need to vent about a thousand different things."

"Consider me your ventilator," Alex said, pausing. "Which doesn't sound dirty so much as stupid."

"I'll forgive you. We should eat at the Deerlightful where you should leave a big tip despite two out of the three owners sucking," I said, smirking. "Cherry pie is on me, but everything else is on you—but not because I'm a woman. Instead, it's because I've got debt up to my eyeballs."

"So noted." Alex nodded. "I may not have Lucien's money, but special agents are unlike other government employees in that we can actually survive off our salaries. I also put everything on my expense account. That allows me to save money for when I have to inevitably go into hiding for all the various crimes I've committed as an agent."

"Thank the Goddess for Uncle Sam's deep pockets," I said before turning to Emma. "Emma, you stand watch outside of the crime scene and bark once for yes and twice for no if anyone is coming toward us."

"Oh, ha-ha."

"You think I'm kidding but we almost got eaten by an eagle-lion." It single-handedly explained why no one wanted to ride them to Mordor. That thing with the One Ring would have been worse than Sauron.

*It really wouldn't have been,* Raguel said.

*Hush you. Just stay on the lookout for evil to kill.*

*As you wish.*

# CHAPTER FIFTEEN

There was a sense of peace walking beside Alex that I didn't quite understand, since he just admitted to being a guy who'd killed a fifty people. Then again, I'd seen just how evil and awful the world could be, so maybe I just didn't care there were a few less monsters. Human or otherwise.

"So were you serious about coming to work here in Bright Falls permanently?"

"Yes," Alex said, taking a deep breath. "They offered me a permanent position teaching magic at Quantico, but I don't have any interest in that."

"Wow, you want to come here that much?" I asked.

"Yes and no," Alex said. "Yes, I love Bright Falls and its environment. Murder is a stranger here and the people are kind in a way I don't feel in Washington D.C."

Wow, did he misjudge this town.

Alex continued. "But, actually, it's also the fact magic isn't easily taught. You either have the knack for it or you don't, and the type of sorcery you do is determined by the person you are. You can't standardize that. The FBI would be far better off recruiting existing magicians and letting them recruit at their own pace."

"Magic is like music," I muttered, remembering Larry's words.

"Yeah," Alex said. "Plus, there's someone in town that I'm very interested in."

"Kim Su?" I asked.

"Ha-ha. You know who I mean," Alex said, showing he did consider me his girlfriend.

That made me smile. "So you're okay with dating a nineteen year old?"

"If only there was a law for when it was appropriate to date someone younger than yourself. Like, say, if they were an adult at eighteen."

"Old enough to kill, old enough to date an FBI agent." I snorted. "In any case, I won't lie to—"

The two of us reached the crime-scene door, but no sooner did we do so than two figures stepped in front of it. The first of them looked like a younger, better-looking version of Dr. Jones with silver-white hair but a face showing him to be in his early thirties at most. He was wearing the typical white suit of an Ultralogist but of a much more expensive and finer cut than the majority of them around us.

The second one's appearance made my blood run cold, as it was the twelve-year-old girl from my vision. She was wearing a white blouse and skirt but had a little blue vest on as well as a headband that gave her a little color. The twelve-year-old girl had auburn hair and freckles, but this didn't disguise the fact there was a crazy zeal in her eyes as well as a magical aura stronger than Lucien's.

I grabbed Alex's arm. "Oh hey, uh, hello, Ultralogy people."

"David," Alex said, looking at the man in front of me. "Judith."

David was notably the name of Dr. Jones's son according to Robyn. Robyn had also said he was a decent person compared to other Ultralogists.

"You're both going to burn in hell," Judith said, looking between us. "You're unworthy before the eye of the Preceptus."

"And a fine hello to you too, little girl," I said, sighing.

"Be kind, Judith," David said, the man said, pressing his hands together as if in prayer but aimed downwards.

"The black knight and the pawn turned black queen are our enemies," Judith said, glaring at us both. "When our father returns from the dead, he shall wreak a terrible vengeance upon them."

Judith then walked off, actually hissing at us.

"She reminds me of a movie star," I said, watching her depart. "Linda Blaire."

Alex looked away, clearly trying not to laugh.

"Judith has the misfortune of having been raised in the Ultralogist family," David said, surprising me. "She's been fed nothing but a steady stream of father's propaganda and his rules since childhood."

"And yet you continue to serve your father's will," Alex said, sounding more confused than condemnatory.

"I believe in the principles of Ultralogy," David said, simply. "I helped write them after all. I just dislike how my father misuses them. As to why I continue serving him, he is my father and we live in a world where any source of hope is a good thing."

"Their wallets would disagree," I said, not having any sympathy for this guy or his religious convictions. "You know your dad is going to come back from the dead, right?"

"Yes," David said, his voice low. "The last time it happened, my elder brother Saul was wiped away. I'm terrified of being next."

My eyes widened. "He possessed his own son?"

"Replaced," David corrected, as if it were just an issue of grammar. "Blood ties make the Eternal Life spell easier to perform. My father has tried to sire children with other cultists so he has a host of other bodies but that is a long term project. I expect him to possess me only begrudgingly because I am unsuitable."

"Unsuitable?" I asked, trying to guess what was wrong with him in Dr. Jones's eyes. I couldn't feel any aura of power from him. He had less magical people than even quote-unquote "normal" people did. Perhaps because his father had sucked it all out of him. "Because you don't have magic?"

"Because I do not like women," David said, sighing. "The Prophet of the Earthmother has some decidedly retrograde beliefs."

Prophet of the Earthmother? Was that coincidence? I briefly considered reading up on their religion before deciding that would make me suicidal. "No offense, Dave, but I think you should drop your Selfosophy card fast. It sounds like a raw deal all the way."

"I could," David said, sighing. "Then my father would kill me. Even if he didn't, though, then who would look after Judith? What little I can do is better than nothing."

"All that is required for evil to triumph is for good men to think the lesser evil is enough," Alex said, sighing. "I didn't kill your father, David."

"No, Huntsman, if you did then he would not be returning." David let out a sigh. "It seems we have a common enemy."

"No," Alex said, pointing to his side and gesturing for David to get out of the way. "We don't."

Charles stepped aside and Alex waved his hand over the police tape, causing it to shimmer like it was a blurred picture. Alex walked through it without breaking it. Blinking, I did the same and it felt like the tape was water rather than an actual physical substance.

Charles watched us enter the room. "I want to help you, Alex."

"Just like you helped Laura?" Alex asked. "She trusted you and she's dead. Did you lift a finger to help her or did you just stay silent when your father murdered her?"

Charles had no response to that and departed.

I walked past it and headed to the location we needed to investigate. The interior of hotel room seventeen was the kind of place I didn't really want to run a black light over because of what I might find. The walls were pea green while the windows were covered with a set of pine-tree drapes that would look tacky on, well, a cheap motel's windows. The bed had numerous maps of Shadow Pine Park spread out over it, black-and-white pictures of Robyn, plus pamphlets as well as poster designs for a 'Save Shadow Pines' project.

The body of Dr. Jones was on the ground at the foot of the bed, a silver knife stuck through his chest, but surprisingly little blood. His expression was one of surprise with his mouth hanging open as well as his eyes staring up at the ceiling. A knocked-over chessboard was on the ground, the only pieces standing up being a white bishop and pawns.

The bathroom door to my side was open and led to a gross interior where an Ultralogist cultist's body was sitting on the toilet, having been shot in the head. It was an ugly image, but nothing I hadn't seen before.

"No dignity," I said, shaking my head.

"Death is rarely dignified," I said. "At least he was on the commode when his bowels emptied."

"Yeah," I said, grimacing. Being a weredeer, I could always smell that happening to corpses. "So you knew that guy, Charles?"

"Laura did," Alex said, sighing. There was a dreamy, mournful quality to his next words. "She was the person who convinced me people should be redeemed, if at all possible, versus killed."

"She sounds like a nice girl," I said, feeling strangely jealous of the late married older FBI agent.

"She was special," Alex said, the regret still heavy in his voice. "I've only known a few people like her. Charles reminds me not everyone will accept the chances people give them. I have no doubt he helped her right up until the point when it became dangerous."

"People who sit on the fence get kicked by both sides," I said. "Uh, Alex, I had a vision of Judith shooting you in the head. Try not to let that happen to you."

Alex paused. "That would be an unfortunate way to die."

I wasn't sure if I could ask him to shoot her if she tried to do it because, murderous little brat or not, it was still killing a kid. "I'm just saying, if you need my Taser then it's an option."

Alex laughed at my statement.

"Not joking," I said.

Alex looked over the maps on the bed, stepping over Jones's body like it was garbage. "So his plan was to find the Dryad and bind it in Robyn's body so he could take her over and wield the powers of a god?"

"That is some *Big Trouble in Little China* supervillain craziness," I said, shaking my head. "But yeah, basically. Eventually, Mother Nature destroys Bright Falls in response. Nice to know actual honest-to-Goddess divine punishment is for stuff like trying to enslave the universe instead of voting Democrat."

"I'm Independent," Alex said, lifting up the white bishop. "I wonder if this means anything? No, it's just finding symbols in things that don't exist."

"Shouldn't you be the white knight?" I asked. "You know, black and white tending to go with the former as bad and the latter good."

Alex shook his head. "Like Johnny Cash, I believe black is the color of the good guys and white is the color of the wicked. One hides behind the light while the other embraces all its many colors."

"That's a beautiful, albeit meaningless, statement," I said, walking forward to examine the body. "Okay, I better get to seeing who killed Dr. Evil."

I may have already mentioned it since I loathed using it in just about any situation involving murder, death, or infanticide, but my Gift sucked. Being able to get psychic impressions off objects was really only useful when you wanted to verify if an object was real or when it was involved in a horrible crime. I had better control over it now than in my teenage years so I wasn't picking up on things like what Jeremy had done on his sheets when doing the laundry, but that was small potatoes compared to reliving people's last minutes.

Reaching down to touch the knife in the man's chest, I heard Alex speak. "You don't actually have to do this, Jane. It's not your responsibility to help me clean up Kim Su and my messes."

"Hey, I want to help," I said, only slightly fudging the truth. "Also, I don't see how the Ultralogists are your fault."

"Kim Su trained my father who trained Dr. Jones."

I blinked. "Is it just me or is your life basically *Star Wars*?"

"Thankfully, I was never involved in a relationship with Lucien," Alex said.

I stared at him.

"Please tell me that's not a mental image you have," Alex said.

"No," I said, lying outright. "Of course not."

I wrapped my hand around the knife and found myself, thankfully, just feeling the impression of the past couple of hours. The knife was enchanted and full of unholy energies that caused the vision to be confusing and dream-like. It was like everything was wrapped through a green filter.

The man carrying the knife was nervous, sick with himself, actually but also determined. He was wearing a thick flannel overcoat despite this being summer. He was also carrying an amulet that made him less likely to be noticed. It was the same kind of weird sorcery that had been used on the griffon, since I could feel the pain inside his body from where it was killing him. The man using the magic knew it was toxic but believed the use of said magic was worth the cost.

He walked up from a green-and-brown jeep to the door, passing by several Ultralogists who paid him no mind before knocking his fist against the door of room seventeen. I could tell the man was African American, but couldn't adjust my perspective of the knife to see his face. The magic was too strong and interfering with my gaze.

The door opened and Dr. Jones answered it. "Oh, it's you."

"We need to talk," a distorted, confused voice spoke.

Jones snorted. "I don't think there's anything you have to tell me I would want to hear."

The knife holder coughed, blood coming up his mouth. "I know what you're up to."

Jones turned around and walked away, leaving the door open. "I think not. Besides, you were happy when I first picked her up."

"You lied to me," he said.

"I lie to everyone," Jones replied. "Besides, I'm saving your precious forest, aren't I?"

"There is no forest without Her," the knife holder said, reaching down into his overcoat pocket and clutching it. I could hear the capitalization in the last of his words. This man had a very close relationship to the Dryad.

Not sexual, something deeper.

Jones went over to his chess board, which was still on the side of the bed, and moved a white knight. "You need to think of the larger picture, friend. We're running out of environment to despoil and becoming an overpopulated hellhole. Not just of humans either. The vampires are breeding out of control now that no one is hunting them and their leaders have lost the right to cull their progeny at will. Speaking as a man who intends to live forever, we need to make sure there's a Mother Earth in the coming centuries. What better way to do that than make the Earthmother a being they can worship? They're so sick of spirit and in need of something to worship they'll flock to Ultralogy and abandon their old gods. A new creed will replace the old that will be sweet, sugary, and in line with modern morality. One that will give them the direction they need to fix this planet's problems."

I was surprised, really, to find out that Jones believed at least some of what he preached. It was still grossly cynical, but I couldn't say it was entirely wrong. Then again, I wasn't a big fan of the public at large myself. It was easy to dismiss the environment in your air-conditioned apartments, but not so much when you had to avoid cars every few miles of your moonlight run.

"I don't disagree with anything you've said," the man said, taking a deep breath.

"Thank you," Jones said, standing up to put his hand on the knife wielder's shoulder.

The knife wielder stabbed Jones in the heart. "But you're not hurting Robyn."

The knife glowed when it entered Jones's chest, causing blood to pour out of his mouth. The weapon's black magic easily tore through the cult leader's defenses and quenched his life. I could see his spirit depart his body before it was dead, though, flying away through the door. The man holding the knife let Jones's body fall before he pulled out a silencer-equipped Desert Eagle and opened the bathroom door, killing the man inside. He felt regret for doing so but was still determined to do what he felt was the greater good.

Then nothing.

The vision ended.

I took my hand from the knife. "Okay, our black magician is working alone. I think. He didn't exactly strike me as a joiner. He's also dying."

"I see," Alex said, taking a deep breath. "His motives?"

"Protect Robyn and the Dryad," I said. "Is it possible the Brotherhood of the Tree still exists?"

"A very good question," Alex said, looking back. "One that will only be answered, I believe, by visiting the Dryad herself."

I nodded then turned around to see the man who'd died in the bathroom. He was standing up, not wearing any pants, with a huge hole in his head. He stretched out his arms and walked toward me.

"Jane," the dead man moaned.

Would you be disappointed to hear I screamed?

# Chapter Sixteen

I pulled out my gun and aimed it at the dead man before firing twice. The bullets passed through the figure and landed against the hotel wall beside the door.

"What the hell!?" I asked, staring as the figure stuck his arms into my face and waved them around.

It felt a bit like a chilly breeze before I walked through the figure, unharmed.

"It's a ghost," Alex said.

"I know ghosts," I said, staring at it. "They look like my grandfather and don't look like they were shot on the commode like this guy."

"Your grandfather is an actual spirit of the dead," Alex said, looking at the moaning creature that turned around to go for me again. "This is more the malevolence and anger of someone left behind. Call it a poltergeist or specter if you need to differentiate it."

"How do I get rid of it?" I asked, stepping out of its way as it stumbled after me again. It was like a immaterial zombie—not very smart. "Also, how does it know my name?"

"Search me," Alex said, frowning. "It may be trying to pass on a message."

"Park, park, park," the specter moaned. "Ranger."

"Uh-huh," I said. "I think it said 'Park Ranger'."

"No kidding," Alex said. "Stick your hand into it and tell it to go away."

"What?" I asked.

"You're a shaman," Alex said, shrugging. "Also, you're much stronger than me."

"In death magic?" I asked.

"Just do it," Alex said.

"All right," I said, jabbing my fist into the specter's chest. "Get ye to the afterlife, Casper."

The specter burst into flames, letting out a silent scream as he did so.

I looked over to Alex. "Is that supposed to happen?"

"Usually it's a ray of light," Alex said, grimacing. "This fellow seems to have gone someplace unpleasant."

A year ago, I didn't believe in Hell. I believed no truly good deity could condemn an innocent soul to an eternity of suffering. That was before I got banished there by the Big Bad Wolf for five minutes (Alex with me). I'd also encountered a number of demons from there since. I wasn't sure how this affected my worldview but it was uncomfortably true that evil existed in a spiritual form rather than just as an opposite of good.

*I could have told you that,* Raguel said.

*Hush you,* I said. *I'm having a spiritual crisis and the last thing I need is an angel butting in with answers.*

*Fair enough,* Raguel said.

Clara and Emma emerged at the other side of the police tape seconds later.

"Are you okay?" Clara asked. "We heard shots."

"It's fine, just a ghost," I said, looking at the door. "I didn't hit anyone, did I?"

"No," Clara said, shaking her head. "You did shoot out an Ultralogist's window, though."

"Thank the gods," I said, taking a deep breath. "Gun safety is an issue when you're faced with immaterial beings."

Emma looked around. "Is the ghost still here?"

"No," I said, looking around. "He's gone down where the goblins go, below, yo-ho-ho."

"Middle Earth?" Emma asked, confused.

I shook my head. "In any case, I think we're done here. Do you have anything to add, Alex?"

Alex lifted up a white king from the chessboard in a handkerchief and looked at it for a moment before slipping it into his pocket. "Yes, I have everything I need. Thank you for letting us view the crime scene, Sheriff."

"You're welcome," Clara said, frowning. "I don't like doing

favors for friends, but I like the idea of cultists and baby murderers even less. Besides, I know you guys are the good guys. Anyone else would have shot me when I was possessed."

Raguel had said we should shoot Clara while she was possessed, but I was glad we exorcised her instead. Not the least because it had obviously come in handy a bit down the line. "We're close to finding out who was responsible."

"Well, make sure you tell me so we can hang them," Clara said, giving a thumbs-up.

"Yeah, because that's not creepy," I muttered, walking to the police tape and just stepping through as it got in my face. I didn't want to spend another minute in room seventeen. Emma helped remove the tape as Alex departed with me.

"Did you find anything out?" Emma asked, joining at my hip.

"Maybe," I said, frowning. "It seems like there could be a remnant of the Brotherhood of Trees in the area."

"You think there's a three hundred-year-old group of druids still secretly living in Bright Falls?" Emma asked skeptically.

"Versus the secret sect of shapechangers?" I asked.

Emma didn't have an answer for that.

My stomach growled. "Listen, I think we're all at our wits' end and need a break. Emma, can you join the hunters and Robyn to keep an eye on them until we're ready to go out into the woods. Alex has said we can get the divining rod to work on finding the Dryad. We need to do that so we can…figure something out. That doesn't involve killing her. So we'll also need some supplies. Do you think you can handle that, Lieutenant O'Henry?"

"You want to hang out with your boyfriend you haven't seen in months and want me to get lost," Emma said, nodding. "Gotcha."

"Evil truth-telling doggie," I muttered, scratching behind her ears.

"This is racist," Emma said, smiling broadly. "Please don't stop."

I didn't for a few seconds. "You know me so well, Prince Woof-Woof. Now go, play."

Emma rolled her eyes. "I'm going to buy the ugliest pair of hiking boots imaginable."

"That means they're effective," I said, pointing to the car across the street. "Only my sister, mother, and all my other female relatives care about sexy hoofware."

Emma departed and, for once, nothing seemed to be going bad. The fact this was a sentiment I had in the middle of two murder investigations as well as a fight against gentrification said just how crazy my life had become.

"Boyfriend?" Alex asked, standing beside me.

"Unless you have a problem with it?" I asked.

"Nope," Alex said, sighing. "My relationships have been a bit unorthodox, though."

"Not much time for socializing in the nuthouse?"

Alex looked down at me, raising one eyebrow.

I winced, realizing this was probably one of the subjects that Alex wasn't actually comfortable making jokes about. Mental health facilities had come a long way since Bedlam House, but I got the impression Alex's place of treatment wasn't one of the nicer ones. I took a deep breath and stretched out my arms. "Would you believe I have no filter on my mouth?"

"Actually yes," Alex said, smiling again. "Of course, that is one of my own flaws. It comes with my atypical brain chemistry."

"It comes with my not giving a flying buck," I said, having embraced my deer pun habits. "I tried to be nice to people and all it ended up as was getting be ground underhoof by the world's herd mentality."

"You already used a hoof pun," Alex said.

"Dammit," I said. "I guess my songwriting career is out of the question."

"Yes, deer."

"I see what you did there," I said, smiling. Said smile left my face when I saw Judith staring at us from the second floor of the Lumberjack Inn, looking in between the balcony bars. It was a glare of death and I wondered what the little troll was plotting. I shouldn't have been concerned about a pre-teen trying to kill me, but I'd already seen her kill the strongest mage I knew so I thought my paranoia was justified.

*Using the innocent as soldiers is a Hell-worthy offense.*

*I could have figured that out on my own, Raguel,* I said.

*Just checking.*

I clasped my hands and looked over at Alex. "So let's get some cherry pie and coffee."

"I actually don't like cherry pie," Alex said.

I stopped in mid-step, horrified.

"Just kidding," Alex said, raising his hands in mock protest. "I do like apple more, though."

"You monster," I said, horrified. "How could you?"

Alex chuckled. "It's good to be back, Jane."

I hesitated to ask my next question. "Are you really giving up a position at Quantico because you don't want it?"

"You're asking me, I assume, if I'm actually coming to live here at Bright Falls because I want to be with you rather than my career?"

"Uh, yes?"

"Partially," Alex said, looking at me. "The truth is, I've had enough of serial killers and monsters to last a lifetime. My entire life has been one long road trip between evil-doer after evil-doer that I don't have enough gas left in me to keep going. I don't want to continue hammering the gavel of judgment without knowing what exactly I'm hammering for."

I felt the back of my head and tried to parse what he said. "Okay, three things that come to mind. First: You can't say evil-doer in a sentence without sounding ridiculous. It doesn't work if you're the president, it doesn't work if you're a wizard. Second, I think the hammering metaphor is a big deal. Three, you shouldn't do things just because of romance because—"

"You don't know if it'll work out?" Alex asked.

"Yeah," I said, biting my lip. "I won't lie to you, though. I actually had a vision of us together when I was twenty-three."

"Given that most of your visions are of horrible murders or the end of the world, that doesn't bode well."

"No, it's not that," I said, surprised at how quickly I corrected him. "It's just that there were other things I saw too. I saw I was a deputy for the Sheriff's Department. We weren't married either. I also felt you were still on the road and this was like, I dunno, a casual hook-up or something."

"Do you think that's predestined?"

"No," I said, thinking about earlier. "I mean, I saved your brother from being killed earlier. The future isn't set. I think. Well, it's sort of set, but it can be changed. I mean, well, I'm not very good at divining things."

"Destiny is real," Alex said, walking up and putting his arm around me. "We are all fated to die one day and nothing can prevent that. The particulars, however, are all up in the air."

"That's not as reassuring as you probably intended."

"Do you want to be a sheriff's deputy?"

This was the first time I'd gotten a chance to talk about it. "I dunno, law enforcement isn't what I expected to do with my life."

"You wanted to be a writer," Alex said.

"Yeah," I said, thinking about the last time I wrote anything. "Truth be told, I haven't touched pen to paper since last October."

"You actually write short-hand?" Alex said, confused.

"What?" I said. "It's not that rare."

"Honestly, I'm surprised people still use paper," Alex said, smirking. "All my writing is done on my laptop."

I grumbled about stupid government expense accounts. "Anyway, I ended up becoming the shaman of the Cervid, or trying to be. Truth be told, nobody really treats me like it. She left some big shoes to fill."

Actually, she'd been a size eight, but that was just another thing I hadn't inherited from her.

"I know you like to help people, Jane," Alex said. "You also have your entire life to figure out what to do with it."

"Because you've lived so much, Mr. Twenty-Six Year Old." I paused. "Actually, you're an FBI agent and apparently used to be the wizard John Wick."

Alex blinked. "Of all my regrets, that's my greatest."

"Did you save people?" I asked. "People who might have been killed by those people in the future?"

"Yes," Alex said, sighing. "But I could have saved more if that was my primary concern."

"Nobody's perfect," I said, sighing. "Besides, I know you, Alex, you're the good one."

"Versus whom?"

I'd actually been referring to Lucien but wasn't about to bring that up. So, instead, I diverted the conversation in the stupidest manner possible. "So what did you think of that whole marriage thing? I mean, where our relationship was headed, wasn't headed—oh

Goddess almighty what have I done?"

I felt my face with both hands, covering my eyes with my palms. We were right beside Alex's FBI provided black Cadillac SUV that looked exactly like the kind government agents used on TV. One thing I appreciated about President Justin Carver was that he didn't scrimp on the FBI's budget. I just hated everything else he'd been elected on, like making sure supernaturals were kept in their place.

"Do you want to be married by the time you're twenty-three?" Alex asked. "Or earlier?"

"Goddess no," I said, responding before thinking. "I don't think anyone should get married before they're twenty-five."

Alex smirked. "I'm not in any rush, Jane. I just enjoy spending time with you. Whether on the phone or in person."

"Thank you," I said, feeling a little better about my situation. "My relationship experience is a bit miniscule."

There had been Bobby Horne and apparently Lucien. I kind of regretted not dating more in my junior year, but I'd had the stupid idea of focusing on my studies. Stupid math and its alluring mysteries. Why did I have to be so good at it?

"I've had a couple before," Alex said. "So don't think I'm completely inexperienced myself."

"Who are they so I can kill them?" I said, half-jokingly.

Alex stopped.

"Uh-oh," I said, pausing. "I asked something I shouldn't have, didn't I?"

Alex paused and looked forward. "I was in a relationship with Diana at one point."

I let that sink in. "Was this before or after we started internet dating?"

"Before," Alex said.

I let out a breath I hadn't been aware I was holding. "Wait, she was married."

"I'm aware," Alex said, blinking. "It shouldn't be one of the things I'm most ashamed of, but it is."

"Did she break it off or did you?" I asked, suddenly filled with a million questions. "Did you break it off or did Jones kill her before you could?"

"I broke it off," Alex said, sighing. "We still tried to be friends afterward but it didn't work out."

Yeah, I could imagine. It was awkward as buck with Lucien after all. Wow, that was an all-purpose useful word substitution there. "I can imagine. Are you here to, like, avenge her or something?"

"I don't know," Alex said, staring down at his car. "I feel like I should be but I can't help also feel like there's a thousand other regrets standing in my way."

"What kind of regrets?" I asked.

"Mixed ones," Alex said, opening the driver's side door. "Do you still want pie?"

"Now I want *two* pieces," I said. "You're still buying too."

"Of course."

# CHAPTER SEVENTEEN

Riding in Alex's car was an experience. It was anything but standard issue with numerous computers that hummed with magic. I suspected could turn into a plane if he pushed the right buttons. I'd always known Alex was into some hush-hush government stuff but whenever I asked him about the Men in Black, he firmly insisted he wasn't among them and considered them "the worst mages in government." Which called into question just how many mages were in the government. Because, whoever they were, they weren't doing a very good job of running it.

The drive to the Deerlightful Diner was about fifteen minutes through traffic, another reason to curse the tourists, and I noted the two buildings beside it had already been marked for condemning in order to build a shopping mall as well as a parking lot. The Deerlightful was a fifties-style restaurant with a ceramic deer on the roof next to the neon sign that advertised it at night. It had been founded by my grandfather and was passed down to his my parents before I'd hoped it would be passed down to me.

I kind of felt hypocritical about that, because I'd never actually wanted to be involved with the family business any more than Jeremy or Jeanine had been. My father loved being a short-order cook and my mother had loved managing the business, but I'd always thought I would end up a writer. Of course, first-time writers made diddly squat unless they were J.K. Rowling, so maybe I'd always been mentally depending on the Deerlightful. Maybe I just didn't want to lose one more thing left from my childhood.

"Do you think I made the right decision pressuring my mother to testify against Marcus O'Henry?" I asked, watching him drive into one of the many vacant parking spots. I hadn't been paying attention to the business end of things, but that wasn't a good sign.

Then again, the places whose employees usually came in here for lunch were now piles of concrete and debris.

"I don't think there's a right answer to that," Alex said, parking the car.

"No, you're supposed to say absolutely," I said, correcting him.

"My mistake," Alex said softly. "I think Marcus O'Henry's trial is a pivotal moment in the integration of supernaturals into mundane society. If one of the leaders of supernatural society can be made accountable for his actions, then it's a giant step for an equal law for everyone. That those with superpowers can live alongside regular humans with the same protections as well as restrictions."

"Except people with superpowers are different from regular humans," I said, looking at him. "The reason the X-Men have their own academy is so they don't eye-blast their fellow students over bullying or because Jean turns out not to like Scott. Vampires live forever, shapechangers have instincts, and mages alter reality by staring. Regular people have a right to be scared and we have a right to be scared of regular people, since they're the ones with the nukes and numbers."

Alex looked at me.

"Which is why you said there's no right answer," I said, taking a deep breath. "But assume, for a minute, I'm a selfish doe-eyed girl."

"Of which you are, partially," Alex said.

"Yes, I am selfish," I said, smiling. "What if I didn't care about any of that and only cared about the fact I love my parents as well as miss them. That I hate the fact that they're missing and their business is falling into the hands of greedy developers, one of who is your brother, who offered to buy it for me."

Alex frowned. "Lucien never does anything unless he expects something in return."

I shook my head. "Ignore that and answer the question. I…need some comfort."

"Comfort or truth?"

"Both if I can have it. Comfort if I can't."

Alex took a deep breath. "Your mother had a lot to atone for. It was something inside her she'd tried to suppress but I don't think she ever successfully did. She could have kept running away from her actions but is doing her best to make amends. I think she did that so she could regain your respect."

"So it is my fault," I said, looking at the ground.

"No, it's your mother's and Marcus O'Henry's. Mine, too, if you want to spread the blame around. After all, you never would have found out if I hadn't become involved in your life."

"You were investigating a murder my brother was framed for," I said, sighing. "Not that he's ever thanked me for getting him off."

Alex put his arm on my shoulder then reached into his jacket pocket before handing me his cellphone. "Here."

"If this is showing me your porn history, I have a suspicion you like adorable petite girls with magical powers."

"I don't keep that on my phone," Alex said, scrunching up his face. "Also, you've made my attempt to give you your mother's number really weird."

"Oh," I said, taking the phone. "You could have given me her number earlier. You gave it to Lucien."

"Your mother wanted to talk to him," Alex said, pausing. "Strangely, Lucien wanted to talk to her back."

"Lucien wanted to talk to the woman who killed his parents?" I asked.

"And brothers," Alex added. "Lucien was spared by your mother because he was a child, though."

It was the ugliest, most confusing part of the whole ordeal for me. My mother had killed four of the Drake family, including his mother, Lucy Lyons, as part of a ritual sacrifice to appease an evil spirit. The rest of the Dragon Clan, all of Lucien's cousins, aunts, and uncles, had been killed by the Darkwater PMC. Modern weaponry versus the breath of dragons.

My mother had been unable to kill the fourteen-year-old Lucien, though. It made the entire thing confusing, as she hadn't been able to fully commit to either side of the battle and just ended up making it worse as a result. I was glad she hadn't killed Lucien, obviously, but I wish she hadn't involved herself at all.

"Do you know what they talked about?" I asked, taking a deep breath. "Aside from me?"

"You could ask her," Alex said. "She's in the contacts."

I stared at the gun and opened my mouth then frowned before handing it back. "I can't."

"You can do anything you want," Alex said.

"Says the guy who prays to Anakin Skywalker," I said, half joking.

"He died for our sins," Alex said, sounding completely serious. "Just in a more roundabout way than most messiahs. I also think he's a Jungian representation of Lancelot while Luke is Galahad."

"Neither of whom existed according to our gun," I said, pulling the phone back.

"In this reality, yes." Alex snorted as if that made sense.

I stared down at the cellphone then nodded. "Next time you're going to have to explain how *The Force Awakens* fits into the cosmology."

"Rey is hot," Alex said, watching me as if the very act of searching through his contacts was adorable. "Kylo Ren reminds me of Lucien on a bad day. I got really mad when a certain character died at his hand."

"They better redeem him in the third movie," I said, passing by names as ANGELJOLIE, DARPA, FBIDIREC, POTUS, MIBHEAD, WSHATNER, and JRRTOLK, before skimming back up to JUDY. "You're going to have to tell me about some of these names."

"You'll have to pay for dinner for that," Alex said.

I tsked. "So sexist."

I then hit SEND in order to dial my mother. "Should I be contacting someone in Witness Protection?"

"Not in the slightest," Alex said, shrugging. "But I think we're a little past the rules."

"And I had you marked for Lawful Good," I said, listening to the phone ring.

"I never understood why Neutral Good got no respect," Alex said. "They should be the ones with all the cool special abilities."

"If you're not Chaotic Good then you're not playing D&D right," I said, thinking of people I could invite for my upcoming *Pathfinder* game. "Loot and plunder in the name of great justice. As several gods intended."

That was when the phone line opened up. It was my mother. I could just by the sound of her breathing. "Hello?"

"Jane?" Judy spoke, sounding shocked. "Is that you?"

"Me or my alternate universe doppelganger," I said, trying not to cry. I would break if my mother rejected me.

Goddess, I felt like a little girl.

Judy paused and didn't respond for a long moment.

"I have a goatee to prove I'm your daughter's evil duplicate," I said. "I'm committing crimes in Jane's name and ruining her reputation."

No response.

"Yeah, well, I guess it was good talking to you, Mom." I was tearing up now.

"I'm so sorry, Jane," Judy said. "I never meant to hurt you."

"I don't understand why you did what you did but that doesn't mean I hate you," I said, pausing.

"Thank you," Judy said, pausing. "That means a lot to me. It will also mean a lot to your father. It wasn't easy for him to love me after what I'd done."

I wonder if she meant the murders or the fact she'd also been cheating on him during them. "Yeah, well, Dad is awesome. I hope he doesn't hate me."

"Your father could never hate you, Jane," Judy said, her voice soft and reassuring. "You were and always will be his favorite. Mine too."

I frowned before wiping away a tear. "You're not supposed to pick a favorite kid."

"Yeah, well, if the others ask I'll tell them they're my favorite but I'm telling you the truth. Probably."

That actually made me laugh. "Are you okay?"

"It's hard being away from you and dealing with the ghosts of the past," Judy said. "Also, your siblings want to sell the Deerlightful, which makes me want to reach across the phone and throttle them."

"I know, right!" I said, pausing. "Why did you give them permission?"

"Because it's the only thing we could give them," Judy said, sighing. "It's not their dream and they deserve a chance at happiness. It wasn't your dream either."

"I'm nineteen," I said, frowning. "My dreams are insane. I don't know where I'm going or how."

"You'll get used to that as an adult," Judy said. "But you've grown for a while now and I shouldn't have hidden that from you.

You're a shaman now."

"Sort of," I said, frowning. "Technically, everyone turns to Aunt Jessica for that."

Judy frowned. "That's unfortunate. She's never going to let me hear the end of that."

"You can tell her off when you get back," I said.

There was another awkward silence.

"You are coming back, right?" I asked.

"It won't be the same in Bright Falls," Judy said, her voice sad and tired. "The secrets I kept hidden are out of now. What I did was unforgivable."

"Well, I forgive you," I said, surprised by my sincerity.

"Thank you, Jane." Judy's voice cracked a bit. "Bright Falls is a place with many spiritual scars and I neglected to heal them. Instead, I focused on exploiting them for my own gain. I trust you to be able to do what you can to make it a better town."

"Yeah, well, now I'm dealing with a bunch of moon-howling white-suited weirdoes led by an immortal conman plus another god," I said, sighing. "But you probably have seen the news."

"Not really, no."

"Oh," I said, pausing. "Listen, I don't want to ask you about business."

"You can, Jane."

I grumbled and grit my teeth. "Mom, is it possible the Brotherhood of the Trees still exists? Because their goddess still does."

My mother paused. "Yes, Jane, it's possible, but only because the druids passed their faith on to us. Their rites became the rites of the Cervid Clan."

"Did you know there was an ancient goddess in the forest?"

The secrets never ended.

"Yes," Judy said. "There's a lot more going on there than you could imagine. Shadow Pine Park is a lodestone."

"A lodestone," I repeated.

"A place where the spiritual veil between this world and the next is very weak. There's several in town."

"No kidding," I said.

"Long ago, many of the Nunnehi and Manitou invited spirits fleeing from the Europeans to the Underwood in order to survive the coming of steel as well as iron. The Goddess of the Forest, what we called the Earthmother's avatar, kept that realm free and pure. All she demanded in return was regular visits from men to renew their link from the land. This was often the sheriff or mayor or both. Sometimes it was Marcus O'Henry or the clan heads."

I paused and pulled out my cellphone to look at it. "Just so we're clear. There's a European and Native American fairy kingdom in Shadow Pine Park preserved by the Dryad. However, her price for keeping it so is a bunch of dudes *screwing* her?"

"Sex magic is one of the most basic of all nature worship," my mother said, discussing it as if it was perfectly normal. Look at the May Day celebration. You would have learned all about this if you'd continued your training."

I pinched the bridge of my nose. "Please just tell me Dad never helped out in this."

"No, don't be ridiculous. The only sexual rituals your father helped in were mine. However, due to bloodline cultivating, I did allow him to sire other heirs with other Cervid Clan women. You have quite a few half-siblings in the other shapechanger communities. I demanded a very high price for—"

"Nope," I interrupted. "Nope, nope, nope. Not listening. La-la-la."

Alex looked away, pretending not to be interested.

"I've told you this before," Judy said.

"I've forgotten whatever you've told me," I said, whistling. "Deleting file. Bee-boop."

"You should meet them sometime," Judy muttered.

I paused, wanting to know the next answer. "Okay, Mom, this has the potential to go very dark, but did you know there were a bunch of newborns left to die by exposure?"

Judy was silent. "Yes, unfortunately I did. After the massacre of the druids by US cavalry and their wizards, the fairies sealed up the region. Travelers still managed to visit the Goddess of the Forest, but we were bound to never step foot in it. The leader of the US wizards, Balthazar Jones, crazed the power of the goddess for himself."

"I've been to Shadow Pines Park, though," I said, wondering how this all went together.

"Yes, but not to the fairy kingdom," Judy said, her voice low.

"The Grove is locked away except for only a few individuals. I spent many years trying to get inside it to no avail, though I did find where the children were left to die and made it so they would be adopted by a good man who knew the truth of the area."

"Andy Taylor?" I asked.

"Yes," Judy said. "He's a park ranger."

I paused, letting that sink in. "So on a scale of one to a hundred, if say a bunch of greedy developers were to bulldoze Shadow Pine Park and the Grove, then what would happen?"

"Probably not the end of the world, probably tens of thousands of deaths," Judy said, sounding worried. "Certainly it would kill all the spirits living inside there and be an incredible blasphemy. Is that what's happening?"

"Nope, not at all," I said, nodding. "Just checking about incredibly unlikely possibilities. Is Dad there?"

So Robyn's dad was probably the guy behind all of this horrible stuff. Dammit.

"No, your father is out grocery shopping," Judy said. "It's hard to keep mushrooms in stock in this part of Alaska. Do you want me to have him call you?"

Alaska? Ouch. Still, good for deer I supposed, assuming it wasn't too cold. We were white-tailed deer rather than reindeer after all. Man, I wished Emma was here for her cavalcade of biology facts.

"No, I'll call back," I said, biting my lip. "I'm on a date."

"Oh, well, say hello."

"Will do," I said, sighing. "Talk to you later."

"Goodbye."

With that, she hung up.

"Thank you, Alex," I said, closing my eyes and clearing my mind. "You have no idea how much that meant to me."

"I have an idea," Alex said, looking down at the wheel. "Ready for lunch?"

I nodded before stopping. "Actually, you want to get lunch to go and find a non-crappy hotel to have sex?"

# CHAPTER EIGHTEEN

Sex with Alex was better than what I'd hoped for. My experience wasn't exactly stellar, but it was with some I cared for deeply, who knew what he was doing, and had the benefit of magic to make sure he could keep up with a woman who had superhuman stamina. The first time was quick, the second time long, and we also took a shower together that I had to concentrate on not becoming a third time.

And failed.

"Wow, Emma is going to be ticked off at me ditching for the afternoon," I muttered, checking my phone. "Especially in the middle of a murder investigation."

The two of us had gone to a smaller, presentable Best Western rather than any of the locally owned hotels. The room was adequately cleaned and while I could smell the previous customers who'd smoked despite the "NO SMOKING" sign along with other smells, I spent a large portion of my time running around in the woods, so that didn't really bother me. I was sitting on the edge of the room's king-sized bed and putting on my bra. Alex was still shirtless and I was admiring the view as he pulled out his button-down shirt.

I admitted to being one of those girls who liked scars. Alex's back had numerous signs of being shot, attacked with some kind of whip, and claw marks that he'd managed to heal over with his magic but not completely. It was like a map I enjoyed exploring and I wished I could ask Alex about them.

"Well, I have no regrets," Alex said, not reacting to the way I was looking. "Do you?"

"Not in the slightest," I said, smiling. "The best things come to those who wait but we've waited way too long."

Alex chuckled. "Yes, well, there is that."

"Something wrong?" I asked.

"I was just thinking of Laura," Alex said.

"Wow, so not what you want to say to a girl after marathon sex," I said.

"No," Alex said, pausing. "I was thinking about how the whole thing was toxic and I wish I'd never gotten involved with her."

"Better," I said, still hurt.

Alex finished buttoning down his shirt and took a deep breath. "The FBI and the wizards there are something of a clique."

"What with being the Men in Black and all," I said, pulling on my shirt.

"The Men in Black operate out of Area 51," Alex said, as if it was common knowledge. "They work for the military and only have FBI advisors. The FBI answers to the Star Chamber and the Hoover Society."

"Pretend I think any of those don't sound like villains in a tabletop roleplaying game."

"The Hoover Society is a collection of mages assembled by J. Edgar Hoover to fight supernatural crime. The Star Chamber is basically the Illuminati, wizards who use magic to get exceptionally rich, but much less powerful."

"Please tell me the Illuminati aren't real."

"As far as I know," Alex said, turning around and tying his tie. "The idea of an all-powerful secret society is ridiculous because the first thing powerful people do when they get together is start fighting for who gets to be on top. That doesn't keep people from trying, though."

"So which do you work for?" I asked, now worrying I'd inadvertently stepped into Fox Mulder's mind.

Conspiracy theories were kind of an irritation to me because we lived in a world where the government was doing unlimited surveillance, puppet regimes, corporate human testing, had an army of drone murder-bots, and had secret prisons where they stuck anyone who irritated them. All of this had been before the Reveal as well. However, the vast majority of conspiracy theorists I met were complete cranks who actually made it easier for the government to get away with things because they were convinced everything was a plot by who knows what. Finding out there were actual magical conspiracies, just small scale, made my head hurt.

"I'm an independent contractor," Alex said, frowning. "Both my parents were members of the Hoover Society, which tells you what kind of people they are. The Star Chamber is split between those who want to wipe out supernaturals like Dr. Jones and those who want to integrate them into society. I'm staying the hell out of their way until they make a decision. There's other cabals and secret magical organizations across the globe but none of them interest me. I self-study when I want to improve my craft or bargain with spirits."

"How's that working out for you?"

"Columbia protected me from a circle of seven who tried to cast me into Hell. I understand the Earth swallowed them up."

"The city of Columbia?"

"The personification of America."

I rubbed the bridge of my nose. "I actually would prefer to hear about your married ex-girlfriend more than continue this conversation."

"There's a picture of her in the trash folder of my cellphone. Laura was a fascinating woman. She was intelligent, beautiful, hard like a diamond, and possessed of a strong sense of self. She was also utterly ruthless and willing to do whatever it required to bring about her ideals of justice. Laura was the one who recruited me into the FBI along with several other mage hunters."

"I was actually kidding about wanting to hear about her."

"Oh." Alex winced. "I sometimes have difficulty telling when people are being literal or not."

"Yeah, yeah," I said, reaching out for his cellphone. "I've heard that before. Gimme."

"Really?"

"Now I have to see her," I said, knowing it was a bad idea. Laura was dead, after all, and Alex had broken up with her before she'd died. It was, in all honesty, a relationship that was done and buried.

Alex handed his cellphone over. "Okay, if you say so."

I checked the cell phone trash and, sure enough, saw a dozen photos of a beautiful Asian American woman in a gym workout tank top and sweats. She was a lot more endowed than I expected and more traditionally beautiful than my type of frame. I couldn't help but compare myself to her.

"Wow, she's gorgeous," I said, frowning. "Unnaturally so. Is she a werewolf? Some sort of unnaturally curvy athletic girl I can blame the looks of on fairy glamour?"

Alex rolled his eyes. "I think I would have noticed if she was a werewolf."

"Might explain some of the scratches on your back."

"Those came from child abuse. My father used to turn me and my sister into cats then force us to fight."

I paused, letting that sink in. "Don't take this the wrong way, but that is almost too insane to be horrifying."

"Kind of hard not to," Alex said, grabbing the phone back from me.

"And you broke up because she was married?" I said, adding a bit of accusation to my tone.

"Among other things," Alex said, frowning. "She was also prone to hiding things from me as well as her husband. Honesty became a stranger and I found that was a quality I wasn't willing to sacrifice."

"So you hate people hiding things from you?" I asked.

"Who doesn't?" Alex asked, picking up on my guilt.

I paused, looking at the ground. "So, uh, now is probably an exceptionally bad time to be utterly truthful."

Alex finished putting on his jacket and looked toward me. "I sense you're going to do it, though."

I felt guilty but wanted to continue our relationship on the right foot. Maybe it was the high of being together for the first time or the fact I didn't want him to reveal something to me without returning the favor. Even so, I couldn't help but believe this was a potential disaster in the making. "I wasn't exactly not-dating before you."

"That's hardly something to upset me."

I didn't meet his gaze. "This will upset you."

I sighed.

"Please don't tell me it was Lucien."

I spun my head toward him.

"God damn that bastard," Alex muttered under his breath.

"It's not really a big deal," I said, trying to underplay it. "I mean, it was my choice."

I closed my eyes.

"Lucien did this to spite me."

"Excuse me?" I said, offended for multiple reasons.

Alex muttered something under his breath. "He knew, Jane. He knew I was interested and he did it anyway."

"Maybe he was just interested himself. Did you think of that?" I asked, wondering why he thought my previous kinda-sorta-but-not-really was only seeing me as some sort of complicated revenge plot.

"Yes," Alex said, pausing. "I suppose you're right. You're a fascinating wonderful woman."

"Thanks," I said, mollified.

"Did it have to be my brother?" Alex asked.

Ouch. "Uh, well, I didn't plan it, but—"

I couldn't help but remember Emma's words about telling Alex before sleeping with him. In retrospect, not only should I have followed that recourse but I should have given him a few days to tell him about Lucien instead of right after. Goddess, I was an idiot.

Alex went to the door. "If you'll excuse me, I need some air."

I closed my eyes, feeling my stomach lurch. "Please, say something funny. Tell me how weird it is Vulcans are the most religious *Star Trek* race despite being devoted to logic or why you think Obi Wan was tricking Luke into redeeming Anakin."

Alex paused at the door. "Honestly, Jane, I'm just not in the mood to talk about pop culture."

He then walked out and shut it behind him.

"Well, frankly, Scarlett, I don't give a damn either!" I said, snapping. "Dammit, I am a stupid, stupid deer."

"Honestly, this doesn't rank that high up there," a voice spoke beside me.

I turned around to see a large White Stag standing there in the middle of the room. It was taller than me when I stood up with an enormous rack of antlers that stemmed from its luminescent white-furred head. Its eyes glowed while its voice seemed to have a reverb, not entirely unlike Raguel's, but gentler.

"Ah!" I shouted, falling off the edge of the bed.

"That's not very dignified behavior for a shaman," the White Stag said.

"How the hell!" I shouted.

"I'm a spirit; I can appear anywhere I want," the White Stag said. "The problem is getting people to pay attention."

I climbed onto the bed. "I haven't seen you since you led me to the lodge in Darkwater Preserve."

"Well, I didn't need to help you until now," the White Stag said. "Also, you're kind of terrible at this shaman thing. No vision quests, attempting to use the bones to gain advice, meditation, or prayer. You do realize it's a job meant to involve interceding between the spirits and humans, right?"

"Yes, I am the avatar. Korra is hot," I muttered, shaking my head. "Listen, I am liaising. I'm going to go kill a baby-killing avatar of the goddess, I worship. It's like an old adage if you meet the Buddha on the road you should kill him."

"You have totally misunderstood that saying."

I paused, climbing to my feet. "Yeah, I always thought it was a bit weird."

"You also can't kill the Goddess of the Forest."

"If I do?" I asked, sighing. "Just in case, you know, she's in the way of the Merlin Gun that wants to kill her."

*Hypothetically*, Raguel said, sitting on the dresser.

"Raguel is bound to a gun for the fact he needs a human hand to tell him when not to kill people since our father said he was too judgmental and unforgiving."

"Our father?" I said.

"Or mother," the White Stag said. "Your preference."

I shrugged. "Mother, please. You didn't answer the question."

"Remember the tornado I sent you a vision about?" The White Stag asked.

"You sent me?"

"Is there an echo in here?" The White Stag asked.

"No, just a big huge reindeer."

"Don't be insulting, White Tail. Admit it, you've been admiring my rack since I came in here."

I snorted. "I guess you aren't the Jesus Stag."

"No, but we're related. Mind you, we're all children of the Great Spirit, so it's not really all that big of a deal."

"Uh-huh," I said, suspecting the stag was trolling me. "So if I kill the Dryad then the town will be hit by a tornado?"

"More like everything in the immediate hundred-mile area will die. She is the force keeping the land magical. Without it, Bright Falls will lose its mystical verve and unleash the thousands of creatures kept in its spirit world."

I stared at him. "Like griffons?"

"Like griffons."

I sighed. "So I have to break my promise to Robyn."

"No, if you do that then you'll be banned from the Spirit World. You need to go there in order to keep her from being kidnapped by Dr. Jones in his new body. Then he'll gain divine power and screw up the world."

I felt my face. "I'm feeling a damned if you do, damned if you don't situation here."

"Pretty much, yeah."

I covered my face and sat down. "I don't suppose you have any advice, all-wise Jesus Stag?"

"Please stop calling me that."

*Gabriel does not like it*, Raguel said.

I opened a space between my two fingers. "Wait, what was that?"

*Nothing.*

"I sincerely doubt that!" I shouted at Raguel.

"You need to convince Robyn to let go of her desire for vengeance," the White Stag said.

"Easier said than done," I said, sighing. "I'm also not sure it's not a legitimate grievance. You can't tell me the Earthmother didn't know she was leaving those kids out to die. She's a frigging goddess."

"Life and death are both her purview," the White Stag said. "Though the Goddess of the Forest's mind has become addled from centuries without much human contact, spirits who spend too much time in one form often become corrupted."

"Yeah, so I've heard," I said, pausing. "I'll think of something. Thanks for telling me."

"You're welcome."

I paused. "Uh, I don't suppose you have any romantic advice for my Alex situation. You know, if you are supposedly all wise."

"Sleep with him again," the White Stag said. "Maybe something involving whipped cream or handcuffs?"

I glared at him.

"Oh right, humans are like that," the White Stag said. "Well, he's motivated by jealousy of his brother and possessiveness. Alex is also quick to blame his brother for anything that goes wrong as well as see the worst in him. You've stepped in some serious lingering Cain-and-Abel stuff."

"Lucien loves Alex."

"I didn't say who was who," the White Stag said. "The fact is Alex loves you or believes he does and Lucien is your friend. It will all work or…or it won't."

With that, the White Stag vanished. No puff of smoke or crack of thunder. One second he was there, the next he wasn't.

"Well, thanks for nothing," I muttered.

That was when there was a knocking on the door.

# Chapter Nineteen

I stood up to walk to the door, hoping it was Alex. It was unlikely he'd decided to come back after five minutes of being steamed, even if he was the weirdest most interesting guy I'd ever met.

*So is the White Stag really Gabriel?* I asked, not sure I wanted to know the answer.

*Yes and no,* Raguel replied. *Spirits are all linked in the great web of being. I am a part of a larger being that is part of a larger being still that is a part of the creator. Just as the Goddess of the Forest is part of the Earthmother, that is a part of life itself. The White Stag is the child of the Forest Goddess.*

"You lost me," I said, reaching the door.

*You are a citizen of Bright Falls, which is a part of Michigan, which is a part of the United States, which is a part of the world. Now imagine that each of those was a sentient being that you were part of. Which they are, because they all have spirits.*

"And you've made the metaphor useless after starting so well," I said, unlocking the door and opening it.

*Yes, the White Stag is Gabriel.*

*Was that hard?* I asked.

*Humans,* Raguel grunted.

The person on the other side of the door was Robyn, who was standing in front of the Millennium Falcon parked in front of our hotel room. The rest of the group had arrived and it seemed like we were having a reunion. I saw Alex walking to the vending machines and getting himself a Mr. Pibb. Oh Alex, how far you've fallen. Not Dr. Pepper?

"So," Robyn said, putting her arms on her waist, "you actually ditched me for a booty call?"

I paused. "Yes, that is exactly what happened."

Robyn stared at me then shrugged. "Fair enough. He is hot as hell. So you doing both or just the one?"

"Crude but inquisitive," I said, letting her in the room.

"I just tell it like it is," Robyn said, sitting down on my bed. "We've got your Hummer full of supplies for our trek through Shadow Pine Park. You know, where you're going to help me kill my mother the goddess. I've bought plenty of gasoline for it. Also, the equipment to make an amateur flame thrower."

I shook my head and sat down beside her. "Listen, I made a promise and I've got your back on this, but if we kill your mother then the entire town is going to be destroyed because she's the spirit of the town."

"The spirit," Robyn said.

"Cross my heart and hope to die," I said, making a circle with my thumb over my heart. It was the local version of the cross. "I would never try to influence your beliefs about the world, but spirits, gods, angels, and other weirdness are real just like vampires as well as werewolves."

"That's hard for to believe," Robyn said, staring at me. "It's a pretty rough world to say there's any kind of divine. Also, you know, science."

"Allow me to show you via repeatable science just what I'm talking about," I said, taking her hand and squeezing it.

Then I showed her what I'd seen when I'd touched Raguel, just like I'd shown Alice.

Seconds later, Robyn was in the bathroom  throwing up.

"Yeah," I said, grimacing. "Just let it all out."

She threw up for about a minute longer then brushed her teeth as well as gargled with the house toothpaste as well as mouthwash.

I looked around. "I probably could have taken a less dramatic tactic with that."

"You think?" Robyn called back.

I grimaced. "Hey, haven't you noticed vampires react to religious figures and names? I mean, it was always true."

"Everything is true so nothing is true," Robyn muttered. "All you've done is make the world more confusing."

"I felt the same way when Alex tried to explain Hawking's theory of the Multiverse," I said. "But yes, your mom is the Goddess of the Forrest."

"And still a bastard," Robyn said.

"Gods are historically not the nicest of people," I said, taking time to explain everything I knew in detail. I didn't scrimp on the part where Dr. Jones wanted to turn her into his puppet-goddess to convert the United States to Ultralogy. I did, however, scrimp on the fact I wasn't sure if her father was the guy who killed Dr. Jones.

Robyn stared forward. "Wow, religions suck."

"I'm sensing you have some issues with organized supernatural worship," I said, taking a deep breath.

"I had a lot of issues with the way my father raised me," Robyn said, frowning. "He's a good man and a loving parent, but it was smothering."

I sucked in my breath. "I feel like today is going to be a day where I make bad decisions by telling people the truth. So, odd question, but is your dad black?"

"That is an odd question," Robyn said, frowning. "But yes, my adoptive father is black. So is my mother."

I opened my mouth to suggest it was possible her father was the guy who murdered Dr. Jones, but I wasn't sure that was a good idea. We didn't know enough to make that conclusion. "Well, that's great for him."

Robyn gave me a sideways look. "You're really bad at this lying thing, aren't you?"

"It helps when your mother is telepathic," I said, sighing.

"Ah," Robyn said. "So what's my dad have to do with all this?"

I sighed. "Okay, well I'll explain it to you."

I told her my theory.

Robyn burst out laughing.

"Oh, yes, this is hilarious," I said, deadpanning.

"My father is many things, but he's not a warlock or a killer," Robyn said, sighing. "He's sixty years old and a pacifist. I've seen him a few times in the past few years but he certainly wasn't a wizard when I was growing up around him. Believe me, I would have known."

"Well, whoever this is really wants to help you," I said, feeling like Robyn probably knew him best. "Also, magic is a lot more readily available than it was a decade ago."

"You've been studying magic for a year; can you do anything?" Robyn asked.

"Yes," I snapped. "Not much, but some things!"

Robyn crossed her arms and raised an eyebrow. "Uh-huh, like what?"

"I know deer-based martial arts!" I said, pausing. "I learned them from cleaning up the shop, manning the register, and getting Kim Su's lunch. Just like Mr. Miyagi!"

"I've known you like a day and already can't tell when you're joking about this stuff."

I nodded. "Probably better that way."

"Oh, and I already figured out Amelia Earhart is Kim Su."

"Yeah, we did a really crappy job of hiding that," I said, grimacing. "Okay, we'll put a pin in the idea that your father is actually an evil wizard who has been trying to kill me and Lucien this entire day."

"Probably a good idea," Robyn said, snorting. "In any case, we can drop by his house if you want. If there's a park ranger who's obsessed with protecting me and is a wizard, then I'm sure my dad will know. Do you want me to call him?"

"No," I said quickly. "Let's just…drop in."

"Suit yourself."

I tried to figure out how to ask my next question. "So, knowing what you know about this goddess—"

"Monster," Robyn said, correcting me. "I don't care if its survival is necessary to keep this town alive, it's still a monster."

"It didn't know what it was doing."

"Doesn't make the kids any less dead, does it? What does happen to kids after they die?"

"We all become spirits," I said, hesitating. "Or so I've been told. I don't really know much about the specifics of life, death, and transubstantiation of the soul. I get the impression it's a lot more complicated than Good Place, Bad Place, though. Which is a strike against the universe according to Kristen Bell."

"You're really kind of crap at this shaman thing."

"No one mentioned it would involve priestess things!" I said, lying. "I can do the murdering-evil-spirits part!"

"Then let's do that," Robyn said, frowning. "Find a way to kill the Goddess of the Forest without destroying this town. In the meantime, we can just make sure Dr. Jones stays dead so she can't be moved."

"You're really set on this killing-your-mother thing."

"Most adoptees wonder whether their parents loved them. I didn't know. But really, now it's about the fact I don't like this crazy goddess. I've lived my entire life under the thumb of other people and I'm going to show I'm uncontrollable. I can't think of a better way than wrecking this talking tree's shit."

"That is a terrible excuse for deicide."

"Have you killed a god?" Robyn asked.

I thought of the Big Bad Wolf. "Maybe."

"Did the world end?"

"No." I hesitated in answering "I think it reincarnated as a less crappy deity. I do feel like bad weather follows me now, as well as insect swarms."

"Like I said," Robyn replied, "I'm willing to hold off on killing it. That's about as much as you're going to get now. You've proven to me that gods exist. Well, I'm not worshiping any nor do I see any sign they're making the world a better place. If they do evil, they should be punished."

*I like her*, Raguel said. *She is a woman of conviction.*

*This is why you were kicked out of Heaven*, I thought back to him.

*I was not kicked out of Heaven. I'm just doing…community service.*

"Okay, we'll hold off on deicide and figure something out," I said, stretching my arms out and offering her a hug.

Robyn hugged me back. "It's nice to have a friend here in town. You're sadly my first one."

I leaned over to hug her, almost immediately being overwhelmed by the image of us making out on a bed.

I pulled away, flushing my face brightly. "Okay, right, let's get going."

Oh God, what the hell was that? I mean, yes, I'd been attracted to some women before, but I was trying to build a relationship with Alex. I also had Lucien waiting in the wings. I didn't need anything else right now.

"You okay?" Robyn asked.

"Yes!" I snapped, jumping up. "I am ecstatic! Let us go to the woods and find the goddess to slay!"

"I thought we weren't doing that yet."

"Yes, that too!" I said, panicked.

Robyn stood up and headed to the door. "Don't ever change, Deer Woman. You are a bright spot of insanity in an all-too-banal world."

"If you think that, you haven't been looking hard enough," I muttered.

Robyn headed through the door and closed it behind her.

"Think unsexy thoughts," I said, immediately thinking sexy thoughts about other people. It turned out thinking sexy thoughts was rather natural after a marathon sex session.

Dammit.

That was when someone else knocked on my hotel room door. "Alex?"

"No," Yolanda's voice spoke from the other side. "It's your friendly neighborhood hunter."

"I'm a deer and a shapechanger," I called back to her. "There has never been any occasion whatsoever between 'friendly' and 'hunter'."

Yolanda snorted in a way I could hear through the door—blame my Cervid Clan ears. "I need to talk."

"About what?" I asked, suspecting it was about that favor I'd promised her.

"It's about that favor you promised me."

Dammit! I hated being right. Well, not usually, but in this specific instance. "Okay, okay, well you can come in."

I walked up to the door and opened it up before letting her in. "Remember, no killing the Pope."

"You are a weird, weird girl," Yolanda said, walking into the room. "No wonder Alex likes you."

I grimaced, wondering if that was still the case. "Yeah, well, I'm just a small-town girl living in a lonely something-something."

"I don't like Journey," Yolanda said.

"Who doesn't like Journey?" I asked, blinking. "That's like disliking chocolate or French fries."

"'Don't Stop Believing' was the song played at my wedding," Yolanda said, taking a seat by the window. "

Ouch. "Well, I suppose that would be enough reason to hate

Journey."

"So you're the girl who finally took down Marcus O'Henry?" Yolanda asked, staring through the window.

"The woman who did it," I said, taking a deep breath. "Alex helped. So did Lucien and his family. Marcus's family, I mean. There were a lot of people willing to come forward once it was clear others were."

"What did he do to you?" Yolanda asked.

"Excuse me?"

"Everyone who has opposed Marcus O'Henry—and there's a long list even if most of them are dead—had some reason to hate him. I was just asking yours."

"He hurt my friend," I said, sighing. "But, honestly, that wasn't why I did it. Dude was an asshole. He had a lot worse coming to him than life in prison but I figured that was a better punishment than just killing him."

"I disagree," Yolanda said, taking a deep breath. "I tried taking him out once. I had another partner, a hunter we worked with sometimes, and I tried to snipe him. In the end, it hit a shield spell and his men tracked us down. I got away. My friend didn't."

"I'm sorry."

"You just walked into his office and got him arrested," Yolanda said.

"Yeah."

"I wish it had been that easy for me," Yolanda said. "I know you don't believe it, but I don't hate monsters."

"The fact you call us monsters kind of belies that," I said. It was a common way of referring to supernaturals but no less hurtful. There had been plenty of people in Bright Falls who'd known of the truth before the Reveal but plenty who hadn't. Both sides included people who hated what I was in school. Even in a town founded by supernaturals, there were those who considered us abominations or freaks.

Yolanda made a face like she'd been punched. "Sorry."

"Hey," I said, giving a thumbs-up. "It's okay. My father says it's important to remember most supernaturals are horrible creatures who eat humans and are pure evil. It's just we're totally the exception. Don't trust vampires or wizards."

Yolanda raised an eyebrow. "Really?"

"Funny how prejudice works," I said.

"Not really," Yolanda said. "Also, awkward coming from the white girl."

"The bisexual biracial girl," I said. "But then again, I can't imagine you've had an Indian headdress dumped on your head during Thanksgiving before being shot with ink-filled water pistols."

Yolanda blinked.

"Kids are cruel," I said, crossing my arms. "So what do you want me to do?"

"I'd like you to help me talk to my dead son," Yolanda said, taking a deep breath. "Alex says you can help."

# Chapter Twenty

I was taken aback by Yolanda's request and took a step back. "You want me to *talk with your dead son*?"

"No, I want you to serve as a medium," Yolanda said, frowning. "You talk to him and tell me what to say."

I narrowed my eyes. "I know how being a medium works. It's just I don't know how—"

Actually, I did know how to serve as a medium but it wasn't from Kim Su I'd learned how to that. No, I'd learned that from my mother. Sort of. While I'd never been able to get the rituals to work before, that was because I'd been crippled with guilt, thanks to the tragic death of my cousin. A death I had no small part in. I'd avenged her death and spoken to the dead since then, but it was still something I couldn't be called an expert in.

"Shouldn't Alex do this?" I asked, looking uncomfortable. "I mean, he is the other death mage around here."

I wasn't quite sure I believed I had the knack for it but again, I had talked to the dead.

"He told me to go to you," Yolanda said.

"Oh he did, did he?" I said, my voice lowering. "That's it, we're totally even for my sleeping with his brother."

"Excuse me?" Yolanda asked.

"Nothing," I said, rubbing my temples. "Okay, I agreed to help you and I'm going to. I need to warn you, though, people change when they become spirits."

"Change?" Yolanda asked.

"Babies are different from teenagers," I said, shrugging. "People don't remain static from the way they die. There's no time in the Spirit World but they change. What they experienced help forms the being they become."

"Explain," Yolanda said.

"They aren't human anymore even if that's their formative years." I shrugged, not quite sure how to put. "My grandfather appeared to me as my grandfather, but he was also a small god. I'm not an expert on this. I'm not even sure it was really him. Some spirits don't answer the call, are unable to communicate, while others become the spirit of mountains or join the great chain of incarnation."

"You mean reincarnation?" Yolanda asked.

"No," I said, unable to put it into words. "Listen, I'm willing to do it. I'll try to contact your son after we're done with the Dryad."

"I want you to do it now."

I closed my eyes. "You're killing me, Yolanda."

"No, which is part of the reason why we're here now," Yolanda said, looking up at me. "It's taken a long time for me to look at shapechangers and see the person rather than the animal. I'm sorry for that, but I need to face my son and tell him what I wasn't able to in life."

"Your son was a shapechanger," I reminded her, though it's not like she could have forgotten. "That may influence how he reacts."

"I don't care. What would you do to talk with the person you most loved but can never talk to again?"

I could only think of my parents, whom I had just talked to. "So if you'll do this, you'll help with the Dryad?"

"I would anyway but I need you to do this for me so I'm going to lie and say I won't if you don't help," Yolanda said, blinking. "Okay, why did I say that aloud?"

I made the horns with my hands. "The power of weredeer charisma. We're disarmingly cuddly."

"You sound a lot like Alex," Yolanda said, frowning. "Which means you make a lot of references I don't get and are perpetually sarcastic. Except I don't think he's ever sarcastic, he's just weird."

"Weird is better than normal," I said, smiling. "It's just another way of saying exceptional."

"I could do with a whole lot less exceptional in my life," Yolanda said, looking over at the windows. "Do you need to get anything before the séance?"

"Please don't call it a séance," I said, taking a deep breath. I walked over to my staff, picked it up, plopped myself in the bed near the pillows and placed my staff over my legs before moving them into a lotus position. "I don't even know if this is going to work, but I have everything I need."

Yolanda took a deep breath. "Is there a Heaven?"

"I'm equipped to talk to your son for you, not to answer those kinds of questions," I said, pausing. "But yes. Hell too. Also, Valhalla. Happy Hunting Grounds. Elysium. Arcadia. There's also places that defy description. Abysses, places of eternal torment, places where there's just an endless series of doors that open up back to themselves. Places that do not allow you to leave but have the two most annoying people in the world trapped with you who hate you every bit as much as you hate them."

"That's not very comforting," Yolanda said.

"It's not meant to be," I said, taking a deep breath. "My mother used to say any miracle that doesn't leave you quivering on the ground questioning your sanity is insufficiently miraculous."

"My dad was a Baptist preacher, he said life was a miracle," Yolanda said.

"Then he knew what I was talking about," I said, thinking about all the times life had reduced me to a fetal ball. If I had a nickel for every time, I'd have a whole twenty cents. Shaking my head, I muttered, "I really need to start studying how to be a priestess as well as a magician if I want to be the shaman of the clans."

"So I guess religion is wrong then," Yolanda said.

"It depends on what questions you're asking. It's like Yoda's cave. The only thing you'll find is what you take with you." Which wasn't true but, again, I didn't want to blast her mind like I had Robyn. I didn't want to leave the bathroom a mess for some poor cleaning lady to clean up. What was with everyone wanting to turn to me for all the answers? Oh yeah, I was the one claiming to be the shaman.

*Raguel, some help here?* I asked. *You know this stuff.*

*I can't advise mortals on religion,* Raguel said. *For the exact reason you're now experiencing.*

*Yeah, well, remind me to follow Michael's advice next time,* I said.

*I will.*

"Is everything a *Star Wars* quote to you?" Yolanda asked, clearly not happy with what I was saying.

"Would you prefer I communicate in nineties fighting-games lingo?" I asked. "I know those too. Dad used to have a half-dozen in the Deerlightful and he regularly upgraded them despite the fact he could only—"

Yolanda raised her left palm. "Stick with *Star Wars.*"

"Thank you," I said, sighing. "Now give me your cell phone."

Yolanda blinked. "Why do you need my cell phone?"

"Because this is going to ruin a cell phone and I don't want to use mine," I said, holding out my hand.

"Oh," Yolanda said, pulling an incredibly cheap-looking piece of plastic from her jacket.

I took Yolanda's phone and looked at it sideways. "I take being a hunter doesn't pay very well."

"It doesn't but it's a burner," Yolanda said, frowning. "Hunting is illegal after all."

"What with it being murder, yes," I said.

Yolanda stared at me. "The third monster I killed was something I don't have a name for. It stored the bodies of people it picked off the street in its apartment basement no one ever entered until I did. They were all grown together on a fungus and it fed off the things that grew inside them. I pulled the fire alarm and burned the entire place to the ground to make sure it stayed dead and didn't spread further. They found a hundred bodies inside, some having been alive since 1913. What do you call that?"

I stared at her. "The universe being a scary nasty place. There was probably a man behind it, though."

"You think that thing was a man?" Yolanda asked.

"I think there's no atrocity that can be done which man hasn't done," I said, looking at her. "I think if you give a normal person claws, magic, glowing eyes, or just a tail then he's going to immediately try and figure out how that justifies him killing everyone without them. I believe, generally, people suck and the supernatural is just another kind of power. That makes them suck more."

"That thing wasn't human," Yolanda said, shaking her head. "Not even close."

"Maybe it was a thinking animal," I said, shrugging. "Which humans are. I believe the good outnumbers the evil in this world despite whoever designed everything intending to be brutal, painful, and harsh. The Earthmother is my goddess and nature is cruel as well as beautiful. It's why I'm not looking forward to facing her."

Yolanda turned around and sat cross-legged across from me. "I never got to tell my son a lot of things. I can't help but think when he was taken that he was brainwashed by the people who did it. By his father. But the thing is, he didn't die in Bright Falls. He escaped from his captors and lived his life elsewhere. I always have wondered. deep in my heart, if he tried to find me again. If he didn't find me or if he found out—"

"You were now killing supernaturals?" I asked.

"Yes." Yolanda frowned. "Alex managed to clear up our past with the authorities but we're still on a couple of terrorist watch lists. I blame the vampires."

"You are really making me wonder if I should be helping you," I said, shaking my head.

"Larry is the charming one," Yolanda said. There was a brief flash of pain on her face and I realized his feelings toward her were requited.

Or had been, once.

"Are you two together?" I asked, clutching her phone and taking a deep breath. It didn't take much to consecrate it. It was weird, but you'd think I'd need a special ceremony or something to "bless" things but no, actually, that apparently just came with my status as a self-proclaimed shaman.

"No." Yolanda blinked then looked away. "We were for a while. A couple of times, actually. However, every time we ended up breaking it off but continuing our partnership."

"Why's that?"

"What's this got to do with my son's séance?"

I gritted my teeth at that word. "Maybe I need to know who you are to work the magic."

Yolanda closed her eyes. "I can't focus on things other than the Hunt. Love isn't something that's going to make us better warriors or help us protect the world. It weakens you, makes you less sharp, and I don't think I could survive losing someone else like I did my son."

"Would you still be able to continue if Larry died now?"

Yolanda didn't respond.

"I didn't think so," I said, holding her phone. "This may come as a great shock to you, but I think it's better to go with love and enjoying life than dedicating yourself to becoming a bigger, better killer."

"We've saved a lot of lives," Yolanda said.

"You've also taken five innocent ones," I said, looking at her. "I think the world improves in a lot of ways. Ways better than killing things."

*I disagree.*

"Shut up, Raguel," I said, over to my gun.

Yolanda looked between us.

"The gun talks," I said, shrugging. "You don't want to know more."

"Okay. Are we ready?"

"Yep! As ready as we'll ever be." I paused. "Except, you know, I need to know your son's name. His true name."

"Jefferson Jones," Yolanda said. "It's my last name, not his father's. That's—"

"Gotcha," I said, feeling like her last name was the right one.

I leaned back against the headboard, closed my eyes, and began picturing all of the various symbols as well as images I needed to work the ritual. None of it was strictly necessary. The trick to magic wasn't in words or gestures but the mind of the bearer. Getting to the right place where you could, literally, reorder reality was something that I'd struggled with for many years. In the end, though, I saw the Spirit World. I then dialed 555-SPOOK then hit Send.

Sparks filled the room as every light bulb inside the room exploded, one after the other. The air temperature dropped to the point I could see my breath. The burner phone displayed a series of nonsensical characters and I knew I'd overdone the ritual. Still, I could feel a presence inside the room.

I just hoped it was her son's. "Here ya go."

Yolanda grabbed the phone and held it to her ear, starting to talk in an animated fearful voice. "Jefferson, Jefferson!"

I tried not to listen in on her conversation but was it was necessary for me to stay due to the fact I was the "battery" for the connection between the Spirit World and this one to stay in place.

What I did hear, despite my best efforts, was pretty much what one would expect of a good mother trying to see if her son was okay. There was much apologizing, much crying, and ultimately Yolanda didn't want to say goodbye when her son did. Instead, the phone just died in her hands.

Yolanda was a mess, her face puffy and snot running from her nose. She didn't wear much makeup, if any, so it wasn't running, but she had the look of someone devastated by emotion she'd kept bottled up for years. I didn't blame her, but it was sad. I briefly considered trying to comfort her before remembering she was likely to go for her gun if I did.

Yolanda stood up and went to the bathroom, cleaning off her face before returning. "Was any of that true or just shapechanger illusions?"

It was so insulting I almost snapped at her. "Lady, if I was going to lie to you, I wouldn't do it this way."

"How do I know that?" Yolanda asked.

"Would you believe me if I told you it was definitely your son or would you doubt anyway?" I asked. "Because I have a cousin named Jerry who refused to believe in magic or weredeer even when he turned into one."

Yolanda blew into a pile of toilet paper. "How did that work out for him?"

"He eventually shot himself in the head," I said, remembering the funeral. "He didn't use silver bullets so he survived as a vegetable until his mother asked for him to be taken off life support. We can starve to death."

Jerry had been an organ donor, too, but they hadn't wanted them because they were afraid they were tainted with whatever horrible disease made shapeshifters into monsters. I hadn't known the guy very well; he wasn't like my cousin Jill, but it had devastated Aunt Jenna.

Yolanda looked down at the useless cell phone. "I guess there are some things we have to take on faith."

"Do or do not, there is no try," I said, shrugging and getting up. I stopped before I exited out the door, though. "I will say, though, I hope your son was in a happy place."

"He is," Yolanda said. "Though it didn't sound like any kind of

Heaven I'd ever heard of."

"What was it?" I asked.

"A shopping mall," Yolanda said. "He runs the arcade."

"Sounds nice," I said. "One man's Heaven is another man's… also Heaven."

"I'm ready to go," Yolanda said. "Thank you."

"Just do your job."

# CHAPTER TWENTY-ONE

I got to exchange a few words with Alex on our way out, but it was clear he didn't want to talk given those conversation points were a grunt of agreement and, "We should get going." I was glad Yolanda had gotten to speak with her son, but I wasn't sure that was going to help us with our current problem of getting to the Dryad. Still, we all got together in my Hummer and Alex's SUV to head out to Shadow Pine Park.

I half expected a manticore or the Flying Spaghetti Monster to attack us on the way, but we managed to get to the crowded park fine. It was surrounded by people who had come to investigate the crime scene and I was briefly worried we would end up going right back into the heart of the media when Yolanda handed over her dowsing rod to Alex. With a similar adjusting of the glyphs, the six of us found ourselves heading in the opposite direction of the murder pit.

Which turned into a long, long hike.

"Are we there yet?" Robyn asked, carrying a heavy backpack as she drank from a quart of bottled water.

"Yes," I said, waving around the dowsing rod. I was standing in front of Larry and Yolanda, who were carrying their own heavy packs. Strangely, Larry was holding a frigging war hammer while wearing a pair of metal gauntlets as well as a medieval-looking belt. Alex was walking behind the group. He leaned heavily on a wooden staff similar to mine. He'd put on a pair of boots but was still wearing his FBI uniform. Emma was in dire wolf form, looking like a combination of wolf and pony as she walked beside me.

"Really?" Robyn asked.

"No," I said, sighing. "Also, that's like your sixth bottle. We're not stopping so you can pee again."

"I'm a plant, I need water and sunlight," Robyn said, putting on a pair of sunglasses and raising her hoodie.

I rolled my eyes. "We need to get your situation resolved. You're way too snarky for this group and stealing my thunder."

Larry laughed at that.

No one else did.

"Where did you even get that hammer, anyway?" I asked, looking over at Larry's weapon. "It looks halfway between a sledge and a maul."

"It's a giant's hammer," Larry said. "Supposedly belonged to a god."

Robyn muttered. "Gods, gods, gods."

Larry said, "Supposedly a Norse one. I think he only existed in comic books, though. Magni or something."

"Magni is a real Norse god," I said, remembering what I read. "His brother is Modi and they're Thor's sons with the giant Járnsaxa."

"I thought Sif was Thor's wife," Larry said.

"In real mythology, human relationships are actually like real-people relationships. Full of ugliness and adultery," I said, pausing. "Of course, real people note that this kind of thing is forgivable and doesn't apply to relationships before people start dating."

Alex grumbled. "I'm not mad at you anymore, Jane. I'm focused on the immediate danger we're facing in the Dryad's defenses. Whoever attacked you in the parking lot and hired Anne O'Henry to kill Lucien is going to be formidable. That doesn't include whatever defenses the original Brotherhood of Trees and the fairies living here have set up to defend their home."

"Oh," I said, huffing. "Well, you could have told me about that versus leaving me stewing this time entire time."

Alex didn't respond, looking troubled.

"Am I missing something?" Larry asked.

"Teen drama," Yolanda said, chuckling under her breathe. "Apparently, mons…supernaturals get it too."

"I am not a teenager." I looked up between the great Douglas firs around us. "I am nineteen. In some parts of the world, that's the age where I'd be taking over the family business."

"Just not America," Larry said.

"Shut up, Hammertime," I muttered. I hated that everyone knew my business in this group and wasn't sure how it could get worse.

"I should probably mention I've told Lucien to meet up with us here. I sense his presence nearby," Alex said.

I spun my head around and stared at him. "*Excuse moi*? You must be speaking French, because I know you didn't just speak English."

Alex's voice was dry. "I am going to have it out with my brother after this is over in the traditional manner. Before that, though, we need all hands on deck."

"What's the traditional manner?" Robin asked.

"We punch and kick each other until we feel better," Alex said without missing a beat. "The way brothers trained in the martial arts do."

"Your brother is a dragon," Larry said.

Alex nodded. "It almost makes it a fair fight."

I tried to hide my explosive anger but failed, gritting my teeth. "You are not going to beat up your brother because of me. I thought you were above this kind of macho crap and my gods, are you really going to—"

Everyone was looking past my shoulders.

"Is there a monster or Lucien behind me?" I asked. "Because I'm really hoping it's the monster."

"Hey!" Lucien said.

"Dammit," I muttered, turning around. "How did you sneak up on us despite my awesome weredeer hearing?"

Lucien was standing there, wearing a red-and-black flannel shirt over jeans that somehow still looked good on him. Like he was a cologne ad in *Backwoods Adventurer*. He was standing by Deana, wearing similar attire, and Gerald who was simply wearing a hoodie as well as pair of sunglasses.

"You were distracted," Lucien said. "Always entertaining, though."

I made a hissing gesture and made the sign of the cross at his attire. Sadly, I couldn't make a symbol of the circle or other ward against evil. "What is that evil you are wearing?"

"Clothing appropriate for the outdoors?" Lucien said.

"It's abominable!" I said, exaggerating. "It's like Alex wearing something other than his suit."

"Hello, Lucien," Alex said, waving from the background. "I'm glad you got my text."

"It's my town," Lucien said, a smug grin on his face. "I have a duty to protect it from evil gods. Also, you promised to knock me into next week."

I didn't like his smile or what it implied. "No fighting between you two. Especially not over me."

"There's plenty of other things I'd like to punch him for and vice versa," Lucien said, not missing a beat. "Though, honestly, you are a girl worth fighting for."

"I will beat the hell out of whomever throws the first punch," I said, pointing between you. "Everybody got that?"

"Promise?" Lucien asked, smiling.

"Ugh." I rolled my eyes then looked at Gerald. "Wait, how the hell are you up and about? The sun is up."

"Insufficiently analyzed science," Gerald said, looking comfortable.

"Magic," Lucien said, shrugging. "I'm sharing my power with him to protect him against the sun. Alex taught me how."

"Great," Larry muttered. "Now you're arming the bad guys, Alex."

"Do you want me to return your hammer to Magni and the giants?" Alex asked.

"No!" Larry said, grabbing the hammer protectively. "We've already set a date for the wedding."

Gerald looked away from the sun and toward Robyn. "I also came here for other reasons."

"To apologize for replacing me with a random high-school girl?" Robyn asked.

"She wasn't random," Gerald said.

"She also wasn't the first," I said, sticking my snout where it didn't belong. "Gerald was with Emma's sister last year."

"That wasn't by choice," Gerald said, his voice low and growly. It was a stark contrast to his usual melodic tone. "She forced me to love her."

I grimaced, remembering that. I'd conveniently forgotten that fact due to my desire to think of Gerald as a perverted old vampire preying on my friend's sister. The fact that Victoria had been possessed during the ordeal made me forget that he'd been a victim in all of this. The way Emma was looking at me also said she didn't think I was being cool.

"I'm sorry," I said, struggling to apologize to the vampire. "You were a victim too."

Emma barked in approval.

"What was that?" I asked. "Timmy fell down a well?"

Emma rolled her eyes. It was adorable even on a giant man-eating wolf.

"Well, between us, I think we can deal with just about anything the Dryad can throw at us," Lucien said, looking around. "Which is good because we really need to tear this place down and build a mall."

Everyone looked at him unhappily.

"Yeah." Lucien took a deep breath. "I know my real estate scheme is D.O.A."

Something clicked in my head and I couldn't help but think about the fact the griffon might have been attacking Alice O'Henry rather than me. Indeed, coupled with Lucien being attacked by Anne O'Henry, I wondered if I'd never been the target at all. It was possible this was all just an attempt to protect the forest from being destroyed. If so, they'd chosen a damn medieval way of going about it.

"Well, I'm glad you're here," I said, sort of.

Gerald put his fist over his chest. "I may not be Sparrow's biological father, but if there's some sort of evil ancient fairy trying to kill him, then I'm going to do my best to protect him."

"What?" I asked.

"I may have misrepresented some things," Lucien said, shrugging.

I looked back at Robyn.

Robyn didn't look at Gerald. "Thanks, but we're never getting back together."

"I'm just worried about you," Gerald said. "I mean, I'm out in the sun for you. That's like locking myself in a nuclear reactor, radiation suit or not."

Robyn didn't respond for a second. "Thanks, I mean that."

"So where is the portal to the Grove?" Lucien said, not paying attention to the lovers' quarrel around me.

I looked back at Alex who was waving the dowsing rod around. "It's around here…yes, that way. Got it."

Alex started marching towards the east and everyone followed without hesitation except for me. It was the kind of leadership that didn't require a display and annoyed me. I wanted to be able to get everyone to follow me.

*They have been. For two hours,* Raguel said.

*I'm pitying myself. Hush.*

*Yes, pity the poor girl with two handsome suitors who love her as well as a small army behind her.*

*If I had three dragons, I'd burn you right now.*

*Sadly you only have one.*

"Trouble in paradise?" Lucien said, coming up behind me.

"Funny," I said. "You know he wants to beat you up?"

"No, he wants to fight me," Lucien corrected. "There's a difference. Alex has got a few wires crossed in his brain that means he never really knows anyone until he has a sparring match with them. It's how he's going to find out whether or not I did this to screw him over."

"First, that's from the *Matrix* sequels we both agreed don't exist. Second, that's not for him to judge."

"It is," Lucien said, shrugging. "I knew you liked Alex and Alex liked you. I just wanted you more so I decided to move in."

I elbowed him in the gut.

"Oomph," Lucien said, almost falling over.

Everyone turned around to look at us.

"Sorry, reflex!" I said, lying. Well, not entirely. It was me reflexively elbowing him in the gut because I was so pissed off.

Lucien just laughed then stood up. "What?"

"That's a shitty thing to do to your brother and me," I said. "There are lines and rules not to cross."

"I've never been good about following rules," Lucien said, looking down. "Besides, as much as I love my brother, he's lost any right to tell me what to do."

I had the feeling I'd wandered into a complicated brotherly dynamic. "What do you mean?"

"When I first moved into Alex and Diane's home, it was a

house divided. He'd just gotten out of the asylum and mastered his powers. They hated each other and stayed on opposite sides of the mansion—"

"Alex is rich?" I asked.

"Not anymore," Lucien said, frowning. "As soon as his family trust hit, he gave it all away to charity."

That was stupid of him. Admirable, but stupid. "So you were his mother's replacement goldfish?"

"Yeah, for her dead child or Alex, I dunno," Lucien said. "Despite being the same age, Alex was always the more mature. He taught me everything he'd learned about the martial arts and we decided to become hunters together when he got back from studying magic with Kim Su. He promised he'd help me find my family's killers and I promised I had his back."

"Was he there when you took down the Darkwater PMC?" I asked, imagining Alex going *John Wick* on everyone. I knew some of this story because Alex had told me but I didn't have Lucien's perspective.

"No. He abandoned me not long before," Lucien said, staring forward. "He decided after we'd torn a big hole in the worst of the Vampire Nation to just up and leave. To become an FBI agent. We'd done an immense amount of good but he decided to go work for the government. It was insulting. Worse, it was a betrayal."

"So you became a crime lord to get back at him for joining the FBI?" I asked, seeing if I was understanding him correctly.

Lucien frowned and didn't meet my gaze, staring forward. "It wasn't like that."

"And I'm just a way to get back at him too?" I hesitated to ask.

"No," Lucien said, quickly. "Not even close."

"But it was a bonus."

Lucien didn't respond immediately. "Jane—"

"Bastard," I said, walking away from him.

I walked past everyone to take up position beside Alex. "Just because you're right doesn't mean I don't warrant a hell of an apology."

"I shall do it with flowers and jewelry," Alex said, stopping.

"Good," I said, pausing. "Wait, are we there?"

"No," Alex said, frowning. "But they're here."

I grimaced. "I hate when people are referred to as a 'they.' It's never good. Quite a bit different from 'George is here' or the guys.'"

"Jane, this is serious."

"You should see me when I'm goofing off."

Emma put a paw on the top of her snout. "Oy vey."

Looking where Alex was pointing the dowsing rod and saw a large grassy clearing in a circle of large trees that included a single one that had been uprooted as if by a storm. It was about half the size of a football field and radiated more magic than any other part of the forest I'd yet encountered. But it wasn't that which disturbed me. It was the fact that I felt other presences coming our way. Many presences.

"Who?" I asked.

"The Seven," Alex said, sucking in his breath and cursing to himself. "I suspected he'd hired them from the pieces on his chess board. They had the impressions of them."

"Should I be nervous about people who are referred to as a number rather than a name?" I asked.

"Yes," Alex said, clutching his staff tightly. "They're a kill squad of seven supernaturals who specialize in extremely hard-to-kill targets. They're coming for Robyn."

"We're not going to let them have her, right?"

"Over my dead body."

"That's what I'm afraid of."

I pulled out the Merlin Gun and hoped it was going to be enough.

# CHAPTER TWENTY-TWO

It wasn't seven people who came out of the trees, though, but nine. The first of them were David and Judith, the same two jackasses from the Lumberjack Inn in their same impractical outfits. However, the presence of Judith was different and stronger now. Indeed, it glowed with a kind of overwhelming power that caused me to feel sick to my stomach. I recognized it was the raw, unholy energy of John Jones without any attempt to hide its true power. The bastard had possessed his own daughter.

"Oh no," Alex said, staring at her. "Jones, you monster."

"Is she still inside?" I asked, not wishing that sort of fate on anyone. Brat or not.

"I don't know," Alex said.

"You can't hold back," I said, not sure if I was asking him to kill a kid if it meant saving his life.

Oh wait, yeah I was.

"Don't ask me that, Jane," Alex said, swallowing the air in his throat. "I killed Samantha. I'm not going to kill another child."

Samantha had been Alex's sister. The one he'd killed trying to save her from their father.

"She's not your sister," I said, grabbing his arm. "I saw you die."

"Some things are worse than death," Alex whispered. "After we all die eventually. Living with that is a worse curse."

I wanted to scream at him, curse him for his stupidity, but my attention was drawn to the rest of the bad guys coming through the trees. They had strong presences, too, almost as powerful as Jones's.

The first of them was a hideously deformed vampire who looked like Count Orlock with a black tattered monk's robe and a smell of death that carried with the wind. I didn't know much about vampires but I knew the really old ones looked less like people and more like demons once they started reaching their thousandth year. Vampires that old, known as Ancient Ones, were supposedly unkillable by any other than another Ancient One.

*Not quite true,* Raguel said. *That is the Visigoth. His name is lost to time and even he doesn't remember it. He kills as a mercenary because the lust for battle is all that quickens his dried, powdered blood.*

Behind them came a pair of beautiful Asian woman who it took me a second to realize were identical—not twins, but actually identical. They wore business suits with one wearing two holsters and the second carrying a staff over her shoulder. There was something about them that put me off on an instinctual animal level.

*Aoki and Aya. They are names for things that have never been human. They are a single demon inhabiting two colonies of spiders inhabiting the skins of humans they wove from many victims.*

I blinked. "Okay, that's going to give me nightmares for the rest of my life."

*Only if you see them at work.*

The sixth figure to exit moved with an enormous thumping that made me wonder how I hadn't heard it earlier. It was a nine-foot-tall stone statue of a long-haired, bare-chested man with a jawbone built into its hand.

*Samson,* Raguel said, his voice pitying. *It is a being like me. A blessed spirit put into an artificial body that it might fight for justice. Visigoth murdered its rabbi master and twisted its glyphs. It will not fight well, but it doesn't have to.*

"How the hell did they move that thing around?" I asked, staring at the golem. "I think you'd notice something like that!"

Emma glared at me. "Shh!"

*The Visigoth controls space as part of his magic. He keeps Samson in his pocket when he doesn't need it.*

Okay, that was both horrifying and cool.

The remaining three of the Seven were a petite blonde in a purple hoodie, a bare-chested Asian man in black sweatpants with a black dragon tattoo on his chest, and a guy who looked like a Hell's Angel biker had eaten a truck driver then taken a mountain of steroids. He also had a straight-up medieval flail hanging over one shoulder, which could best be described as like nunchucks but end was huge with spikes.

*Kate Madison, the fire elemental. She is a serial killer and arsonist. Visigoth bred her from psychics he captured and forced to mate until he sired her himself. Karl Chang is a distant cousin of Lucien's and Dragon Clan royalty.*

*Any chance he'll be friendly?* I mentally asked Raguel.

*No. He considers Lucien a half-breed insult to the family since his mother was a cougar shifter.*

*I'll keep the cougar jokes to myself,* I said. *Also, we need to work on the racism among shapechangers.*

*Humans are proficient at creating nonsensical categories to demean each other.*

"Agreed," I muttered. "Who is the last guy?"

*Steve Caldwell, the lone wolf. He is a werewolf who has devoured many others of his kind to gain their power.*

Another servant of the Wendigo spirit. Great. "Real bunch of winners Jones has gathered. You know, I was joking when I compared him to a supervillain but this is some straight up Masters of Evil deershit. What's next? Inviting us all to a fighting tournament?"

"I was thinking more Sharks vs. Jets," Emma said, her cute voice contrasting to her giant wolf appearance. "You know, the two of us rumbling."

I looked over at her. "Real-life gangs don't dance, Emma."

"Some of them do," Alex said, keeping his eyes on the group as it gathered around the fallen tree. "Those are the ones you have to watch out for."

Judith, or John Jones in her body, stepped in front of the group and spoke up to us. Her voice was a strange amalgamation of the Ultralogy leader's and his daughter's. "You've been an incredibly annoying presence in the past few hours. Give us Robyn and live another day."

Robyn stepped in front of the group and flipped him the bird. "Hey, body-stealing nutjob, I quit your stupid religion!"

"You were never welcome in it," Jones said, sneering, which had less effect when it was coming from an adolescent. "The entire purpose of your life was to serve as a host for the Dryad. It is the only meaning your otherwise wasted life of excess and stupid decisions will have."

"I'm glad my dad killed you!" Robyn said, revealing she wasn't as confident of her earlier statement as I'd thought.

Wow, I was easily fooled.

Jones smiled. "He'll be made to pay for his treachery. Many times we met when you joined my religion, him begging for me to take care of you and agreeing to anything so I didn't destroy you. Somewhere, somehow, he found a spine as well as the ability to work dark magic. You are going to cooperate with me, though."

"Why the hell would she do that?" I asked, putting my hand in front of Robyn before she jumped down to strangle a little girl. That would solve a lot of my problems, admittedly, but leave her exposed to the Seven.

"Because if she doesn't then I'll come right back here with another host for my goddess," Jones said, gesturing to the woods. "Your little boy, Sparrow, was left with your parents. I sent my people to acquire him for the faith."

"Bastard!" Robyn screamed.

The trees around us started to uproot themselves.

"Your child is fine, Robyn," Alex said, staring down at Jones and lifting up the white chess piece he'd pocketed from his board. "As soon as Jane identified her father as involved, I texted Lucien to make sure the boy was all right. He's somewhere safe along with your mother. David even gave me a warning of how to get past your spies watching the roads."

Alex tossed the chess piece down in front of Jones.

Jones spun around and stared at his son/brother/whatever. "Traitor!"

David narrowed his eyes. "You killed my sister."

"Not yet," Jones said, lifting his small hand into the air and calling forth a bolt of lightning that struck his son in the chest, sending him spiraling to the ground.

I didn't know if David Jones was alive or dead, but I had to admire the guy for standing up to his father. Too bad it had taken the possession of his little sister to do it. I just wish Alex and Lucien had left me in the loop.

"Not cool," I said, to him.

"Never make arrangements like that without telling me," Robyn said, growling as a glowing aura surrounded her.

Six of the trees continued to uproot themselves as they grew arms from their branches and became increasingly anthropomorphized.

"You have my word," Alex said, putting his hand over his chest. "I will never make those kind of arrangements without you or Jane again."

Kate Madison lifted up her hands and caused the six animated trees to catch fire around us. It caused Robyn to fall to her knees and scream as if the trees' pain was her own, but she just focused through it and pointed at Jones' host.

"Kill that son of a bitch!" Robyn shouted.

I'd never actually been in a mass battle before. It hadn't been on my bucket list of things to do, either. However, no sooner had Robyn made the command than both sides made a move to attack. That went to show I really did need to establish myself as the leader. I would have gone directly after Jones and maybe prevented everything from going to complete hell.

"That's all right, ignore the shaman," I muttered, lifting up my staff and slamming it against the ground.

I unleashed every bit of stored magic inside the staff at once, calling forth the storm glyph that caused clouds to cover the area in seconds before pouring down rain. I, perhaps, overdid it because I'd been hoping to put out the flames of the trees with a drizzle and ended up more with monsoon season.

A cascade of water poured down upon us and blinded me even as everyone still charged at one another. Lighting cracked in the air along with thunder. Kate Madison's fires, indeed, went out, and that meant we had a slightly better chance of survival, but I wondered what I could do to help in this battle.

*Have faith in yourself, Jane. You are more dangerous than you know.*

I tried to believe that. Of course, it would have been easier to believe if not for the fact I had to turn into a deer to duck out of the way of Jones pulling out a wand then firing glowing balls of hellish fire at me.

"You are not going to *Avada Kedavra* me, Hermione!" I shouted.

Alex engaged Visigoth in battle and it was hard to tell who was winning, since the two thousand-year-old vampire moved faster than the eye could see. Alex was friends with spirits of light and wind that allowed him to move every bit as fast. In the brief moments I saw them stop when one exchanged a blow. During the fight, Alex's body glowed with sunlight he used to punch the ancient undead thing with the force of a mountain. They blinked in and out all around the clearing, like they were characters in an anime.

Lucien, meanwhile, turned into his twenty-foot-long dragon form and breathed fire that ignored the torrential downpour around us, only to have that fire wash over a similarly sized black dragon. The two grappled like kaiju, smashing into one another, biting, and slashing. It was a contest to be decided by pure strength and made me sad in a way, since there were so few dragons left in the world.

I tried not to scream as the two spider-women exploded into a mountain of spiders that grew into ones the size of cars, filling the area with things from Tolkien's nightmares. Emma killed one another a single blow then another as Yolanda pulled out her shotgun to fight. That was when I forced down my fear, dodged between them, and charged at Jones before head-butting her across the field.

Should I feel bad about doing that to a little girl? I asked Raguel.

*Yes.*

*Too bad!* I proclaimed.

I didn't get a chance to respond, though, because the Visigoth appeared right in front of me with Alex held above him in one hand. I should have known Alex had been throwing everything he had at the Ancient One. The millennia-old vampire looked triumphant, but there was a sadistic gleam in his old eyes that made me realize he wanted to watch as he killed someone I cared about.

Loved.

I turned back into a human woman, holding the Merlin Gun in front of me, and aimed at his head. "Put him down!"

The vampire laughed and spoke with an inhuman gurgle I could barely understand through his fangs. "A gun, you think you can threaten me with a gun. Wait, that's the—"

I put every bit of magical energy I had into the Merlin Gun and fired a single bullet that slammed into the forehead of the vampire. The creature dropped Alex on the ground. Its head started to glow yellow then orange as the blessed bullet burned away its brain. Its head finally exploded as the rest of its body disintegrated into flaming ash. Ancient Ones could only be killed by another one of their kind—but the Merlin Gun was, apparently, an exception that proved the rule.

*The first sacking of Rome is avenged. King Alaric has paid for his crime.*

"Yeah, well the Romans were kind of asking for it," I muttered.

*Says the woman living in one of Rome's spiritual descendants.*

While the Merlin Gun was capable of focusing the power of any wizard to a tremendous level against what it perceived as evil, what was evil, it still needed one to provide the *oomph*. As much as Alex said I was stronger than any wizard, I couldn't help but note that had taken almost everything I had. I collapsed to the ground even as I felt an immense amount of fear and confusion radiate out in a spiritual wave. The Visigoth had been the Seven's leader, so his loss was an immense one. Sadly, none of them seemed to be the type to retreat either as they all believed they would be shown the same mercy they had shown others—which was to say none.

"Goodbye," Jones's voice spoke behind me.

"Crap," I said, only capable of looking over my shoulder to see the little girl once more. Jones was no longer holding a wand, but instead the gun from my vision. He'd used up all of his magic, it seemed, getting rid of the storm around us as well as destroying all of Robyn's living trees, as I saw nothing but burning stumps behind him where they'd been. Jones wasn't aiming the gun at Alex, though, but me.

Jones contorted his little girl's smile into one of deranged satisfaction, only to shake fiercely and collapse to the ground.

Behind him, Robyn was holding my Taser in hand. "Sorry, I hope you don't mind, but I picked this up from your room."

I glared at her then Alex, who was getting up. "See, I told you to Taser her."

Alex didn't respond, though, instead focused on the battle still going on between the dragons. Karl Chang had gained the upper hand on Lucien and was clutching his back between his arms, squeezing him to death.

Alex knelt down, lifted his palm up, then propelled himself forward with telekinesis before smashing the dragon across the battlefield into Samson the golem. The dragon's body broke in half then turned back into its human form.

I stared at him. "Okay, you are teaching me how to do that."

Larry hurled his magic hammer at Samson with more force than was humanly possible, causing the stone golem to shatter into a thousand pieces. The stone statue spoke something in Hebrew I didn't understand.

*He said thank you*, Raguel translated.

With that, the battle was over, as Deana, Emma, and Gerald had killed most of the spiders. Kate Madison, unlike her fellows, had been smart enough to flee into the woods. Stephen Caldwell, the biker, had knelt down in surrender with his hands over his head. We'd won with no casualties! Yay! Then I saw Yolanda on the ground, twitching. She'd been bitten by one of the spiders and they probably would have been lethal at a normal size.

"Shit!" I said, running toward her.

# CHAPTER TWENTY-THREE

Alex and I both rushed to Yolanda's side while Lucien shifted back to his human form. Yolanda was writhing in pain and I knew, in an instant, the demon inhabiting the spider twins had made their poison so it dealt death slowly.

"Damn it," I said, coming to her side.

"Is there anything you can do?" Larry said, grabbing her hand and holding it tight.

"Alex?" I turned to him.

Alex placed his hand on her stomach and closed his eyes. "I can keep her alive and dull the pain, but her time on Earth will end the moment I stop. The poison is all in her blood."

Yolanda stopped thrashing about but still looked to be in pain. Her breathing was labored and I could see sweat coming from her forehead, as difficult as it was to see with her clothes soaked like everyone else's, including my own.

Larry looked over to Gerald. "Surely you can do something."

"No," Yolanda hissed. "I am not going to become a monster."

"I could not change her with her blood poisoned as it is," Gerald said, standing in the back. "I'm sorry."

Larry growled at Gerald, clearly seeing it as a betrayal, despite the fact they barely knew each other. He was also ignoring Yolanda's wishes.

"Let me help," Jones's voice spoke from the back as Lucien stood over the girl with a gun pointed to the back of her head. It wasn't the most pleasant thing to see but I reminded myself "she" was a century-old psychopath wearing his daughter's corpse.

"Right," I said, turning back to her. "Fat chance."

"I know the magic to transfer the disease to another," Jones said, chuckling. "Death can be pay for life. You know this. Alex knows this."

"I'll do it," Larry spoke up, quickly. "I'll give my life for you."

"F...that, Larry," Yolanda said, in between pained breaths. "You are not dying for me. You need to live."

I pitied and envied the hunters at the time. They'd managed to create a bond unified by countless missions together. It was a bond that was always going to end in death, though, because there were only so many times you could wrestle with Death before you lost. I didn't want it to end for her like this, though. Strange as it may seem, I had started to respect the hunter and had forgiven her for the fact that she was an angry bigot. Maybe the fact she was on "my" team was all it amounted to, but that was enough.

"That's not your choice," Larry said, holding her hand with both of his now. "I would do anything for you."

"Oh, spare me," Jones said, laughing. "People die, that's what they do, and the only ones who matter are the immortal."

"Alex can do it," Lucien said coldly.

"What?" Jones said, looking back.

"Lucien," Alex whispered. "Don't ask me—"

"Do you want to save your friend or not?" Lucien said. "I've seen you do it before."

"Please, Alex," Larry looked over to him.

"All right," Alex said, lowering his gaze.

I looked over at Jones. "Awesome. Goodnight, Jones."

"You wouldn't dare kill a child," Jones laughed.

"You're right," I said, standing up and then leaping in the air before kicking in Jones's direction. "SPINNING DEER KICK!"

Despite making a *Street Fighter II* joke, I was entirely serious about the spell I was working. I'd recovered enough to do one more. It was the only one I knew other than how to read objects. It was also an ability I'd used only once before to defeat the Big Bad Wolf. It was the power of exorcism.

The blow struck out against Jones and knocked his ghost clean from the young girl's body. I saw Jones's translucent form hover in the air for a second before disappearing. The look of snide contempt on his face was unmistakable even as he faded away. Judith collapsed like a doll which had its strings cut, plopping face-first into the muddy ground before her. Lucien bent down to check her pulse.

"Is there any chance he's permanently dead?" I asked Alex.

"No," Alex said, still holding his hand on Yolanda's side while giving everyone orders to make circles, marks, and glyphs around her. "However, he will be trapped in the Spirit World for a while."

"How long was a while?" I asked, looking around. "Because he didn't stay dead for more than a few hours last time."

"We should draw protective circles around his daughter and son," Alex said. "At least that will force him to seek out the others. He can take any of his followers, though. It's just harder."

"She's alive," Lucien said, standing up. "I think she's got her soul still, too."

"There's an unusual sentence," I muttered, looking over to the fallen soaked form of David Jones. "Is he alive? I mean, he got hit by lighting."

David lifted his hand up and waved it a bit.

"Well, that answers that question," I said, wondering if I was willing to sacrifice his life to save Yolanda's.

*That would be murder*, Raguel said.

*Oh, that would be murder*, I thought, rolling my eyes.

*Yes.*

Okay, fair enough.

"Can you help her?" Lucien asked.

"Yes," Alex said, taking a deep breath. "I'm going to need Robyn's hand, though."

"Like hell!" Robyn said, pulling away.

"I promise you no harm will come to you," Alex sad, his voice serene. "I want to try and take power from the whole forest, though, rather than trying to kill someone for it to work. It is the gift of life you've been blessed with, Robyn Taylor, and something you can give to the rest of the world."

"I've heard a lot of holy men talk stuff like that," Robyn said, staring at me. "Usually before they ask to fuck me."

"I have someone else for that," Alex said.

"You better be talking about me," I said.

"Yes, Jane, I mean you," Alex said.

"Just checking."

"Monogamy is overrated," Lucien muttered, looking over his

shoulder as he made protective circles around the fallen Jones family members. "Honestly, more people should work in groups. Frankly, one should never knock threesomes before—"

"Please stop talking," Alex said.

"Right," Lucien muttered. "By the way, I wasn't referring—"

"Silent as a monk who has taken a vow of silence," Alex said, holding out his other hand for Robyn.

Robyn, reluctantly, put her hand in Alex's. "This isn't going to hurt, is it?"

"It will, yes," Alex said. "I am asking you to endure it for the life of a stranger."

"All right," Robyn said.

"Ugh," Yolanda said, choking. There was a defiant look on her face and I saw she was struggling to maintain it despite everything. "Just heal me or let me die, because this in-between thing is really sucking."

What happened next could only be described as a combination of a miracle and an abomination. The screams of both Robyn and Yolanda filled the air while I saw Alex's eyes produce tears of blood. The air filled with magic and there was a rush of the wind before Yolanda jolted up then vomited what seemed like a stomach full of black fluid. The fluid caught fire on the ground before going out almost instantly.

Robyn pulled her arm away from Alex's. "Holy crap, could you warn me next time you're going to do something like that?"

"I did warn you," Alex said, sighing. "It worked, though."

"What would have happened if you hadn't?" Larry said, going to check on Yolanda.

"Yolanda would have died and then one of those spider women would have hatched from Yolanda's body to wear her skin," Alex said, frowning. "We got all of the spiders, didn't we? They're hosts for the demon otherwise."

There was the sound of rifle fire nearby.

"Yeah," Lucien said. "Alice is going to get them all."

"You trusted the crazy mercenary lady with a gun?" I asked. "The one who tried to kill you?"

Lucien nodded. "She promised we were fine."

I stared at him, waiting for some sign of sarcasm. "Okay."

Deana looked at me. "It seems my new master is not the only one who has an exaggerated sense of a promise's value."

"A man is only as good as his word," Lucien said, looking at Alex. "Though some promises clearly mean more than others."

"So you didn't have to kill anyone?" I said, turning around to look at our prisoner. Steve Caldwell was lying facedown on the ground, his body burnt to a crisp from the inside out. It was like someone had set his blood on fire. "Oh."

Alex sighed. "I was hoping not to, but it didn't work out."

*He was a murderer many times over.*

"I know," Alex said, surprising me. I hadn't realized he could still hear Raguel when he spoke. "That doesn't make it any easier."

"Well it should," I said, looking around.

Larry looked over at the burnt corpse then at Yolanda. "I don't care what he did. I'm glad he did it."

Alex stood up and looked around. "We are reaching the last leg of our journey. All we have to do is find the entrance to the Grove."

Robyn waved her hand like it had been burned then pointed behind Lucien. "There it is?"

I looked where she was pointed and squinted. I could just make out a shimmering circular gate that seemed like an optical illusion in the sunlight streaming through the trees. A rainbow from my impromptu storm was nearby, making the clearing look peaceful and serene despite the numerous dead bodies scattered about.

"Huh," I said, taking a deep breath. "That was easier than I thought."

"You call this easy?" Larry asked.

Yolanda slapped him across the shoulder. "So what do we do now?"

Alex looked over to it. "Robyn can bring people through the gate, but I don't think the rest of us will be able to go. The curse here is very powerful and only she can break it."

"How do I do that?" Robyn asked.

Alex shrugged. "Take someone through the gate and confront the Dryad. Ask her to do it."

"Before or after I set her on fire?" Robyn asked.

"Before, preferably," Alex said.

Robyn nodded, seemingly missing the joke (if a joke there were).

"Jane, I'd like you to accompany me. Can I take anyone else?"

"If you can hold their hand, yes," Alex said.

"Then you, Handsome Agent Man," Robyn said, pointing to you. "Sorry, Gerald, but I need a wizard here."

"I understand," Gerald said, looking down.

Robyn paused before responding. "I'm glad you came, though, Gerald. It was hard when you disappeared. You were one of the few people who were ever nice to me."

"You were a far better survivor than I ever was. I owe you for the lessons you taught me," Gerald said.

"You still owe me for child support," Robyn said, pointing at him.

"Absolutely," Gerald said, smiling. It was one of the few times I'd ever seen the vampire display such emotion.

Alex took several deep breaths and cupped his hands in prayer, or maybe he was just performing martial arts breathing exercise. I couldn't tell which, if not both, he was doing. "I'm not sure how much help I'm going to be. I exhausted much of my power fighting the Visigoth. Still, you have every bit of my remaining strength."

"Anyone else know anything about magical groves or supernatural hoodoo?" Robyn asked.

I looked over at Lucien.

"Not as much as he does," Lucien said, shaking his head. "I'll keep any surprises from following you in."

"Thanks," I said, giving him a thumbs up. "I'm willing to forgive for earlier."

Lucien arched his eyebrow. "What the hell did I do wrong?"

"Ugh," I muttered, heading to the gateway. "This is why men are going to eventually be replaced by the inexhaustible android."

"I feel offended," Alex muttered, standing beside Robyn.

"You will be spared when the revolution comes," I said, pointing to him. "You and Ryan Reynolds."

"Why not build the robots to look like Ryan Reynolds?" Robyn asked.

"Ooo," I said, smiling. "You going to be okay with this group, Emma?"

I was hesitant about leaving Emma behind, not because I didn't think she'd be safe with this group, but because I didn't like going into the heart of the supernatural without my best friend. I honestly thought it might be better to take her along than Alex.

"Are you going to be okay with this group?" Emma asked, trotting up to my side on all fours.

I scratched behind her ears. "I absolutely promise not to be killed. If I am, you have the right to be upset."

Emma growled at that.

"Who's a good girl? Yes you are, yes you are!" I said, smiling before giving her a kiss on the snout. "Seriously, if I die, I want you to find out whomever Jones reincarnates into and eat them."

Emma whined. "Can't I just kill them?"

"No, I expect full digestion," I said, pointing at her. "Eat him. Got that?"

"All right," Emma said. "I'll eat him...or her."

"Good," I said, patting her on the head.

"You know I only let you do this, right?" Emma said, grumbling.

"Absolutely."

I turned around and took Robyn's hand as Alex took the other. It felt right to have the three of us together and I saw events in the future with us involved.

I saw the image of us in New Detroit at some kind of mixed martial arts tournament where my brother was fighting a werewolf. The three of us were in the stands, watching him. That confused the hell out of me, because Jeremy was a mechanic.

I saw a golden-haired man wearing a yellow tracksuit staring down at the three of us in a biker bar, bodies lying across the ground, and pointing at Alex. I saw an—honest to Goddess—*ninja* dressed in black attacking me with a sickle chain on a rooftop. I saw Robyn kissing Lucien, which made me jealous.

I shook that image away before the three of us stepped through the gateway. We found ourselves in a forest that felt like a truer, more real version of Shadow Pine Park. The trees were larger, standing taller and wider than the ones in reality. The air was cleaner and fresher, lacking all of the traces of smog that was ever-present in the United States for those who had the nose to smell it. I saw a squirrel the size of a medium-sized dog dart past us carrying a nut along with a path lead down toward a light I could only describe as heavenly.

"Wow," Robyn said, staring at the place. "I can feel everything."

"Yes," Alex said, taking a deep breath. "Plato called this the Realm of True Forms. Native Australians Dreamtime. The Cervid Clan call it the Great Forest or Underwood."

"What do you call it?" I asked.

"Home," Alex said, sighing. "When I was trapped in the Bedford Asylum, drugged up to my eyeballs, I learned to project myself here. It was the only way to stay sane."

"You had a really crappy childhood," I said, not sure how else to respond.

"There were some good times," Alex said, pausing. "Like when my father sent me every summer to Hong Kong to study with Kim Su. Those were good times."

That was when I heard a gun cock behind us. "Don't move."

I looked over at Alex. "Well, that's unexpected. I was thinking more Aslan than getting mugged."

"You never know," Alex said, unconcerned.

I had a suspicion who was holding us at gunpoint. There was only one person, really, left in this sordid mess.

Robyn turned her head to look at the man behind us. "Dad?"

Okay, that was actually *not* whom I was expecting.

# CHAPTER TWENTY-FOUR

I turned around to face the man from my earlier vision, the one who'd "killed" Dr. Jones and his bodyguard on the commode (such an undignified way to die—no wonder he became a ghost). Andy Taylor was wearing the same clothes from earlier, a hoodie over a pair of thick gray Michigan Forest Ranger pants.

He was a black man in his mid-fifties with slightly graying hair as well as thick, round cheeks that reminded me a bit of Lawrence Fishburne. He had a goatee and mutton chops that looked like they belonged in the seventies. Andy Taylor was holding a gun on Alex while looking at Robyn.

Robyn stared in shock. "I didn't want to believe it was true."

"You shouldn't be here, Robyn," Andy said before a furious fit of coughing over took him, causing him to lower his gun.

I grabbed for it first and wrestled it away from him before pushing him back.

"Hey!" Robyn said, growling at me. "That's my dad."

"Don't have him point a gun at me!" I snapped back.

"You'd survive," Robyn said, looking at the weapon before frowning. "Right? I mean, unless it was silver bullets."

"I do not want to test that theory!" I shouted.

Birds the size of puppies flew from their nests in nearby branches. Apparently our fight was disturbing the idyllic peace of the region.

Andy continued to cough before falling to his knees, Alex going to his side to help. "You're very sick, Mr. Taylor. You should not have used the magic you have."

Andy tried to fight him off but just waved his arm a bit in Alex's direction. "I'll do whatever I have to."

"A philosophy that has caused the destruction of many a great man." Alex put his hand on Andy's chest before both started to glow.

Magic came from the Spirit World and was much stronger here. I could feel it in my bones, in my heart, and all throughout my body. I wondered what sorts of miracles were possible here and whether I could learn to harness that power in the real world.

*No,* Raguel said.

*Spoilsport,* I thought back to him.

"Your father is dying," Alex said, standing up and offering his hand to the fallen park ranger. "I'm sorry."

"What?" Robyn said, her voice cracking. "What the hell?"

Andy looked at Alex's hand as if it was diseased before climbing up. "This doesn't change anything."

"We're not here to defile the Grove," Alex explained. "Jane is the new shaman of Bright Falls and the intermediary between the spirits as well as man. I am an enemy of Dr. Jones and am working to put a stop to the Shadow Pines Project. Peacefully, though, not through assassination."

"Dad, what the hell is he talking about?" Robyn asked. She had lost all of her usual snark and was in full panic mode, clearly still processing the blunt pronouncements Alex had given.

"I tried nonviolent ways," Andy said, coughing a few more times. "I wrote letters, I attended meetings, begged, borrowed, and stole. Nothing worked. Alice O'Henry owns this town and has the local crime boss in her pocket too. There was nothing an ordinary man could do in that sort of situation."

"Stop ignoring me," Robyn said, balling her fists. "What is going on?"

"He's the Guardian of the Grove," Alex said, as if it was the most natural thing in the world. "The last of the Brotherhood of the Tree, or perhaps the first of the new, depending on when he found the Dryad. He attacked Alice with the griffon and Lucien with an assassin, though I have no idea where he found her. He also killed Dr. Jones and his colleague."

"He's basically those guys from *Indiana Jones and the Last Crusade,*" I explained to Robin. "You know, the ones with the fezzes who didn't do much to slow the Nazis down from getting to the Holy Grail. Which, as we saw with *The Ark of the Covenant,* probably could protect itself. You know, Indy didn't even need to be there in the first movie."

"Wrong," Alex said. "If Indy wasn't there, Marianne would have died in Nepal."

"Oh right," I said, having never thought about it that way.

"Guys," Robyn said, taking a deep breath. "Shut up, please."

I went silent.

Huh, so that's what that felt like.

"Dad, is this true?" Robyn asked.

Andy Taylor stood up and took a deep breath. "Yes, though I don't know anything about a Brotherhood of the Tree. The Goddess mentioned it several times, but it's meaningless to me. I found her when I was twenty-one and walking through this place. She showed me many things and made me her priest. I'd always loved nature and the world, felt it was divine, but it wasn't until her I could put a face on it. She may not be God, but she's certainly an angel."

*Not even remotely*, Raguel said.

*Not now*, I said.

"An angel who abandoned babies to die," Robyn said, her voice dripping with confusion and betrayal. "Her own children. Me."

"No," Andy said, covering his face. "It's not like that. It was the fact I found you and took care of you that opened the Grove to me."

"So you aren't Robyn's biological father," Alex said.

Both Andy and I looked at him like he was an idiot. I mean, I loved Alex (wow, that was a bit premature) but it was pretty obvious they weren't biologically related.

"Seriously?" I asked.

"It's possible," Alex said, frowning. "Unlikely, but possible. You wouldn't think Lucien was half-Japanese or you—"

"Please stop," I said.

"No," Andy said, looking down. "I don't know who her father was. She lets whomever she wants through the gate. Though, seeing as you're here, it's clear it also opens up for you, Robyn."

"God, Dad, you're a pacifist," Robyn said, taking a step back. "Were a pacifist! Now you're a murderer!"

"The Grove needs to be protected," Andy said, his voice low. "The Goddess of the Forest brought you to me and later your son. I had to protect her and the other things here. Things that don't exist in nature anymore."

"Like the griffon you forced me to kill," I said, looking at him.

"Because I don't think there's many of those left, even here."

Andy had been ignoring me for the majority of the conversation but I could tell those words struck him like a kick to the face.

"Where did you get the magical tools to work your sorcery?" Alex asked, speaking even more like a comic book character than usual. "Your body is full of residue from improper use. I don't think that's your doing, though. Whoever sent you the tools to bind magical creatures sent you improper instructions. Like a faulty radiation suit."

"Don't talk to my father like that!" Robyn said, turning her back to us. I could sympathize with her situation. She wasn't acting that dissimilar to how I'd responded to discovering my mother was a killer.

"I can help you, Mr. Taylor," Alex said, looking at Robyn then back to her. "I can burn out the black magic from your body and heal some of the damage."

"You'll be dead within the hour, otherwise," Alex said, his voice cold.

Robyn spun around and stared.

"I—"

Alex stared at him. "You have betrayed your oath to the Earthmother. You have blasphemed and brought the taint of Hell to her holy place. You have killed the creatures under your charge. You can feel how this place rejects you. It does not reject us or your daughter. Accept our help and that you are not carrying the burden to protect this place alone or submit to pride and die a blasphemer to everything you have loved. Including your own daughter, who looks on at you in horror and confusion rather than love."

Andy didn't say a word for a moment. "I have been a fool."

"No kidding!" Robyn said, staring at him. "You lied to me! All this time! You knew where I came from and you hid it from me! There were times I thought I was going insane and you pretended it was all in my head."

Andy's eyes were close to tears. "I did what I thought was right. If people knew what was here, what Robyn was capable of, they'd send government teams to tear it apart. To slice her open and find out what was inside of her. Even after the Reveal, people don't know what to do with the holy."

*Or the damned,* I thought, but I didn't say that. "Yes, because her being ignorant of who she was worked out so well. What with the running away from her home, getting involved with an evil cult, and wanting to kill her mother."

Robyn glared at me then her father. "What she said. Also, I should have been the one to say it."

"Sorry, was just trying to move the conversation along."

"Wow, and I thought I was rude," Robyn muttered.

"Sorry," I said, grimacing. "I blame the fact I've almost been killed like three times today."

"Please," Andy said, lowering her head. "Forgive me, Robyn."

"If you let these people help you," Robyn said, walking over to him and grabbing his hands. "They're good people. Something I never say about anyone. Even if I want to punch the deer girl right now."

I nodded. "It's a fair cop."

"All right," Andy lowered his head. "I don't like it, though."

*Well, in an hour it won't matter,* is what I *wanted* to say, but didn't, because I have some tact.

Not much, but some.

Alex placed his hand on Andy's chest again. "Robyn, I would like your help again."

"This is getting irritating," Robyn muttered.

"Don't blame him, you're the demigod," I said. "Plant Wonder Woman."

"Do you communicate entirely in pop culture?" Robyn asked. "I mean, you're like Buffy with a side order of venison."

"Don't say venison," I said, lowering my voice to dangerous levels. "Only we can use that word."

Robyn looked slightly cheerier and put her hand in Alex's. "This will heal my dad, right?"

"Yes," Alex said, frowning. "Somewhat."

There was a hint of remorse in Alex's voice and I knew that whatever he was about to do wasn't going to fix Robyn's dad completely. Given Alex could cure cancer at the top of his game, that struck me as tragic, but I'd felt what it was like to be inside Andy Taylor's body. The taint of black magic had seeped into his blood, lungs, and soul. It seemed there were no free lunches, even when there was magic involved.

This time, though, there was no scream of pain or sounds of agony from anyone in the spell. The forest seemed to respond to Alex's request and channel energy through Robyn to Alex to Andy. All three of them glowed in unison and there was a scent of verbena in the air that burned my nostrils. After a second, Alex pulled his hand away from Andy and Robyn.

"It is done," Alex said, taking a deep breath.

Andy took several deep breaths. "I can feel the difference. The air, the moisture against my skin, and the spirit running through my soul are all sharper. The anger has lessened, too, though I wonder if that's because my daughter is back."

"So everything is cool, huh?" I said, trying to put a positive spin on things.

"We are not cool," Robyn said, clearly searching for something harsher to say. "We are not cool at all."

Andy lowered his gaze. "I'm sorry for lying to you, I truly am."

"You could try apologizing for trying to kill my friends," I replied. "Also, being an actual murderer."

Alex cleared his throat and mentioned something about the beam in one's own eye versus the plank.

*He says you're being a hypocrite*, Raguel translated.

"Oh really?" I asked, turning to Alex. "Just because I wanted to kill Jones and killed a bunch of guys in the forest, I should ignore… Okay, yeah, actually I get what you're saying. Forget it."

"I'm glad you're alive," Robyn said, looking to Alex. "What's going to happen now?"

"It is not my place to judge you," Alex said, his words coming from a place of authority beyond his role as an FBI agent. "I will not protect you from the mortal authorities but I think you'll find them less inclined to judge you than you might think—assuming they even bother to investigate the case. My brother is more reasonable than you'd imagine and has no wish to further endanger this place. Alice O'Henry? Well, pray she never discovers you were responsible rather than Dr. Jones. She is even more ruthless than her father."

"I knew Marcus O'Henry," Andy said, his voice low. "I thought him to be an honorable man, but everything they've accused him of makes me think otherwise."

"Yeah, he hurt his kids and grandkids. Screw that guy," I said simply.

"Where did you get the items you used?" Alex said. "You need to divest yourself of them."

"Points for a man who uses the word 'divest' in a sentence," I said.

Andy reluctantly removed a chalice from his jacket pocket. It was copper lined and made of stone, but felt wrong to look at. I could feel the unnatural energy surging from it and knew someone had decided, *Oh, I know what I'm going to do today. I'm going to make a Satanic Grail.* That is not something a person does unless they're on drugs, seriously messed up, evil, or all three. He also pulled out a small Bible-sized notebook that was bound in coarse leather that I felt contained even more black magic than the Satanic Grail. Alex picked up the objects and somehow put them in the pocket of his jacket that couldn't hold them.

"I got these in the mail with instructions," Andy said, looking guilty. "The book told me how to summon and control spirits as well as incarnate them into the natural world."

"And you just thought that was a great idea," I said, appalled at his lack of perspective.

"Do you know how many spirits are in the Grove?" Andy said, looking at me. "There are things here that do not exist in nature anymore. Not just mythical creatures but ones that went extinct long ago. I wouldn't be surprised if I found a T-Rex here if I looked long ago enough."

I had no idea what that referred to. "You decided to do this all by yourself, without any help?"

"I knew the shaman," Andy said, accusingly. "She was not a teenage girl."

"Robyn, may I punch your father?" I asked.

"No!" Robyn said, before looking back to him. "Does my mother know?"

"Yes," Andy said. "Wilma is a priestess of the Goddess. Do you really want to kill her for what she's done?"

"Wouldn't you?" Robyn asked.

It spoke volumes about our situation and the Taylor's religion that he didn't have an answer. "Jones's spirit is still a threat to the

Grove," Alex said, keeping us surprisingly on track. "We need your help to save her."

Robyn didn't answer to that.

"Jones is dead," Andy replied, crossing his arms. "I killed him."

"Rather than explain that he's an immortal wizard, I'm going to simply state we're going to visit the Goddess of the Forest right now whether you want us to or not. Also, I'm going to pistol whip you if you don't."

Andy looked down at me. "I'd like to see you try, little girl."

That was when Robyn waved her hand and a pair of roots reached out from the ground to wrap around his legs. "You're going to stay here, Dad."

"Robyn!" Andy said.

"Goodbye, Dad," Robyn said, turning around to walk toward the light. "This is not over."

I looked over at Alex. "Should I still pistol whip him?"

Alex looked at me then him before shrugging. "I don't care."

I smirked.

# CHAPTER TWENTY-FIVE

"Are you okay?" I asked, walking beside Robyn as we followed a dirt path to what seemed to be Heaven itself.

"Nope," Robyn said, taking a deep breath. "I am most definitely not okay. I'm in frigging Oz, my father is a crazy eco-terrorist, and I'm off to see a god I don't believe in who happens to be my mother."

"Religion is annoying when it's true," I said, repeating a statement I'd once heard one of my college professors say. He'd been quite irritated with the Reveal and had quit his lucrative gig on the talk-show circuit to become a hippie in Bright Falls.

"I'm still not sure any of this is real," Robyn said, frowning. "This could all be a hallucination, waking dream, or a bunch of aliens playing tricks on me."

"Aliens are more believable than spirits?" I asked.

"Duh," Robyn said. "One has flesh and blood."

"Spirits, ghosts, and souls are matters of physics, not biology," Alex said, gazing around. "Though I have often taken note everything we see and experience is filtered through our consciousness. That, in its own way, makes us each a deity. Religion is, in a way, just reverence for anything we choose to give it since all of reality is a miracle."

"That's stupid," I said. "No offense."

"Some taken," Alex said.

Robyn laughed. "Yeah, well, just assume I'm an agnostic. I believe what my own eyes tell me but I see no reason to worship it. It's pretty, but so was Disneyland when my parents took me there. You don't see me worshipping Cinderella."

"You remind me a great deal of Gerald," Alex said, leaning heavily on his staff. He'd pushed himself to the limits during this mission. It was the biggest evidence he was telling the truth about me being stronger since I felt like I could start throwing fireballs all around this forest.

*Why would you want to do that?* Raguel asked.

*I didn't say I did,* I replied mentally. *Just, you know, if I wanted to burn the forest down, I could.*

"You know Gerald?" Robyn asked.

"Yeah," Alex said, sighing. "We became friends after the Victoria O'Henry case. Gerald believes there's nothing man was not meant to know and there's nothing science cannot explain. He also disdains any sort of reverence for the universe."

"You're wrong," Robyn said, shaking her head. "He has an immense amount of reverence for the universe. He just believes we have to fight it because it's such a cold and hostile place. What good in this universe comes from people not gods. I admire that strength of will."

"Well, we can agree to disagree," Alex said. "I believe the universe is a test but filled with as much good as there is evil."

"I believe I'm hungry," I said, shrugging.

Both of them looked at me.

"Sorry," I said. "It's just I think you sound like Jeremy when he gets high but without the fun part of snacks or getting high."

No one responded to that.

"Oh yeah," I said, nodding. "I dropped your mike."

"You're saying that phrase wrong," Robyn said, looking annoyed.

"I dropped your mikes, oh yea," I said, making finger guns at them.

Alex smiled and we continued on into the forest. It was the sort of place I wanted to become a deer and trot around for a few hours, especially as I hadn't gotten my morning run out. However, that had the potential of being an extraordinarily bad idea.

Paths in the Spirit World were important, because when you were in a place that was potentially infinite, you could easily wander into a place where your mind would keep you occupied forever. Plenty of stories across the globe talked of people entering the Spirit World, only to return months or even centuries later. It was basically like the movie *Inception*, only you didn't have to be asleep for it to happen.

Paths, like the one we were on to the light, were representations of our mind's desire to reach a destination. If you fell off of them or were, Goddess help you, pushed, then you lost your tether. As such, it was always important to pay attention to the road because not only did it lead to your destination, but it also was a way back home. The Grove might not be dangerous as it was a place designed for human beings to visit their god, but I wondered how wild the magic might have grown with a century of abandonment.

"So, still interested in killing the Dryad?" Alex said.

"Not sure," Robyn said, sighing. "But, yeah, I'm actually more pissed off now. Abandoning me and my kids in the woods is bad enough. Abandoning my father and leading him to crazy town? That's even worse."

"Your father knew what he was doing," Alex said. "In the circles of mages I run in, they're called Green Men. People who become the chosen defenders of natural places and receive supernatural powers for it. The druids may be gone, but it seems she was hardly helpless."

"And yet there's still the murder pit," I said. "All I'm thinking of is the fact that she's not aware of what happened to her children. The Earthmother I worshipped wouldn't do that. She's a goddess of love."

"I thought that was Aphrodite," Robyn said.

"There's…more than one goddess," I said, confused about how to explain. Truth be told, I worshipped pretty much whomever I felt like I needed the help of at the moment. It was a benefit from having the belief all gods were real thanks to the "Your Mind Makes It Real™" nature of the Spirit World. I could probably find the Flying Spaghetti Monster around here if I looked hard enough.

"I'm just trying to wrap my head around how many gods there are supposed to be. Which are real and which are fake?" Robyn asked, mirroring my thoughts.

"That is a question which ends up answering itself," Alex said. "The search defines it."

"That's not a real saying," Robyn said. "It also makes no damned sense."

I just shrugged away her complaints. "Of course it is, he just said it. Also, let the deer woman enjoy the Grove. Let us the sunlight dry our clothes."

In fact, we were already almost dry despite the fact that the air was cool. The mysterious light was warm but not hot and yet the closer we got, the more I felt comfortable. There were few signs of the monsoon I'd brought down upon us, and it actually seemed like my clothes had been through the wash now.

Approaching it made everything feel more real.

"Well, you'll have your answers soon enough," Alex said, sighing. "We can determine then if the Goddess of the Forest is still a deity or has become a demon."

"If she's a demon?" I asked, not liking where this was going.

"We do what we must," Alex said. "Banishing her back to the Earthmother so she can become part of her again should be less damaging than outright destroying her, though."

"I'm cool with that," Robyn said. "Assuming it's the best we can do without causing the destruction of the town by tornado."

"I'm hesitant at the should be," I said, noticing Alex's equivocation. "He's pretty precise in his language, weird as it may be, so I'd like to know the odds."

"Never tell me the odds," Robyn said, grinning.

"Only Alex and I get to make *Star Wars* references," I said, shaking my head. "Don't steal our thing."

Alex waved a hand in front of him. "Like eighty percent chance."

"That's a twenty percent chance of me not being happy with this plan," I said.

"The only guarantee in life is death," Alex said.

"That is really bad way of convincing me this is a good plan," I said, shaking my head.

"Sorry," Alex said.

One more thing occurred to me, not related to our present situation. I couldn't help but remember how sick using black magic had made Andy. The problem with that was a lot of black magic had been thrown about recently, and not just by the bad guys. "Alex, you said black magic did a number on Robyn's dad."

"It did, yes," Alex said, looking down at the rich brown soil beneath our feet. "All magic is dangerous, doubly so if you're borrowing power rather than using your own. Black magic is the worst since it's the magic of death and destruction."

Robyn stared at me, like this was an unwelcome question.

"Really? You want to bring this up now?"

I ignored her. This was bigger than her feelings or even my promise to her. "What about Lucien? You? Me. I know Lucien uses black magic all the time. He's got a portal to Hell in his club. Is that something we should have been worried about? Like a toxic-waste dump he built a dance floor over?"

I was still mad at Lucien for what he'd done and using his relationship with me to hurt his brother. I mean, who the hell does that? I'd forgiven him, mostly, and I didn't want to see him hurt. Then again, I'd known he was using the power of Hell for his spells. What did I think was going to happen?

*You are growing wiser*, Raguel said.

*I'm not sure realizing demonic power is dangerous is growing wiser*, I said.

*It is if you didn't know before*, Raguel replied.

Alex paused before responding. There was a brief flash of pain on his face before he shook his head. "No, Lucien can use black magic without hurting himself."

"That's…good," I asked, wondering what Alex was alluding to. "Why?"

"His mother was possessed by a demon when she gave birth to him," Alex said. "It's probably why he was able to open the portal to Hell to rescue us last year."

"There's a Hell now?" Robyn asked, chiming in. "I'm still getting used to not being pissed off about benevolent gods and there's a Hell."

"There's a lot of hells," I said, wanting to get into that example of why the universe sucked even less than the fact her father had seriously screwed himself with his actions. "The hell of being skinned alive, the special hell for people who talk in the theater, and the hell of being stuck with your in-laws for all eternity are just some of them. The universe is full of countless places where enhanced interrogations never end because no one asks any questions."

The discovery that Hell wasn't a metaphor and that there really were places where people were tortured for all eternity had been one of the worst moments in my career as a shaman. No just god or goddess would create a place of endless suffering. What did that say about them that they not existed but in glorious multiple dimensions?

*Do you have an answer, Raguel?* I asked.

*No,* Raguel said.

Great.

"Hell exists. Okay, now I'm stuck in the Cthulhu mythos," Robyn muttered, again mirroring my thoughts on the subject. I knew there was a reason I liked her.

"No, in the Cthulhu mythos, the monsters don't care about humanity," Alex corrected, running his hands on the tree branches as we walked past them. "In this universe, there are many spirits that actively hate humanity and want to destroy us or feed off of our suffering. They are the enemies of the world and are as powerful as the gods of good, at least as far as I've seen. It's a Manichean universe, not a traditional benign theism."

*Is that true, Raguel?* I asked.

*No. It is also not false. God is all and all is good but this universe belongs to mortals and they may destroy it.*

*Wow, that was not the answer I was hoping for,* I said.

*It answers all questions because you are the one they are being asked.*

*Thank you, Mr. Miyagi. That makes no sense.*

*You asked.*

Robyn was silent. "Oddly, that makes the universe make a lot more sense."

I shook my head. "Back to Lucien being a demon."

"Half-demon," Alex said.

"He's a *demon* dragon?" I asked.

"Yes," Alex said. "The Drake family was not the nicest bunch of people in the world. To them, black magic was just another tool."

Great. "What about us?"

"Black magic is harsher," Alex said, softly. "It will enact a price on us to work it but, for you, I think it is a gift that will only make you stronger. For me, not so much."

"Did you hurt yourself curing Yolanda?" I asked, panicking. As glad as I was he saved her, I didn't want him knocking years off his life for her either.

"Only by making myself more like my father."

That was a statement full of portent but what it was portending (is that even a word?), I couldn't say. "Well, speaking as the ADD-suffering weredeer, I'm glad you did it even…ooo, what's that shiny thing over there?"

I wasn't joking, at least too much, because we finally entered the nimbus of the light and found ourselves someplace else. It was a place beyond the forest, with no trees or anything but a warm light. In this place, I saw a sight I didn't expect.

A unicorn.

An honest-to-Goddess, stallion-sized unicorn with a single curved horn rising a foot in the air. The horn served as the source of the light. The creature was beautiful, clearly male, and possessed an aura about it that prevented me from approaching. I'd always assumed unicorns were a myth, I know that's stupid of me, but I'd assumed they were based on the Chinese kirin or Zeus's magical goat. I mean, some things weren't real. Mermaids weren't, at least as far as I knew. Yet, here I was, standing before a creature straight out of Peter S. Beagle's imagination.

"Huh," I said, staring at the sight before me. "That's something you don't see every day."

"Okay, I'm back to being skeptical," Robyn said, looking at the creature. "A unicorn, really?"

"What's wrong with unicorns?" I asked.

"You don't find them...silly?" Robyn asked. "I mean, they're not even the coolest supernaturals. They're just a horse with a horn."

I stared at her. "You are like the worst person in the world to take to see things. I bet you complained at Disneyland too."

"Of course I complained at Disneyland!" Robyn said. "Have you ever been there? Lines, screaming babies, and bad food. That doesn't have anything to do with the fact I think unicorns are lame. Unlike, say, dragons."

I glared at her, suddenly intensely jealous. I furrowed my brow and stared. "You like dragons, eh?"

"What?" Robyn said, confused by my expression.

"I'm standing right here," the unicorn said. It had a Midwestern accent and sounded annoyed.

I did a double-take. "The horse talks!"

"Like Mr. Ed," the unicorn said. "A horse is a horse, of course, of course."

"Who?" I asked.

The unicorn replied drolly. "I've been here awhile. What year is it?"

"2018," I said.

"Yikes," the unicorn said, stretching its neck. "I've been here since 1965."

"Uhm," I tried to figure out how to ask my next question. "This is going to sound like a stupid question—"

"Then you probably shouldn't ask it," the unicorn said.

I took a deep breath. "Were you always a unicorn?"

"Oh, that's not a stupid question," the unicorn said. "No, I'm Dave Johnson. I used to be a mechanic in Detroit. Man, I bet that's bigger than New York now. The auto industry will never die! Rock and roll forever."

"Yes," I said, clenching my teeth. "Detroit is awesome now. No vampires at all."

"Vampires?" Dave said. "Lady, are you okay? There's no such thing as vampires."

Okay, I was ready to punch the horse. "How did you get to be a unicorn?"

"Oh, the Goddess made me one," Dave said, acting as if it was the most natural thing in the world. "I told her about them one day during our conversations about the world then she mentioned they didn't exist naturally in the Spirit World. So she made me one."

"Uh...huh," I said, feeling deflated. I'd been suffering a crisis of faith since feeling the Goddess of the Forest's viewpoint on her children.

This wasn't helping.

"No, it's groovy," Dave said, waving his head around. "Whenever she wants to get busy, she turns me back into a human. Me and Andy are good friends about that."

"Oh Lord," Robyn said, feeling her head.

"Lovers are often jealous, but religion is an act where all can share in the same adoration," Alex said. "That's from *The Bridge of Birds*."

"Never heard of it," I said, looking at Dave. "So if you're not busy grossing out Robyn, could you let us go see the Dryad?"

"Are you my father?" Robyn asked, sounding horrified.

Oh Goddess, I hadn't even thought of that possibility.

"Possibly!" Dave replied, shrugging. "There used to be another guardian, but he got killed. Someone told a crazy cult leader about this place."

"I see," Robyn said, frowning. "Well, I'm the daughter of the Dryad and I want to see her."

Dave looked between us. "Yeah, sorry, we've got a protocol for that."

"A protocol?" I asked, feeling more ridiculous every second.

"Yeah," Dave cleared his throat. "You must pass three tests in order to visit the Grove."

"Are you fucking serious?" I asked, stunned we were really going through this. "I'm not about to tell you the air speed velocity of a swallow. African or otherwise."

"Nope," Dave replied. "Don't worry, though, no one has ever passed the first."

"Which is?" Alex said, clutching his staff tight as he started muttering protection spells.

"Me trying to kill you," Dave said before charging.

I could see it now on my tombstone: "impaled with extreme prejudice."

# CHAPTER TWENTY-SIX

So I killed the unicorn. Yeah, that sentence doesn't come off well no matter how you phrase it. I felt all of my magic disrupted by the creature's alicorn (that is what you called the horn—I learned that from *Dungeons and Dragons*) while it charged directly at me with it. That resulted in me drawing my gun and aiming right at its head before pulling the trigger. If I'd been a human woman, then I would have been killed immediately, but I had weredeer reflexes that made us the fastest shapeshifters alive.

I didn't use the Merlin Gun, though, but accidentally drew Ranger Taylor's gun instead. You know, the one I'd confiscated from him while he was coughing up a lung. I don't know if the Merlin Gun would have been any less lethal but I did know steel-jacketed rounds like the kind in his Desert Eagle XIX L6 had enough iron content to slay even a strong fairy creature.

Which it did. Specifically, the bullet went right into the head of Dave and the unicorn derailed in mid-charge to collapse right at my side. It took a few seconds to register what had happened, and then I leaned over to check to see if the Guardian was alive or dead. Seeing the big hole in its head and not knowing where a pulse was on a horse, I concluded, yes, I had killed a life-sized My Little Pony. Friendship was not magic.

"Oh crap," I said, grimacing. "I am totally going to Hell for this."

"You killed my father?" Robyn said, appalled. "I mean, my biological dad?"

"Your dad isn't a unicorn!" I snapped, really not wanting to have done that. Then I turned to Alex. "He's not, is he?"

"No," Alex said, staring at the body. "Absolutely not."

"How do you know?" Robyn said, staring down at the corpse.

It was a legend popularized by Hollywood that transformed

people turn back into their original forms after they die. This wasn't true, I'd learned from Kim Su, and made sense, as body modification via magic was as permanent as plastic surgery. Illusions disappeared when you killed the mage behind them, but this was clearly the form Dave Johnson would have to be buried in. You know, if unicorns were buried and if there was ground in the empty white void we were currently located in.

"I can use my Blood Sight to see you are unrelated," Alex said, waving his hand. "Your actual father, Tom Parkins, is sadly deceased."

"Oh," Robyn said, calming down. "That's good."

*Is there such a thing as Blood Sight?* I asked Raguel.

*No.*

*Is there a Tom Parkins?* I asked.

*It's the name of an Anglo Hong Kong friend of Alex's. He died saving Alex's life.*

*Is Dave actually Robyn's biological father?* I asked.

*Does it matter?*

I decided not to press the matter further. "Yeah, well, I don't think killing the Guardian was what we were meant to do."

"No, we were meant to die," Alex said, looking around the void around us. "Unfortunately, I suspect that's not going to keep us from having to endure the other two tests."

"Assuming Dave didn't just make up those," I said, still uncomfortable with the fact that I'd killed the man. Killing the man was hitting me a lot harder than the other people I'd taken down over the past couple of years. Maybe it was sympathy for a fellow sometimes two-legger, sometimes four-legger, or maybe it was all the memories of playing with my Twilight Sparkle doll growing up.

Yikes.

That was when the white void we were located in started to darken. I couldn't see myself, Robyn, Alex, or anything else. Suddenly, without warning, I started fall into a dark and terrible abyss that consumed me whole. Then I was drowning.

I was once more in water and held my breath as I was overcome with terror. I didn't even like to take baths and would not swim unless someone's life depended on it. Because when I was a pre-teen, I'd taken my cousin Jill to Darkwater Lake and gotten her killed. The lake had been inhabited by a literal monster, a kelpie, who'd killed her as punishment for ignoring the "No Swimming" sign. Maybe.

To this day, I didn't know if I could trust my own memories. Had she really drowned at the hands of the kelpie or had the kelpie been summoned by my own guilt? To give me a personification of my horror so i could kill it? I didn't remember any kelpie for a decade after the event and only remembered fighting one after my shaman powers had awoken in a traumatic way last year.

In the darkness of the water that I couldn't breathe or see in, I felt the presence of the long-dead kelpie around me. I'd destroyed it, but its disgusting weeds caressed my body, taunting me with its existence. I could hear my cousin's screams echo through the water and wanted to swim toward her so I could rescue her. But I couldn't. Not because she wasn't there. This was the Spirit World, after all. No, I couldn't because she was already dead.

I reached for the Merlin Gun, wanting some sort of comfort to provide a barrier against the darkness, but it wasn't with me. No, I was naked in the water and even more vulnerable, as I'd been stripped of what little defense I had against the horrors within me. If this was the second test of the Dryad, it felt sadistic and evil.

"No," I said, opening my mouth and letting the water pour down my throat. This was not real. It was not justice. I drank the water and turned it into magic within me then focused all of the power I'd used to exorcise Jones' spirit from his daughter to blast away everything around me. I was in the Spirit World so I could control my environment. I was the god here, not the Dryad.

*Obey!* I mentally screamed.

Lights flickered on and I was no longer drowning in an immense blackness. Instead, I was in a teenage boy's bedroom. Thankfully I was once more dressed and could feel the Merlin Gun in my pocket. I wasn't even wet anymore. That was good, because I wanted as few reminders of Darkwater Lake as possible.

I could tell it was a teenage boy's bedroom because there were discarded men's t-shirts, jeans, and underwear on the floor. The walls were covered in posters of Bruce Lee, Chuck Norris, *Star Trek VI: The Undiscovered Country*, and the 2003 *Daredevil* movie with Ben Affleck and Jennifer Garner. That explained a few things about his choice in costumes for Halloween. There was a vague smell of pot in the air and I saw the CD player on the dresser beside the bed had stacks of punk music alongside, I kid you not, Linkin Park.

"God, this is Alex's room as a teenager, isn't it?" I said, looking around. "This is an immense opportunity for blackmail."

I walked over and checked under the bed. Yep, there was a bunch of soft-core porn magazines underneath. I was tempted to look around for a journal or a computer to see if it was as full of emo-deep musings, but decided that would be an invasion of privacy. All of my good-natured snooping came to an end, though, with a young woman's scream.

"Oh crap," I said, realizing if I had been forced to relive my worst nightmare then this was probably Alex's.

Running out the door, I found myself on a balcony overlooking a massive mansion's entrance hall. I'd known Alex's family was rich, but I hadn't expected Hilton-rich. The place had a giant marble floor, chandelier, two grand staircases, and a frigging statue of Mars just down the hall to the right of me. The balcony on was covered in blood and I followed it to see the sight of two fallen figures next to a fourteen-year-old boy who was huddled in a fetal position by them. The first of the two was a beautiful black-haired girl about Alex's age who looked a bit like Kim Su, while the other was an incredibly handsome well-built blond Eurasian man in a white suit who looked like he'd thrown up two gallons of blood.

Alex's sister, Samantha, and his father, Phillip Tzu.

The boy was Alex.

He'd tried to save Samantha and ended up killing her with his powers.

Shit.

"I'm sorry," I said, walking to Alex's side. I didn't know if the child was really him or if it was just a representation. He shuddered away from my touch.

"He needs to face this alone," a voice spoke behind me.

I turned around to see Kim Su, wearing an all-white tracksuit and carrying a sheathed Chinese *jian* sword over her shoulder.

"Are you actually here?" I asked.

"Yes, unfortunately," Kim Su said. "I sensed you two entering the Grove and decided to project myself. I was hoping you two would stay out of this but clearly I was mistaken."

"Yeah, well, ignoring child murder isn't really how I'm built," I said.

"Part of why I like you," Kim Su said, walking over to him.

"Yep," Kim Su said. "If I'd known what Phillip was doing to his kids, I would have killed him myself. Child or not."

"You're Alex's grandmother?" I asked, stunned. It made sense now that I thought about it. How else would Alex have sought out the world's oldest, most reclusive wizard and found her when so many other sorcerers could not have?

*That and he's a quarter Chinese*, Raguel said.

"How?" I asked, ignoring Raguel. "I mean, Alex's father's name is Tzu and…oh."

Kim Su said, "It's how you pronounce it since Chinese doesn't have an alphabet. Mind you, I've had plenty of names over the years too. Phillip preferred giving himself the name of the Shang Dynasty's rulers because he was always an egocentric little shit."

I stared at her. "That explains a lot, I suppose. Do you have many kids?"

"None living," Kim Su sighed. At that moment, despite looking younger than me, she seemed very old. "I stopped having them as soon as I could magic away my potential for pregnancy, but the urge to have them occasionally hit me once every few centuries. Usually it ends in pain and misery. Either they don't get magical powers and get sucked into the regular world's misery or they do get powers then die horribly trying to do the right thing."

"Which was Phillip?" I asked.

"The latter, if you can believe it. His dad was a missionary who was my type, stupidly idealistic and an outsider. He died trying to talk to the people who came to kill him and his converts during the Boxer Rebellion. Not that I'm a fan of colonialism, mind you, but I exterminated every one of the son of a bitches involved. I raised Phillip by myself and that may have been a mistake since my millennia of cynicism rubbed off on him. As soon as he learned glamour from one of my fairy friends, he set out to fix the world. He became able to be anyone he wanted and influence the minds of others since he was one of those humans who viewed people as objects, rather than people. The world was his oyster and he guided it."

"He's done a crap job," I said, looking over at Alex. "He's also a terrible parent."

Kim nodded. "Phillip killed every wizard who stepped between him and becoming leader of the Star Chamber as well as made J. Edgar Hoover his puppet. Why no one questioned why a huge racist like Hoover had a Eurasian secretary is a matter for the history books. Blackmail, money, and political ties got him more than spells ever did. Phillip brought down presidents and manipulated wars to bring about his idea of peace. I taught him the best way to do that was bash skulls and he took the lesson to heart. Still, I loved him and overlooked alliances with the Vampire Nation, Red Sky, and the Crowley-ists."

"Why did he hurt Alex?" I asked, having to know. "He can't have learned it from you."

"No," Kim Su said. "He learned it from experience when his first three magic-less families died of influenza, being cursed to death by a rival's magic, and the Vietnam War. I taught him pain was the best way to awaken magic and he wanted children who could do sorcery, so he inflicted that on his children in hopes of awakening it."

I stared at her. "Alex is really powerful. So…it worked?"

"Yes," Kim Su said, her voice low. "He would have had it easier marrying a weredeer."

"I'm glad he's dead," I said.

"Is he?" Kim Su asked.

I blinked. "You mean—"

"Jones was his student, one of many, and I doubt a sleazy former used-car salesman like him could have deduced how to become a body thief. I can't prove it one way or another, but I think Alex just killed his current host. He didn't take Alex's body because he was too strong even then. Either that or he respected the act of patricide."

"Great," I said, taking a deep breath. "Alex can't find out about this."

"Too late," Alex said, standing up. He was no longer a child but in his adult form with a depressed look on his face.

"Goddess dammit," I muttered. "Listen—"

"I'm fine," Alex said, looking down at his dead sister's corpse before kneeling to close her eyes. "There's nothing in this place I don't relive every day anyway."

I didn't respond immediately. "Yeah, okay."

Alex picked up his staff off the ground, looked at it, then broke it over his knee before tossing the pieces away. "I have spent too long making deals with other people for power. I must rely on my own strength now."

That was a little weird. "Alex, about your dad—"

"I've known he's been alive for a lot longer than either of you," Alex said, his voice deep. "It's why I studied to be a mage and went hunting with Lucien. I hoped to draw him out by tearing through the worst of the creatures of the night in hopes of finding him. It wasn't until later that I discovered it was not in the shadows I'd find him, but the light."

That sounded both awesome as well as irrelevant. "Focus, Alex, we need to find Robyn and get to the Dryad."

"Yes," Alex said, lowering his gaze. "Save the girl, save Bright Falls. Find Jones and beat him until he tells me where Phillip is."

Okay, maybe Alex wasn't entirely over what had happened to him here. Wait, that was a stupid observation; of course he wasn't.

"We'll deal with it," I said, reaching over to put my hand on his shoulder. "There, there."

Alex frowned. "That's really condescending, Jane."

"Sorry."

Kim Su looked at Alex with a pitying voice in her face. "Revenge is not a path I recommend. It's an old statement that when you seek it, you should dig two graves."

"I'm not interested in revenge," Alex said, crossing his arms. "My father was a pathetic awful human being and probably still is. I seek him not because killing him will make me feel better, it won't erase all the horrible things he did to me as well as Samantha, but because I worry he's out there still doing it. What is the point of having all the power in the universe at your command if you can't keep others with power from misusing theirs?"

"Safety," Kim Su said without hesitation.

"Safety isn't enough," Alex said. "I have to make up for what I've done."

"It was an accident," I said, looking to Alex. "Your sister would understand."

Alex got a bitter expression on his face. "I tried contacting her once. Part of the reason why I don't talk to the dead anymore."

I hesitated. "What did she say?"

"She could have survived my father's actions and what I did to her was worse."

Damn. "Remind me to punch her if I ever see her spirit."

Kim Su looked horrified by my statement but also stunned into silence. There was also a sense of amusement she was trying to suppress.

"Yeah, I'm the master of crossing the line twice," I said, not feeling any guilt for what I just said.

The mansion faded around us and we soon found ourselves back in the white void from before. Much to my surprise and relief, I found Robyn waiting for us. She had a sour expression on her face and looked deep in thought.

"Hey," I said, raising my hand. "I hope your test wasn't super traumatizing."

Robyn looked up at me. "I'll tell you mine if you tell me yours."

I opened my mouth then closed it. "Fair enough."

Robyn nodded then turned to Alex. "How are you, Agent Dreamy?"

"Ready to set fire to a tree," Alex said. "Regardless of the consequences."

His eyes were narrowed into deadly fury and I could tell the personal nature of the second test had broken something within him. Hopefully not permanently.

Robyn smirked. "How about you, Ms. Earhart?"

"It is no longer my place to serve as the guardian of the gods," Kim Su said, gesturing forward. "Do as you wish."

A door appeared behind us.

# Chapter Twenty-Seven

I wouldn't put it past Kim Su to give us a door that led to New Jersey then slam it shut behind us so she could move the Dryad to someplace safe. I loved my mentor, but she was a tricksy one and fully capable of pulling a fast one on people she ostensibly loved or cared for. So when we emerged in an Eden-like garden that didn't so much glow with magic as was magic in a physical form, I was surprised.

The Grove, an apt name if I ever heard one, was an enormous garden of enormous beautiful trees all encircled a much smaller but more beautiful green-leafed maple tree. The maple tree was next to a pond as covered in leaves that floated against the water. A spectacularly beautiful woman with chestnut-colored skin and long, flowing green hair was sitting naked by its trunk.

It was difficult to describe just what was about the Dryad that made her so lovely as she wasn't any extreme in form. She wasn't too tall, too short, athletic or buxom, but possessed a kind of balanced form that seemed to contain the whole of the world. To look upon her was to look upon the Earth and that was enough.

The Dryad, or Goddess of the Forest, was looking at a Monarch butterfly the size of a puppy and waved her hand over it. The butterfly transformed into a wolf then loped off into the forest. That struck me as a bizarre abuse of nature. Then again, if you were faced with someone who could legitimately argue that she *was* nature, would you tell her she was wrong? It was impossible to not fall a little in love with the woman just by looking at her and I was filled with a warm worshipful adoration that made me want to my knees before her.

I looked to my companions and expected to see the same level of reverence but instead found Alex frowning as if he was about to step in the ring at a mixed martial arts tournament. Robyn's expression didn't look any better and I could tell this was an encounter she'd been looking forward to for a while. Kim Su looked irritated and came up from behind to pass us, heading to the front.

We all ended up stopping behind Kim Su as she took a position in front of our group and stood between us and the Dryad. I was annoyed to realize the goddess wasn't even looking at us, instead staring at some ants that were an inch long and building a hill in front of her.

Kim Su cleared her throat into her fist. "Goddess of the Forest, I, Kim Su, Holder of the Akashic Record and Chosen of the Earthmother who is your mother, do address you. I beseech an audience in the name of the Spirits Above the Universe. I speak before the Shaman of Bright Falls and Chosen of Raguel, Third Grandmaster of the Intercepting Fist as well as Warden of the Sun, plus your daughter, who is Beloved by the Trees."

I leaned over to Alex. "Did you know we had any of those titles?"

"Yes," Alex said softly.

"Cool," I said, unsure what else to say. I'd never been a Chosen before.

The Dryad didn't respond for a moment. "Do I know you?"

Kim Su frowned. "I helped the Brotherhood of the Trees create you. I beseeched the chance to bind your avatar to this world so the magic of the United States wouldn't die or be corrupted. So there would be a place for shapeshfiter and fae in this part of the world. I've saved you from literally dozens of threats over the decades."

The Dryad concentrated for a moment. "Sorry, no."

Robyn muttered something indecipherable but I suspected was an encouragement to get on with the judgment.

Kim Su looked embarrassed. "You gave birth to Robyn here. She was raised by your loyal guardian Andrew Taylor. Your orders got Dave Johnson killed trying to keep her from meeting you. You know, the unicorn?"

"The unicorn is dead?" the Dryad asked as if hearing a neighbor had lost their cat. "How unfortunate. I shall have to make another."

Kim Su looked surprisingly frustrated. She balled her fists and looked furious. "There was a time when this would have meant a great deal to you."

"Time?" the Dryad asked. "That is something this world has a great deal of and a thing I'm often confused by. Beginnings, middles, and ends. I prefer things to function in cycles. There is a spring and a fall, yes, but they simply give way to each other before coming back around."

That was what I'd felt when I'd touched the bone fragment: apathy and boredom. She possessed an aloofness that didn't care for humanity any more than a beloved pet at best or an annoying insect at worst. Humans were mortal, fragile creatures which were more interesting in the moment than the long term. We might die, but there were always more of us to replace the ones who'd fallen. I wasn't going to find any spiritual enlightenment here—no matter how pretty she was.

Robyn stepped forward, her hands raised. "You gave birth to me. You gave birth to my brothers and sisters who were all left to die. You could have saved them. You could have raised them all yourself. Their deaths are on your head."

"Life is not a gift, young child," the Dryad said. "It is not a punishment. It simply is. You are not a person given this world, you are a part of it. You may be born or you may die in the womb. You may live a long life or you may perish. Each of these things enriches the cosmos and provides its own consequences for reality. The problem for you is that you think of yourself as important when we are all just trees in a much larger forest that carries on without us."

Okay, the fact she could articulate all of that eliminated the last bit of sympathy I possessed for her. "People are not just trees. People are people and you should have empathy for them. You should care what happens to them."

"Open the cocoon of a butterfly and it will never be able to fly," the Dryad replied. "Death, disease, starvation, and hunger are as much gifts to you as pleasure as well as thought. Indeed, thought has ever been a curse of human beings. Better you should rely on instinct and not trouble yourselves so much."

Robyn raised her fists then lowered them, tears streaming down her face. "We're nothing, aren't we? Just the result of you screwing a bunch of guys to amuse yourself."

The Dryad had gone back to looking at her ant hill. "I am bored of this conversation. You would not exist if I did not mate with mortals and life is my gift as well as my curse to you. It was your destiny to survive while your siblings did not. Take the power that is your birthright and use it to grow powerful. Mate with the mortals around you or do not. It is your choice to grow as you see fit and spread your branches. I have no interest in it."

"Screw it," Robyn said, taking a deep breath then looking at me. "I don't know what I was looking for here but this isn't it. You don't have to fulfill your promise to me."

"I am ready to banish her," Alex said, his body filled with a kind of lethal energy I hadn't felt when he'd faced the Visigoth. "She is a goddess not worth worshipping and it's better if mortals find another."

Kim Su looked down, defeated. "I wanted this to be different. To give mortals a taste of the divine they could rally behind."

"I know," Alex said. "Help me."

She didn't answer.

"Your power will allow us to do it quickly," Alex said, looking at me. "The Grove will cease to exist and the spirits can move on to another part of the Spirit World. Bright Falls will be diminished, but it still has many magical places, some linked to the Grove, some not. It will continue to be a special location for decades to come until it is not."

"Worth it," Robyn said.

Between the three of us, I was certain we could banish Queen Bitch Tree. That didn't seem like the way this should end, though.

"No," I said, taking a deep breath. "Let me try something."

"It's over," Robyn said, her voice defeated. "I'm fine, really."

"I'm not," Alex said, his gaze narrowing. "Power and immortality does not make a god."

"No," I said, reaching over to take Robyn's hand. "Trust me."

"Why does everyone want to hold my hand lately?" Robyn said, confused. "I mean, hey, you're cute—"

"Just give me your damn hand," I said, not in the mood. Drowning will do that to you.

Robyn did so.

"Thank you," I said, taking a deep breath.

"Jane, what are you doing?" Kim Su asked, looking hesitant to stop or help me.

"Making use of all your training," I said, looking at her. "You know, what I've been practicing for a year on."

"My training is bunk!" Kim Su said, raising her hand. "Why do you think Alex went off on his own?"

Kim Su wasn't telling the truth, but I appreciated her distraction. It made it easier to read Robyn. I'd been able to read corpses before but never a living person. I'd always thought it against the "rules" of my power, but I realized now the biggest thing blocking my power had been I'd thought there were rules to magic. There weren't. People imposed rules on magic in order to make sense of it but like classical music's rules weren't the same as grunge; it was really the feeling behind it.

I found myself feeling Robyn in a way I'd been unconsciously feeling Alex for a time now. I picked up her feelings of anger, outrage, and loneliness. I'd picked up her desire to be her own woman. I picked up the fear that had blossomed in her heart as a child that she'd never been good enough for a mother she'd conjured in her mind—a mother that the Dryad had lived down to every misgiving about. I managed to copy virtually her entire life and put it in a little glowing spark in my free hand that I stared at.

"What is that?" Robyn asked, looking confused. "What the hell did you just do?"

"Probably something stupid," I said, looking at the glowing star. "Pretty much the story of my life."

Robyn looked at me with a smile that surprised me. It was one of the few times I'd ever seen her genuinely happy looking. "Jane, I've seen enough of your life to know you have never done anything stupid."

"I agree," Alex said, looking at me.

"Thanks for the pep talk," I said, walking over to the Dryad. "But I don't need one."

The Dryad looked up. "I said begone."

I put the spark against her forehead. "You can smite us with your smiting after we give you a taste of just what hell you've put your daughter through."

Kim Su started to speak. "Jane—"

But it was done.

The Dryad's eyes, previously emotionless pools became all too human before her mouth opened in an expression of mixed shock as well as horror. Then, almost as if she'd never existed, she was gone. It was a flicker of light like the kind that occurred whenever I shifted from human to deer form. She was there, then not.

The Grove changed around me, going from a beautiful eternal summer to a depressing fall, all of the leaves having fallen from her tree. The trees around us also looked like they'd lost their vital spark. The magic hadn't died, hadn't even weakened really, but it felt different. I'd changed it and the goddess who embodied it.

"What have you done?" Kim Su said.

"No goddeer clue," I said.

Robyn looked at me then the bare tree before shrugging. "I don't know what you did, but I'm glad you did it. It doesn't make up for what she did, though."

"Vengeance is a thorny path," Kim Su said. "Something-something, pretend I said something wise."

"I like you, Kim Su," Robyn said, obviously having figured out who she was. "You're a truly awful mentor."

I looked around the Grove for some sign of the Dryad. After a few minutes of looking around, I decided to give up. "Well, I think we've accomplished what we set out to do. We still have to find Jones's ghost and put him a containment unit with the Stay Puft Marshmallow Man but I think this is enough for one day."

"Oh, I heartily disagree," Jones's voice spoke from the other side of the Grove.

A gunshot rang out seconds later.

I turned around to stare at the sight of John Jones in his original form, white suit and all, carrying a coal-black gun I recognized as a modified LeMat revolver from the Wild West era. My father was obsessed with old guns like this and said as a signature Confederate weapon, it was the perfect bad-guy weapon.

The gun made me sick looking at it, as it seemed to pulsate with an aura about it that reminded me of the time I almost drowned, seeing Alex suffering, and all the fears I had about my mother never returning home. I didn't need my supernatural senses to know there was a demon inside the gun since I recognized the horrible feeling I was experiencing as the same one I'd had around the Big Bad Wolf.

Jones, himself, looked bemused at my presence and there was

a triumphant grin on his face I didn't understand. It took me a second to notice he looked slightly different with the lines from his face gone and a few inches taller. His aura was raw and powerful despite its corruption and I could tell this was his astral form. Not quite a ghost as I'd thought, but his soul unbound from a physical form with probable full access to his magic.

Crap.

"Grandmother!" Alex shouted, distracting me.

I turned around to see the fallen form of Kim Su, my master, holding the side of her stomach as a terrible black stain was growing next to her kidneys. It reeked of demonic magic, and I meant that in a literal way. I could smell sulfur, brimstone, rot, and a dozen other terrible smells coming from the wound.

"Oh hell," I said.

*The Devil Gun. Hell cannot create so it must imitate what greater individuals have made. I wondered why Phillip believed Jones could defeat Kim Su,* Raguel said. *It turns out he has sent a piece of the Morningstar with him.*

All of which would have been a lot better to know a few minutes ago. I wasn't stopping to think about it, though, because I was pulling the Merlin Gun and firing at Jones. "You son of a bitch!"

None of the three bullets hit him. Instead, they stopped in midair and dissipated.

Crap.

Jones laughed. "Remember, these guns rely on your power to destroy others. I am a very old and powerful wizard. I am like Harry Houdini and David Copperfield. You, my dear, are doing card tricks at children's parties."

I shot at him again, weakening myself when I should have been trying to find another way to dispatch him.

"I wouldn't underestimate her," Alex said, trying to cleanse Kim Su's wound as best he could. The fact she wasn't dead told me Jones wasn't quite as powerful as he thought. Still, I didn't have any doubt the gun couldn't finish her off. I wasn't going to let that happen.

"Give me Robyn," Jones said. "You've apparently killed the Goddess of the Forest, but the magic is still here and I can bind this place to her. It'll be better than nothing."

"Like hell, Jonestown," I said, not exactly doing a great job with my comebacks. I kept the Merlin Gun trained on him. "There's not a damn thing you can say to me that would make me do that."

Jones kept the Devil Gun aimed at me before making a circular gesture with his other hand. Instantly, Robyn's father, Andy, appeared by his side. He was bound much tighter in the roots than Robyn had left him, but also had numerous burns on his face. It indicated he'd been tortured.

"She will come if she wants to see her father again," Jones said, softly. "Tell you what, I'll make it easy. You can give over her or Kim Su. I don't really care. Either one will please my master."

Yeah, this wasn't a good situation.

# CHAPTER TWENTY-EIGHT

"I'll do it," Robyn said, stepping forward.

"Like hell you will," I said, keeping my arm in front of her.

"I'll do anything to protect my dad," Robyn said, her voice calm and resolved.

I glared at her. "Okay, genius, what exactly would prevent numbnuts over here from killing us all once he's got you? Because the first thing I think when I think of John Jones is not trustworthy. Actually, it's the Martian Manhunter, but evil asshole is the second."

"I give you my word," Jones said, slick like a serpent.

"Goddess dammit," I said. Why did so many supernaturals have to be men of their word!

With that, Robyn stepped forward, her hand raised.

"Yes, come to me," Jones said, chuckling. "I'll even give you what you most desire in the world, Alex. I'll tell you where my master is presently located. You will find a hefty bribe that shall soften the blow for Robyn's loss as well, Ms. Doe."

"I don't sell out my friends," I said, staying close behind Robyn. "Not for money, not for anything."

"You'll find the benefits of being a wizard outweigh moral compromises like that," Jones said, getting a distant look in his eye. "I've done unimaginably terrible things my younger self never would have believed himself capable of doing. Some because of my master's influence, others because of the way the magic influences me. Magic is power and I wanted more of it to do good until more became my good."

"My heart bleeds," I said, having crossed halfway across the area between me and Jones.

Alex was still at Kim Su's side, muttering a prayer that caused the black blood to turn white and dry up, like powder. Alex was some sort of priest in addition to being a mage and that seemed to have some benefit against the Devil Gun's magic.

"Not another step," Jones said, lifting the Devil Gun and aiming it at my head. "Look what you've done to this place, Jane. You think I'm evil? This place has stood for a century as a bastion of what is pure and good in this world. A purity sullied and destroyed by mankind. We're a plague, you and I, along with other humans. It's why we need to be controlled and transformed into something better."

I stopped in my tracks, but Robyn kept walking with her head down low. I believed, in that moment, that she was fully prepared to die to protect her father. I admired that in her, even as I looked down to Ranger Taylor and saw him trying to speak. I believed he was willing to sacrifice himself for her as well but couldn't speak because of a spell muffling any noise.

"You killed your own kids," I said, having no sympathy. "I'm pretty sure humanity isn't the problem so much as people like you."

Robyn reached Jones's side before kneeing him in the balls then giving him a solid punch across the jaw that allowed me to assume my deer form then bash him in the stomach then kick him in the head. My attempts to trample him came to an abrupt end as his hand glowed and Alex tackled me out of the way, my body still four legged, right before he blasted a ray of blinding heat up toward the sky.

I turned back into my human form and lifted up the Merlin Gun before seeing the Devil Gun on the ground nearby Jones. The magician's eyes darted to the gun on the ground before I turned my gun from him to his weapon then pulled the trigger.

"See you in Hell," I said, watching the Devil Gun explode into a shower of light and smoke. Jones's hand was only a few inches away before he pulled it back.

"You fool, that weapon was irreplaceable!" Jones shouted, stretching his hands out as a glowing bubble appeared around him. It was straight-out-of-a-comic-book magic and I wondered how much he could do here where reality was determined by thought.

"Yeah, I'm sure your master will love it," I said, pulling back and aiming the Merlin Gun at him. "Why did you send all those tools to Robyn's dad? Did you think he'd kill us or were you just trying to mess with him?"

I was actually distracting him because I had no idea how the hell I was going to hurt him given he was a much more powerful wizard than anyone else here and he'd already taken out Kim Su.

"I had nothing to do with that," Jones hissed. "Do you think I'm stupid enough to give someone who hates me the magic to kill me?"

"Yes?" I said, mostly trying to distract him long enough to come up with a plan to kill him.

"Fire of the Sun!" Alex shouted, stepping in front of me and a column of bright light shot from his hands before smashing into Jones's shield.

Robyn fell back behind us, crawling a bit from the sight. "I'm in a comic book."

"You're just noticing that *now*?" I asked, watching Jones struggle against Alex's strike.

"I am your superior in every way," Jones said, grunting as if he was trying to hold back a tsunami with his mind. "While you were learning to punch things or languishing in a straightjacket, I was one of the most powerful wizards in America. I have tens of thousands of followers ready to give their lives to me."

"You're in another dimension far from your slaves," Alex said, continuing to blast well past the point he should have exhausted himself. "But you've already lost. Jane killed you before this battle began."

"What are you—" Jones started to say before the ground opened up beneath him. "No!"

Massive roots reached up from the ground and wrapped around his arms, legs, and even neck before dragging him down. Jones's scream echoed in my ears as he found himself swallowed by the ground before it sealed up above him. It was a nightmarish scene I wouldn't have wished on my worst enemy. After a few seconds, there was nothing but an empty patch of ground where Jones had once stood. He'd been buried alive.

"Goddess," I whispered, looking at the sight.

"An awful end," Alex said, putting his arms around my shoulder. "But a deserved one."

I looked behind me at Robyn, expecting her to be the party responsible for Jones's horrible end. Instead, I saw her wearing an expression every bit as horrified as mine. She hadn't been the person responsible. Turning my head, I saw Kim Su was still laid out on the ground and looking expressionless. Then I saw Robyn, again, and did a double-take. This Robyn had red and gold colored hair and a gown of leaves covering her nakedness. There was a sad expression on her face, but one that was also hard and angry.

The Dryad had returned.

"Oh crap," I said, taking a step back and debating using the Merlin Gun on the new Robyn.

*Don't,* Raguel cautioned. *Let us see what fruits your actions have borne.*

The other Robyn, the Dryad, stretched out her hand toward the spot where Jones had been buried alive then waved it from side to side. A small sapling tree grew from the spot and I felt the Grove's magic grow stronger and wilder.

"He wanted to be a god ever since he stopped believing in them," the Dryad said, sounding exactly like Robyn. "Now he can be one. It will require a new life, though, in a new form. Perhaps he will gain sentience again and be a spirit worthy of the power here. Perhaps he will not."

Robyn looked at her, an angry look on her face. "Back again?"

"Yes," the Dryad said, walking to Andy's side and placing her hand against him. "You have done an excellent job cleansing the wound, but I will give him more help. He will be strong right up until the end of his days."

"Which will be soon," Alex said, frowning. "He turned to black magic because you didn't help him."

"I am sorry," the Dryad whispered. "I forget when a god takes flesh in the penumbra between worlds, they become a part of it. You reminded me of what it was like to know pain, suffering, and regret."

"What is she talking about?" Robyn asked. "Also, why does she look like me?"

"I kinda-sorta gave her your memories as a way to tell her what you'd been through," I said, looking over my shoulder.

"You did what?" Robyn asked, staring at me.

"I know!" I said, trying to play it off. "I didn't even know I could do that!"

The Dryad stared forward. "I am sorry."

"Too late!" Robyn said, looking at her. "Sorry does not begin to cover what I have been through."

"I know," the Dryad said. "I see this world through your eyes now. It will last until my winter years. I will do what I can to try to make amends, though. Your memories gives me perspective as my past fulfills the hole in your heart. A world that has never rewarded idealism or wanting to believe in something bigger than yourself."

"What the hell are you even talking about?" Robyn asked, confused.

"You're basically Forest Jesus!" I said, embarrassed and surprised by what happened.

"You ruined my life," Robyn said, staring at the Dryad. "You ruined my father's."

"I gave you your life," the Dryad said, holding Andy's head in her lap. "I also know the mistakes you've made. I lived them and know why you're really running away from New Detroit. You have the power to change the world, daughter, but you'll have to change who you are. Those around you have sacrificed of themselves to give you that opportunity."

"How much have we sacrificed?" I asked, going to Kim Su's side.

"Not dead yet," Kim Su said, coughing between breaths. "Being immortal has its advantages."

"She will heal to full recovery," the Dryad said. "I cannot say the same for everyone else."

I took a deep breath. "So what did you do to Jones? I mean, did you really turn him into a tree?"

"Yes," the Dryad replied. "Take the sapling with you and plant it elsewhere. It will make Bright Falls stronger or create another sacred place that will strengthen magic as a whole in the physical world."

"I'm not sure that's a good idea," I said, remembering what she'd done to Dave Johnson. "Magic has as many downsides as it has advantages."

"Much like life," the Dryad said.

"So you just get away with everything because you look like me now?" Robyn said, still angry, and I didn't blame her in the slightest.

"I have suffered and will suffer for what I have done," the Dryad said. "So much so even you will be able to call it justice."

"How's that?" Robyn asked sarcastically.

"Thanks to you, I know what it is to love a child and the pain of their loss," the Dryad said. "I gained those feelings too."

Robyn opened her mouth to reply then closed it. There was a curling of her lip that told me she knew exactly what the Dryad was talking about and felt it was a punishment well-deserved. I wondered how much her choice to give up Sparrow was motivated by a desire to do right by him versus the fact she knew she couldn't care for him—and hated herself for it.

Alex walked over to the fallen plant and pulled it up after digging around its roots before handing it over to Robyn. "It has been a pleasure meeting you, Ms. Taylor. If you ever need a job, I think you'd do wonderful as an associate to my business."

"What do you do?" Robyn asked.

"I kill monsters," Alex said.

Robyn smiled. "I'll think about it. You should treat Jane right."

"I fully intend to," Alex said, nodding. "Otherwise she'd kill me."

"You got a brother?" Robyn smirked.

I tried to be less jealous and failed. Mostly. "So, Kim, you going to be all right?"

Kim climbed to her feet and looked at her stained shirt as well as the hole there. "The Earthmother made me immortal and it'll take more than an archangel with daddy issues to put me down."

"It's the mistake of being a mentor that went out into the field," I said, shaking my head. "Every teacher who does that dies or turns evil because that's the only way the student can stand on their own. Obi-Wan Kenobi, Gandalf—"

"Gandalf came back, though," Kim Su said.

"Yeah, and the story was kind of ruined for it," I said. "Way to remove the dramatic tension."

Kim Su gave me a hug. "Jane, don't ever change. You're truly a breath of fresh air in a world of pleasant smoke and mirrors."

"I'll try," I said, frowning. "But I think I know a good deal more about how real magic works. You make the spells yourself. You aren't taught them."

Kim Su put her hand on my shoulder. "You've past the biggest test to becoming a true mage. Refining your technique and learning to manage your powers is what you have before you now."

"You'll still be there to sponge off my free labor, right?" I asked, a bright smile on my face.

"Oh yes," Kim Su said, patting me on the shoulder. "Of course. I'll also happily teach you some of the hundreds of ways a small woman might pummel the crap out of larger men. Also poor peasants with rich, armed warriors. It's pretty much the origin of all martial arts."

"Yes, Sensei."

"*Sifu*," Kim Su corrected. "Or teacher, since I didn't originally speak Chinese."

"What language did you speak?" I asked.

"Caveman grunts," Kim Su said, smiling. "We weren't lucky enough to have a cave, though."

"I don't believe you're that old," I said, glad to see she was all right. My mom would be returning soon, but Kim Su had become the grandmother I'd never had. You know, despite the fact that she looked like she should be listening to boy bands.

"Ook-ook," Kim Su grunted. "That means 'Fire bad, tree pretty'."

"Dad, we should go," Robyn said, looking down at Andy. "If you still want to associate with me instead of Galadriel here."

Andy looked up at Robyn. His voice lacked its earlier pain and confusion. "I'll be along in a bit. I think we should talk tonight about everything I've kept from you. One thing I want you to know, though, I've always been proud of you but what you've done here is good. You're a better guardian than I ever was."

Robyn looked over her shoulder. "Yeah, bad news, that Dave Johnson guy was killed by—"

"Jones," the Dryad said. "I'm sorry about your friend's loss."

Andy closed his eyes. "I understand. Thank you for avenging him."

I started looking for an exit. "Open sesame? Arch? Computer end program?"

Kim Su waved her hand and a door appeared beside me. "Take the rest of the week off. You've earned it."

I looked over at Alex and Robyn who were exchanging glances about the Dryad's lie. I gestured for them to come over.

"Yeah, I did," I said. "I think I'm good for the rest of the year personally."

"If only that were your choice," Kim Su said.

I still had some questions, like who was the person who armed Andy Taylor with all that black magic as well as what we were going to do with the Ultralogists but things were mostly wrapped up.

As Alex and Robyn came to me, I looked over at them both. "Are you guys good?"

"I doubt Jones will be telling me where my father is," Alex said, frowning. "At least not anytime soon."

Robyn looked down at the plant in her arms. "I'm cool. If she really does have my memories, then I doubt she'll be leaving any other kids to die. That's really all that matters."

"I don't suppose either of you have a way to keep the Deerlighftul in the Doe family's hands?" I asked. "Because, really, that's what's most important here."

"You could ask Lucien to buy it for you," Alex said, deadpanning.

"Oh hush, you!"

# Chapter Twenty-Nine

The three of us exited out the gateway to find our friends as well as allies still present. Deana was standing off to one side by Gerald, looking sullen as always, while Lucien was chatting with Larry and Yolanda. Emma was standing guard right beside the gateway and I had to give her credit for somehow managing to look both adorable as well as fierce. The place smelled awful, the result of unburied dead and Emma being a very big wet canine.

"We're back!" I said, waving as we came through the portal.

Emma turned back into a human instantly and hugged me. She was still soaking wet, her clothes too, which made no sense to me but magic was like that. I let her hug me then hugged her back.

"What happened?" Emma asked.

I patted her on the back. "Oh nothing. Jones got turned into a plant, so he's not only merely dead but really most sincerely dead. We also killed a unicorn."

Emma pulled back. "You what?"

"Yep!" I said, cheerfully. "All in a day's work for Deerdevil: the Doe without Fear. I am looking forward to getting myself a big fat steak at the Deerlightful."

"I thought deer were herbivores," Robyn said, chuckling as she held the plant that was our former enemy. I wondered how much of a temptation it was for her to dash it on the ground.

Probably a lot.

"We're opportunity omnivores," I reassured her. "Not at all just because I love a good steak and could never resist one if it's put in front of me."

"I'm a vegetarian," Emma said cheerfully. "You know, when in human form. Not when I'm in wolf form. That would be weird."

"Which is wrong and unnatural for a werewolf," I said, mock

glaring at her. "Shame, shame, shame."

Emma rolled her eyes. "What happened with the Dryad?"

I paused, trying to figure out how to distill that into words. "We're cool. Are we cool, Robyn?"

"We're as cool as when you asked thirty seconds ago," Robyn said, frowning. She looked back to the gate. "Is my father going to be all right? You've been cagey about just how much damage was done by the black magic since you cleansed him."

Alex lowered his head. "He damaged much of his body and spirit with the use of black magic. I've purged that from his system and can maybe teach him a few things to extend his lifespan, but nothing that will keep him alive indefinitely."

Immortality seemed like a crap shot in this world. Everyone who had the potential to live forever died. Well, except Kim Su. So far.

"How long does he have?" Robyn asked, closing my eyes. "If we're optimistic."

"Five or six years," Alex said, no judgment in his voice. "He could have lived for centuries otherwise."

"You didn't need to add that part, chief," Robyn said, taking a deep breath. It was clear she was devastated by the news. "Is there anything the Dryad can do? I mean, if she is me, then she'd do anything."

"I don't know." Alex's voice was pained. "The person who sent the magic did so with the intention of making it the antithesis of the Earthmother so he couldn't be easily healed."

Robyn looked a bit teary eyed and I didn't blame her. "At least Sparrow will get to know his grandfather."

I paused. "Are you going to be okay? I mean, financially. I've got your back if you want any help. I think this horrible nightmarish experience has really been a bonding experience for us all."

"I'm free of some of my enemies," Robyn said, frowning. "I also have friends here in Bright Falls. I just need to find a job and spend some time with my son."

Emma put her hand on Robyn's shoulder. "I'm exceptionally jealous of how cool you are, but if you need a job then I'll happily get you one as a blackjack dealer or something similarly sexy."

"Blackjack dealers are sexy?" I asked.

"Have you seen those vests?" Emma asked, blushing. It was

weird finding out your best friend's fetishes but I supposed that was what friends were for.

I snorted. "Well, I can only offer you a job waiting tables. You should take the job at Emma's casino."

Robyn smirked. "I dunno, I'm not sure being around that much money is a good thing. I kinda-sorta may have been fired from my last job for stealing."

I grimaced. "I suddenly regret offering you a job."

Robyn laughed, not realizing I was serious.

"How is Yolanda going to die?" I asked, glancing at Alex. "I mean, you were cleansing her of black magic venom too."

"She should make a full recovery," Alex said, looking over at them. "One of the benefits of healing with black magic."

Robyn opened her mouth then closed it. "Right, I shouldn't ask the question on my mind."

I assumed her question was 'can you murder some dudes to restore my father? Preferably people who have it coming.'

"No," Alex said, sighing. "I'm sorry."

Robyn didn't say anything else. I knew what question she was going to ask. Could Alex heal her father by killing someone else. Probably. That wasn't a road Alex would walk down, though. I doubt he would have done it if not for the fact I'd asked him to heal Yolanda that way. I didn't regret doing so but I knew the cost of asking. I just didn't care.

Alex put his arm around me. "You did an amazing thing, Jane. Not many people get to look upon the face of their god."

I wasn't sure if it made more faithful or less faithful. Eh, at least I had other gods to pray to in case I wasn't feeling particularly charitable. I sighed, "Yeah, I suppose there's that. By the way, what's our situation?"

"Our situation?"

"We good, bad, or ugly?" I said, pausing. "Because if I have a choice, it's Clint Eastwood."

"Clint Eastwood it is," Alex said, frowning. "I also could have handled things better."

"Well, if you slept with Jeanine, I'd have deer-kicked you out a window," I said, pausing. "Which is unfair and a double standard but I totally would have."

Alex smirked. "She's not my type."

"Not a big fan of tall, buxom, gorgeous women?" I asked.

"I'm a fan of you," Alex said.

We kissed.

"Ugh," Emma said, looking away. "Gross."

Robyn put her hand around Emma. "You know, I've got some friends who would absolutely love you. One is a werefox."

"Really?" Emma asked. "How's that work?"

Robyn grinned.

The next thirty minutes or so was spent cleaning up the battlefield as much as possible. Lucien burned the bodies with dragon fire and we made sure every last one of the spiders was destroyed. Kate Madison was a no-show but, honestly, given how we'd treated Steve Caldwell, I didn't really begrudge her escape.

I did find, however, that Judith and her brother had woken up and were sitting on a log nearby. Neither of them was saying much, so I decided to be the one to handle their situation. Despite the fact that Jones was dead, I wasn't about to forget David had been involved and was still a potential enemy. I wouldn't put it past the Ultralogists to try and turn Judith into their new leader either. If she wasn't brain dead from having her soul kicked out.

Walking over to them, I waved to Judith first. "Hey, kiddo. We're probably still going to Hell, right?"

Judith didn't respond. Instead, she just stared forward with a vacant expression. I suddenly felt like a dick about the brain dead thought.

"Yikes," I said, cringing. "So, what will happen to her?"

"Her soul was parted from her body by my father possessing her," David said, shrugging. "I'll try to have Alex summon it back, or you if you want to try, but in all likelihood she's gone. Her body is likely to generate a new soul, though. It happens sometimes with traumatic brain injury or other actions that result in the soul moving on before the body recovers. I will welcome my new sister to the world and teach her better than my father."

"That…" I tried to respond but found myself at a loss for words. "That opens a lot of theological questions."

"Thankfully it's my job to answer them," David said, his expression one that didn't match the horror of what he was describing. He looked calm and relaxed rather than someone who had just lost his family. "Is my father truly dead?"

"Yes," I said, not wanting to get into the specifics. "He got introduced into a much greener and pleasant-looking fate than the Nazis in *Raiders of the Lost Ark* but still close enough for government work. As powerful as wizards get, you don't want to mess with gods."

"Said by the woman who killed one," David pointed out.

"Yeah, well, every rule has an exception," I said, frowning. "We need to talk."

"I am at your disposal, Shaman of Bright Falls."

There was a time I would have been happy to hear those words from anyone, friend or foe, but they didn't have quite the same ring now that my mother was coming back. Also, having dealt with two gods and a wayward archwizard, it didn't feel like I had quite as much to prove. The fact David was transparently trying to flatter me also bugged me. Wasn't he supposed to the Token Good Guy™ of Team Ultralogist?

"You're going to have to face justice for your crimes," I said, staring at him. "Even if you warned Alex about it, you helped your father do all sorts of evil…badness."

"Evil badness?" David asked.

"Listen, I'm still new at this," I said, frowning. "I'm not great speeches. You defrauded millions of people with your corrupt church."

"I wish to return to it," David said, staring at her. "I can reform it and make it a legitimate religion. There are many truths about the world my father hinted at or denied. Ones I can reveal. Things that would be of comfort to the living about the dead as well as otherworldly. I would also not require worshipers to beggar themselves."

I stared at him. "Honestly, chief, I'm not sure it wouldn't be better for Ultralogy to dry up and disappear."

"That's not really for you to decide but those who worship its tenets."

He had me there. I also was painfully aware there wasn't exactly much I could actually do to him. I mean, we could link him to the attack in the forest, but unless we wanted to expose the fact we'd killed a bunch of people here, it wasn't like we could arrest him for it. I wasn't a police officer, either, which never seemed like a bad thing until now.

*Can I kill this guy?* I asked.

*He has committed no murders. He has stood by and let them happen, though.*

*I notice that's not a yes-or-no answer.*

*The corrupt are a harder thing to judge than the openly monstrous. Yet, ironically, they often do more harm.*

I took a deep breath. "Yeah, I'm not comfortable shooting you for sins of omission."

"Thank you," David said, lowering his gaze. "However, let me make restitution."

I stared at him. "How's that?"

He pulled out his checkbook, a little soaked but only on the edges of the actual checks.

"You want to *bribe* me?" I asked, opening my mouth in horror.

"No," the man said. "I want to pay wergild without anyone actually being dead. I have already done so with Alex and will do so with the others. I will also pay restitution to the victims of the church as well."

"Listen, pal, there's nothing—"

He handed me over a check for two hundred thousand dollars.

My eyes widened. "Uh—"

"I will also purchase out your family's stake in the Deerlightful Diner from your siblings to give to you. Enough to let them live their dreams and you to have your family property. Your diner can be a kitsch tourist trap in the middle of the new downtown."

I opened my mouth to growl at him then found myself not speaking. "I can't believe I'm thinking this. I'm sorry, Raguel."

*Mortals are flawed. Arthur and Merlin made many such deals for better as well as for worse.*

I rubbed the bridge of my nose. "Screw it. You're not a terribly bad person and I need money to live."

"Thank you," David said, sighing.

"I'll be watching you, though," I said, lying. The truth was, as soon as he left Bright Falls, he was no longer going to be my problem.

We both knew it.

"Good luck, Ms. Doe," David said, smiling. "You have a great number of enemies but it is my hope you'll be able to deal with them."

"Yeah, enemies," I said, muttering. "I still have no idea who sent all that magical bric-a-brac to Ranger Taylor."

"Probably the same individual who sent the Grand Temple of Ultralogy a number of boxes of evidence showing Agent Timmons was involved in a dozen assassinations of slavers, vampires, and cannibal monsters. The same people who clued him in to believing Kim Su was taking up residence here in town."

I stared at him. "Excuse me?"

"I'll show you the evidence and we'll destroy it together," David said, his expression remaining inscrutable. "It was my payment to Mr. Drake for his cooperation. If I'd offered to help Agent Timmons, he would have turned me down."

"Who sent it?" I asked, ready to put a bullet in his head. I was not going to respond well to blackmail, especially of friends.

"Marcus O'Henry," David said, not sounding scared in the slightest. "The former master of Bright Falls is the name of your enemy."

I went still. "He's locked up in the Super Pen, watched twenty-four seven."

"That is no deterrent to those who have magic or money," David replied. "I suspect it was more the latter than the former."

I decided I would pay a visit to Marcus O'Henry after all of this. "You mentioned getting rid of blackmail material on Alex was what you paid Lucien. What about Alex?"

"He simply required me to explain something else," David said, frowning. "That Agent Laura Lee escaped with my help. The person my father killed was a glamoured follower. My father never questioned it in his arrogance."

I stared at him. "So you sent someone else to die in her place."

"Yes," David said. "I never claimed to be a good person. My actions were motivated by a desire to destroy my father, though. I suspect now that he has been dealt with, Laura will come out of hiding. Hopefully with her help I can remove any potential predators who will challenge my leadership of the church. People with supernatural abilities who will question my ascension given they were my father's lieutenants. I can turn them over to Laura in exchange for keeping our tax-exempt status. We've survived worse scandals."

"You're an awful person," I said, shaking my head. "I don't think Ultralogy is going to get any better under you."

"Perhaps," David said, smiling. "Nevertheless, my ambitions are more modest and I prefer to be a source of comfort rather than simply a parasite. You don't have to worry about Alex and Laura, I don't think. Anyone can tell by the way he looks at you that he loves you."

"You don't get to talk about Alex and me," I said, staring at him. "Also, leave Robyn alone."

"She's welcome to return to the church," David said, stretching his arms out. "Certainly we could use a woman who can perform genuine miracles."

"Or I'll kill you," I said, gnashing my teeth.

"Of course."

A better person would have returned the two hundred-thousand-dollar check or told him he could take his money and shove it. Unfortunately, a lot of better people didn't have bills to pay or a home they were hoping their parents would have when they returned. I hated myself for deciding to keep the money, but I would get over it.

*You are not a bad person, Jane.*

"Yeah," I muttered. "I just do bad things. I have one planned right now."

*Oh?*

"You'll like it," I said.

With that, I walked away. We'd saved the day, killed the bad guy, prevented the destruction of a beautiful pocket of magic in the world, and maybe made the world a slightly less crap place. There was only one thing left for me to take care of.

Marcus O'Henry.

# Epilogue

It took a lot of effort to get myself a visit with Marcus O'Henry in the so-called Super Pen in South Dakota. Knowing people like Alex helped, but it turned out I had to sign like sixteen confidentiality agreements and also undergo three background checks. In the end, even that wasn't enough and Alex had to contact a guy called the Revered Elder of the Seventh English Rite in order to make it happen. Frigging Star Chamber.

Even so, that actually made it quite a bit easier to skip past the paperwork of being a supernatural trying to visit the supernaturals-only prison without getting locked up by the incredibly racist guards within. I wasn't officially there so I didn't have to talk to people beforehand, sign in, or be recorded when they finally moved me to the transparent steel box they were keeping O'Henry inside of.

The thing was roughly the size of an apartment with a couch, television set, specially prepared meals, bathroom with shower, and a bed that looked much comfier than mine. The fact it was transparent and watched at all times (except now) did little to calm me. It bothered me that while the Super Pen was supposed to be a super-max run by dirtbags, money talked even here.

Marcus O'Henry was wearing a orange jumpsuit but somehow still managed to look dignified. He was one of the older werewolves in the world, well over seventy, but still looked to be about forty. It was the nature of shapeshifters that we were more likely to die of violence than old age, though my grandfather had been an exception.

Marcus was a handsome man with a slight resemblance to Michael Douglas and that had helped him become the "face" of shapeshifters in the Reveal. The fact he'd already been leader of the werewolves in the United States and had influence over the ones on three other continents hadn't hurt. It was what made his trial so important, since it showed shapeshifters were willing to abide by the same restrictions as we did.

"Ah, the traitor," Marcus said, turning around to face me. "Did you enjoy the gift I sent your way?"

"I'm glad we're avoiding the part where you pretend you weren't responsible and going straight with being the Kingpin behind bars," I said, walking up to him. Wow, I was on a roll with the *Daredevil* references. "Mind you, Vincent D'Onfrio could probably intimidate me through transparent steel. You? Not even close.""

"This conversation is already boring me," Marcus said, frowning. "I prefer communicating with adults rather than women barely out of training bras."

"Ageist and sexist," I said, nodding. "Nice. In any case, Marcus, yes, I figured out it was Barzini all along. That's a reference to *The Godfather*, by the way."

Marcus narrowed his eyes. "I take it Taylor and Jones are dead?"

"They're neutralized, let's just say that," I said, not wanting to give him reason to go after Andy.

"How did you get all that magical hardware out to them?" I asked.

Marcus shook his head contemptuously. "You really thought my arrest would be the end of it? My daughter may have seized my assets, but I still have influence. Also, I never let her know about where I'd stored all my finances."

"You super-rich people are why it's a trickle in trickledown economics and not a river," I said, shaking my head. "Always hiding money so nobody else can spend it."

"It's why we're super rich."

He had a point there. "So what was the point of it all?"

"A reminder," Marcus said, shrugging. "My daughter needed to understand that if she wants to increase the family's wealth then she's going to have to ask permission first. Destroying the Shadow Pine Project was as easy as influencing her into going after cursed land in the first place. Her advisors are still my people and they listen to me. Did you think she came up with the fact she needed the Deerlightful Diner on her own? No, that was my little touch."

"Wow," I said, staring at him. "Evil is petty."

"Less so than you think," Marcus said. "I know where you, your brother, and your sister live. I could have you eliminated at any time. I wonder how your mother would react to that? I think it would cause her to recant her testimony."

I rolled my eyes. "Really? That's where this is all headed? You wanted to show off so you could intimidate my mother and other witnesses?"

"It's already worked," Marcus said, smiling. "Half of the witnesses have either run away or been eliminated. You should have hidden, little deer."

"Your plan failed," I said, sighing. "The Shadow Pines Project may have failed, but Alice has already arranged for the state government to reimburse her for the land and has bought the crappy town next to Bright Falls, Deer Park. They're re-zoning it to be part of Bright Falls. Lucien has even gotten the money from the vampires in New Detroit to build an airport there."

Marcus's expression slightly changed, becoming the beginning of a sneer, but he didn't show much else in the way of tells. "You shouldn't be dealing with vampires. They are a disgusting race of demon-blooded degenerates."

Technically so were we, but I didn't feel the need to protect the reputation of vampires. "You dealt with vampires before. You knew the Reveal was coming and that's how you murdered Lucien's family."

Marcus snorted. "The Drakes were stuck in the old ways. They had to die. As for the vampires, they respected me as an equal."

I doubted that was the case but, admittedly, I only knew one vampire and I treated him like crap. "I also dealt with the attempt at blackmailing Alex. David gave me the little storage unit where all of the information was located and I burned it to the ground. There was a lot of evidence in there, irreplaceable stuff."

Marcus smiled a—and I hate to use this term, but there was no other way to describe it—wolfish grin. "Do you think I'm restricted to what he actually did? That was just a taste of what I could do. I can make him a pedophile, a serial rapist, a terrorist, or worse. His past as a hunter was just convenient because he was actually a murderer of our kind."

"Only the ones who deserved to die," I said, looking at him intently. "In retrospect, I think he made a mistake leaving you alive."

"You can't kill the Devil."

"You're not the Devil," I said, reaching into my pocket and pulling out a little doll made of sticks, pieces of a business suit I'd found in one of his Pinewood closets, and hair, which he'd shed copiously on the suit. It was tied together with a ribbon and I'd spent all night making it with Kim Su's help.

Marcus paused, looking hesitant for the first time in our conversation. "You brought a voodoo doll to kill me?"

"That is a prejudiced comment against a fascinating religion," I said, waving the doll around. "This is sympathetic magic, not in any way related to my spiritual beliefs. But yes, I'm going to kill you with it."

"You wouldn't dare."

I pulled out a long metal pin and jabbed it into the heart doodle I'd made on the doll. "Man, you just don't know who you're dealing with, do you?"

*We cool here, Raguel?* I asked. The Merlin Gun was miles away, but I maintained my connection with him.

*He is a murderer of children. This is in addition to thousands of other crimes worthy of death, from slavery to rape. I do not think him capable of following through on repentence, even if he were so inclined.*

"Wow," I said, shaking my head. "I didn't think I was going to enjoy killing you more, Marcus."

Marcus grabbed at the steel of his cage, banging his head against it while trying to choke out his next words. It was a pathetic site, really, and disturbingly satisfying. Marcus had proven himself a monster many times over and it filled with a sense of righteous revenge to destroy him. I felt a bit like Raguel in that moment and I wasn't sure that was a good thing.

I jabbed the needle in further, twisting it. "You threatened my family. You threatened my boyfriend. You beat the crap out of your granddaughter—my best friend—for most of her adolescence. You are pretty much the worst kind of person. One who has every kind of advantage and yet still kicks the people underneath him. So, really, from the rest of the human race...fuck you."

"Red Sky," Marcus said, falling to his knees and running his fingers against the wall. "Red Sky!"

"Oh God, this is one of those conspiracy movie scenes where you try to buy your survival with some piece of information, isn't it? There's a problem with that. I wouldn't believe anything you had to say."

Still, I didn't drive the pin in for the third and final time necessary to kill him.

"Red Sky is the organization that gave me the resources to arrange all of this," Marcus said, blood leaking from his mouth. The black magic I was working on him was a lot stronger than just a heart attack. "They're trying to put the genie back in the bottle. They want to bring all of the supernatural races under their control as well as eliminate the groups that resist. They've got their hands in crime, politics, and everything. Wizards, vampires, and more all pay homage."

"Uh-huh," I said, snorting. "I'm going to call deershit."

*They are real*, Raguel said. *A weapon created by the Star Chamber that has since taken on a life of its own.*

"Want to tell me more?" I asked.

*Not yet.*

"Huh," I said, looking at him. "I guess you aren't so influential after all. So when your resources all dried up, you sold out your own race to another faction of us? And I'm the traitor?"

"It was a mistake coming out. Human beings will never accept beings with supernatural power if they can't get that power for themselves. Red Sky will force the supernatural back under wraps over the course of centuries. It's been done before."

"I see," I said. "Well, I don't think that's going to be a problem you have to worry about."

"Your family will be one of the least they will have destroyed," Marcus said, clutching his chest. "It's better than the alternative."

"Which is?"

"The Star Chamber," Marcus said, falling flat on his back. "They'll kill us all."

I waited for him to say more, but he didn't, just lay there. "Is he dead?"

*Yes*, Raguel said.

I paused. "That was remarkably less satisfying than I expected it to be."

*Executions rarely are.*

"Do you think I have to fear this Red Sky group?" I asked.

*You have killed one of their henchmen and disrupted their plans. They will eventually come for revenge, but their plans are usually made through proxies and henchmen. You may not see where the next blow comes from.*

"Great," I muttered. "I have enemies I can't even see."

*All humands have that flaw. Though it is especially appropriate in this case.*

Why? I asked.

*The Red Sky are ninjas.*

I paused in putting away the doll. "Wait, what the hell was that?"

*I can say no more.*

"You better say more. Frigging ninjas—are you serious?" I turned around to see Alex was standing behind me.

He was wearing his suit and carrying his staff, which made me think he wasn't here in any more of an official capacity than I was. "Hello, Jane. Talking about the Red Sky?"

I blinked and looked at him. "Yeah, they're—did you know there were ninjas out there?"

"Of course I did," Alex said, looking at Marcus's corpse. "Why wouldn't I?"

"I swear," I muttered, shaking my head. "This world just keeps getting weirder and weirder."

"They were the people that destroyed the Department of Supernatural Security by introducing them to demons," Alex said, walking up to the window. "I see you used my favor to get close to Marcus O'Henry in order to kill him."

"You got a problem with that?" I asked, defensive.

Alex looked down at his feet. "Perhaps I was naïve, believing it was possible to take down the worst of the world without killing. Those who hide behind money and power. I don't want to be just a killer, though."

"Yeah, that's why you're in the FBI."

"I'm not anymore."

"What?"

"There was always going to be a consequence for my refusing to teach at Quantico but I thought it was going to be something I could manage," Alex said, frowning. "Little did I know they were going to let me hang for my past as a hunter. With that taken care of, they've sought another means of showing displeasure. They've brought my mother back into the FBI to serve as their resident magical expert. Her price was seeing me cashiered."

I blinked. "So I take it we're not going to meet the parents anytime soon."

"No," Alex said. "The Men in Black have offered to take me in as well as the Star Chamber."

"You hate the Men in Black."

"I do," Alex said. "The offer came from Laura, though."

I narrowed my eyes. "Oh, it did, did it?"

"Yes," Alex said. "I would get to live in Bright Falls and only have to do a few operations a year. Mostly, my job would just be there to be on-call if there's a greater crisis and serving as a consultant to younger agents. I said I would have to clear it with you, though."

"I don't want you working for your ex or these guys unless somehow Will Smith and Tommy Lee Jones are actual agents."

"They promised they'd protect your family from any and all threats. Your parents could come home."

I cursed under my breath. "Dammit, that's why I'm here in the first place!"

"I know," Alex said, putting his hand on my shoulder. "However, they remain vulnerable since Marcus wasn't the man behind it."

*Dammit. Dammit. Dammit.* "What's the Star Chamber's offer?"

"A billion dollars, a Fortune 500 company, and a seat at the High Table of Elders. I'd have to marry their Third Queen of the Fifth Heaven, though. It's part of their breeding project."

"Stick with the Men in Black."

"What I was thinking." Alex gestured to the door. "That's not all of it, though."

I sighed. "Of course."

"The Men in Black have heard about your abilities, but not from me. They want you too."

"How much do they want me?" I asked, wondering if I could still squeeze out of this somehow.

"Significantly more than me," Alex said. "I suspect more for being asked to read objects every now and then more for wetwork, though. They don't know you as the wonder wrecking ball you are like I do."

"Yeah, I'm a real Miley Cyrus," I said, holding the sides of my head as if in pain. "Yeah, well, if it protects my family then I'm up for it."

"Good," Alex said, sighing. "Your allotted time is almost up. We should get going. When they find Marcus's body, this place will descend into chaos. My friend in the Star Chamber made sure no one will remember our entrance, but I'd rather not be here when they notice his heart attack. No sign of you on the security footage either."

"Sure," I said, looking to his side. "Is it too early post-murder to tell you I'd like to get lunch? Maybe see a movie afterward?"

"Maybe wait until we're outside."

It turned out I was a cold-blooded killer. I was surprisingly okay with that.

No one messed with my town.

# About the Author

C.T. Phipps is a lifelong student of horror, science fiction, and fantasy. An avid tabletop gamer, he discovered this passion led him to write and turned him into a lifelong geek. He is a regular blogger and also a reviewer at The United Federation of Charles.

## Bibliography

*The Rules of Supervillainy* (Supervillainy Saga #1)
*The Games of Supervillainy* (Supervillainy Saga #2)
*The Secrets of Supervillainy* (Supervillainy Saga #3)
*The Kingdom of Supervillany* (Supervillainy Saga #4)
*Esoterrorism* (Red Room, Vol. 1)
*Eldritch Ops* (Red Room, Vol. 2)
*Agent G: Infiltrator*
*Cthulhu Armageddon* (Cthulhu Armageddon, Vol. 1)
*The Tower of Zhaal* (Cthulhu Armageddon, Vol. 2)
*Lucifer's Star*
*Straight Outta Fangton*
*Wraith Knight*
*I Was a Teenage Weredeer* (Bright Falls Mystery Series #1)

Curious about other Crossroad Press books?
Stop by our site:
http://store.crossroadpress.com
We offer quality writing
in digital, audio, and print formats.

Enter the code FIRSTBOOK
to get 20% off your first order from our store!
Stop by today!

www.ingramcontent.com/pod-product-compliance
Lightning Source LLC
Chambersburg PA
CBHW060423180626
46817CB00007B/2642